Anonymous

East Norfolk Election - The poll for a Knight of the Shire for the Eastern Division of the county of Norfolk

SALZWASSER
VERLAG

Anonymous

East Norfolk Election - The poll for a Knight of the Shire for the Eastern Division of the county of Norfolk

Reprint of the original, first published in 1858.

1st Edition 2023 | ISBN: 978-3-37514-876-8

Verlag (Publisher): Salzwasser Verlag GmbH, Zeilweg 44, 60439 Frankfurt, Deutschland
Vertretungsberechtigt (Authorized to represent): E. Roepke, Zeilweg 44, 60439 Frankfurt, Deutschland
Druck (Print): Books on Demand GmbH, In de Tarpen 42, 22848 Norderstedt, Deutschland

EAST NORFOLK ELECTION.

THE POLL

FOR

A KNIGHT OF THE SHIRE

FOR THE

Eastern Division of the County of Norfolk,

TAKEN ON THE 29TH DAY OF JUNE, 1858,

WITH A

COMPLETE LIST OF THE REGISTER OF VOTERS.

CANDIDATES:

HON. WENMAN C. W. COKE 2933

SIR HENRY J. STRACEY, BART. 2720

NORWICH:

MATCHETT AND STEVENSON, PRINTERS, MARKET-PLACE.

1858.

EAST NORFOLK ELECTION.

At the General Election in March, 1857, Sir Edward North Buxton, in conjunction with Major General Windham, were returned as members for the Eastern Division of this County, without a contest. At the time of the Election the health of Sir E. Buxton was in a delicate state, and it was stated by his brother, who represented him at the Nomination, that he would be obliged to be absent from England during the prevalence of the easterly winds in the spring of the year. At the latter part of May of the present year, Sir E. Buxton, not feeling so well as usual, obtained leave of absence for a fortnight from his Parliamentary duties, and retired to his residence, at Colne House, Cromer. His medical attendants felt that he was in a very precarious, if not absolutely dangerous, state—suffering as he did from an attack of *angina pectoris*—but in about a week there were symptoms of improvement, and only two days before he died there were hopes of his ultimate recovery. On the 10th of June, however, great prostration of strength manifested itself, and at an early hour of the morning of Friday the 11th, he expired in the presence of several members of his family.

A few weeks previous to this event, when the Derby Ministry were vainly attempted to be thrown out on a no-confidence vote, arising out of a dispatch of Lord Ellenborough, which censured a proclamation of Viscount Canning for confiscating the soil of Oude, Sir H. J. Stracey had publicly intimated that, in the event of an election, he should offer himself as a candidate for the Eastern Division, which he had represented for two years prior to the dissolution of 1857. Accordingly, on the death of the late member, Sir Henry immediately published his address, and on the following Saturday (the 19th June) he addressed the agriculturists at the close of the business in the Corn-hall, Norwich. In his address Sir Henry Stracey avowed himself to be desirous of giving "his support to Lord Derby's government, believing that there was no statesman of the present day of greater administrative ability than his lordship."

On Tuesday, the 15th, an address appeared from Colonel the Hon. Wenman Coke, a brother of the Earl of Leicester, declaring his intention to contest the Eastern Division, should a poll be demanded. His address was brief, and confined to an announcement of his intentions, and a declaration that "his political opinions were in accordance with those of his late father, whose name was ever associated with the progress of civil and religious liberty, the advancement of agriculture, and the best interests of the people."

On Wednesday, the 16th, a meeting of the Conservative party was convened by circular at the Swan Hotel, Norwich, the Earl of Orford presiding, for the purpose of selecting a Conservative candidate. In consequence of numerous rumours which were in circulation to the effect that Mr. H. N. Burroughes felt annoyed at not having been asked again to become a candidate, that gentleman attended the meeting for the purpose of declaring, that he had no intention whatever to solicit any such honour at the hands of his former friends. On the motion of Mr. Fellowes, M.P.,

seconded by Sir S. Bignold, a vote of thanks was passed to Mr. Burroughes, for his valuable
- services during twenty years of his Parliamentary life. It was then, on the motion of Mr. Fellowes,
M.P., seconded by Lieut.-Colonel Fitzroy, resolved "that this meeting pledges itself to use every
exertion to secure the return of Sir H. Stracey to Parliament as one of the representatives of the
Eastern Division of Norfolk." The third resolution was a vote of thanks to the Earl of Orford
for his able conduct in the chair.

On the following Friday, on the motion of Sir W. Hayter, a new writ was moved in the House of
Commons, and the next day the High Sheriff (S. Lyne Stephens, Esq.) issued a proclamation, fixing
the day of nomination for Saturday, the 26th of June, and the polling for Tuesday, the 29th. At the
nomination Sir H. Stracey was proposed by E. Fellowes, Esq., M.P., and seconded by Lieut.-Col.
Fitzroy; the Hon. Wenman Coke was proposed by W. E. L. Bulwer, Esq., of Heydon, and
seconded by H. R. Upcher, Esq. The shew of hands was declared to be in favour of Sir H.
Stracey, when a poll was demanded by Mr. Coke's proposer. At the close of the poll on Tuesday
afternoon, the numbers were, for the different polling places, as follows :—

	STRACEY.	COKE.
NORWICH	820	774
YARMOUTH	572	495
NORTH WALSHAM	463	520
LONG STRATTON	489	521
REEPHAM	179	348
LODDON	197	271

The official declaration of the poll was made on Thursday, July 1st, when the numbers, as
stated by the High Sheriff, were—

The Hon. Wenman Coke 2933
Sir Henry Josias Stracey, Bart. 2720

Majority for Coke.................. 213

THE
EAST NORFOLK POLL AND REGISTER.

⁎ *The Names of those who did not Vote, or who have been Registered more than once, are given at the end of each Parish.*

NORWICH DISTRICT,

COMPRISING THE PARISHES OF

Acle.	S.	C.
Andrew William, Magdalen-street, Norwich		
Baker Benjamin Heath, Acle		
Blowers John, Costessey		
Cobbold Alfred, Ipswich, Suffolk		
Crowe James, Great Yarmouth		
Drake Spencer, Acle		
Dunt Adam, Acle		
Dawson Thomas, Acle		
England John, Acle		
England Robert, junr., Acle		
England William, Great Yarmouth		
Evans Edward, Surrey-street, Norwich		
Evans Benjamin, Acle		
Furrance George, Acle		
Fowler William Dan, Acle		
Gales Daniel, Acle		
Holmes John, Acle		
Hunn Joseph, Acle		
Hunn James, Acle		
Harding John, Acle		
Herwin Samuel, Woodbastwick		
Jay George, Norwich		
Knights Samuel B., South Walsham St. Mary		
Mallett Joshua, Acle		
Newton Richard, Acle		
Niker Henry, Great Yarmouth		
Porter William, Acle		
Riches John Worship, Acle		
Skoyles John Brown, Blofield		
Tills Charles J., Acle		
Worship John Lucas, Riverhead, Kent		
Winter James John, Heigham, Norwich	25	7
Andrews William, Magdalen-street, Norwich		
Boyce Daniel, Acle		
Cobb J. W., Mount Pleasant, Eaton, Norwich		
Dunt James, Acle		
England George Jarrett, Freethorpe		
Faulke Robert Cooper, Acle		
Fane Christopher, Moulton		
Morse Charles, clerk, Thorpe, Norwich		
Nolbrow Matthew, Lakenham, Norwich		
Randall Henry K., Acle		
Rix Henry, Norwich		
Spooner Wm., clerk, Elmdon, Warwickshire		
Ward Robert, Acle		
Wigg George, Acle		
Worship Starling Day, Gray's Inn, London		

Arminghall.	S.	C.
Clarke Joseph, Tuck's-wood, Lakenham		
Parker George William, Arminghall		
Waters Edward, Arminghall		
	3	0
Attlebridge.		
Bird John, Attlebridge		
	1	0
Barford.		
Blyth William, Barford		
Bond Samuel, St. Swithin's, Norwich		
Burton James, West Pottergate-street, Norwich		
Everett James, Barford		
Gaff John, Barford		
Greeves Henry, Lakenham, Norwich		
Hanworth George, Unthank's-road, Norwich		
Hipperson Thomas, Barford		
Hubbard James, Melton Parva		
Ling Henry, St. Giles', Norwich		
Lee Robert, Barford		
Norton William, Colton		
Smith James, Barford		
Sayer David, Marlingford		
Tice Richard, Barford		
Wilkinson Henry Joseph, St. Giles', Norwich	12	4
Franckling Henry, clerk, Rose-lane, Norwich		
Harrison Robert, junr., Bintry		
Hunter John, Barwick		
King Arthur, Barford		
Nash Samuel, Barford		
Priest George, Newmarket-road, Norwich		
Wild F. R., St. Peter's Mountergate, Norwich		

Barnham Broom.	S.	C.
Barnard John, Barnham Broom		
Cranness Howlett Thomas, Barnham Broom		
Child Thomas, Barnham Broom		
Davy Walter, Barnham Broom		
Gapp Edmund, Barnham Broom		
Gurdon Edward Rev., Barnham Broom		
Jacob Richard, Barnham Broom		
Knights Robt., Paragon-st., Heigham, Norwich		
Laskey Robert, Barford		
Loyterton Michael, Barnham Broom		

B

	S.	C.
Riches Thomas, Barnham Broom	—	
Roberson William Newton, Barnham Broom	—	
Wrigglesworth John, junr., Barnham Broom	—	
	8	10
Child Robert, Barnham Broom	—	
Child David, Barnham Broom	—	
Elliott Norris, Barnham Broom	—	
Harvey John, Hethersett	—	
Turner William, Barnham Broom	—	
Wigglesworth John, Barnham Broom	—	

Bawburgh.

	S.	C.
Cross Thomas, Bawburgh	—	
Crow George, Bawburgh	—	
Howlett John, Bowthorpe	—	
Muskett Jos. Salisbury, Intwood	—	
Tyler John, Bawburgh	—	
	1	4
Claydon Chas. Thos., Hadstock, Cambridgeshire	—	
Cole William, Costessey	—	
Gurney Daniel, North Runcton	—	
Mathews Walter Franks, Bawburgh	—	
Page Robert, jun., Bawburgh	—	
Parker Jeremiah, Heigham, Norwich	—	
Parish W. Sir, Gloster-place, Portman-sq., London		

Beeston St. Andrew.

	S.	C.
Barnes Orlando, Beeston St. Andrew	—	
Bowen Thomas, Beeston St. Andrew	—	
Howlett Harcourt, Beeston St. Andrew	—	
	2	1

Beighton.

	S.	C.
Fellowes Rev. Thomas Lyon, Beighton	—	
Fowler William, Beighton	—	
Howard James, Beighton	—	
Read William, Beighton	—	
Read Robert, Beighton	—	
Thirkettle Christmas, Lingwood	—	
Warnes John, Beighton	—	
	6	1
Burroughes Rev. Jeremiah, Lingwood	—	

Bixley.

	S.	C.
Coleman Geo. Lovick, Unthank's-road, Norwich	—	
Sowter James, Bixley-place	—	
Sowter John, Bixley	—	
Tidnam Robert, Thorpe Hamlet, Norwich	—	
	1	3
Clare Charles, Bixley	—	
Parker George, Bixley	—	
Seaman William, Bixley	—	

Blofield.

	S.	C.
Allen John, Blofield	—	
Baker John, St. Catherine's-plain, Norwich	—	
Bane Joseph Emmerson, Blofield	—	
Benns Thomas, Blofield	—	
Borton Rev. W., Thornton le Moor Lincolnshire	—	
Bowen James, Blofield	—	
Brooks William, Blofield	—	
Broom John, Blofield	—	
Browne William, Blofield	—	
Bulley Robert, Blofield	—	
Bussey James, Blofield	—	
Clarke William, Blofield	—	

	S.	C.
Codling William Henry, Blofield	—	
Crane Robert, Gatehouse, Highgate, Middlesex	—	
Eade Peter, Blofield	—	
Edrich William Skipp, Lingwood	—	
Elliss John, Blofield	—	
Fisher William, Blofield	—	
Freeman James, Cross-street, Heigham, Norwich	—	
Gibbs Alfred, Blofield	—	
Gostling James, Blofield	—	
Goulder Robert, Blofield	—	
Goulder Robert, junr., Yarmouth	—	
Goulder Christmas Catlen, Rackheath	—	
Gowen Benjamin, Blofield	—	
Howlett William, Market-place, Norwich	—	
Kent Alfred, St. Gregory's, Norwich	—	
Long Robert, Blofield	—	
Osborne William, Blofield	—	
Page Joseph, Briggs-street, Norwich	—	
Palmer Charles, Blofield	—	
Patterson Henry, Blofield	—	
Postle Jehosaphat Davy, Blofield	—	
Postle Thomas, Strumpshaw	—	
Reynolds Noah, Blofield	—	
Scott William, Magdalen-gates, Norwich	—	
Skipper William, Thorpe Hamlet, Norwich	—	
Spanton John, Blofield	—	
Swatman Edward Lane, West Winch	—	
Thrower John, Blofield	—	
Tuck Rev. R. G., Wallington rectory, Hertfordsh	—	
Tunmore John, Blofield	—	
Turnbull Rev. Thomas Smith, Blofield	—	
Woodrow John, Blofield	—	
Wright R., Unthank's-road, Heigham, Norwich	—	
	26	19
Boatwright J., Shirley-common, Croydon, Surrey		
Boatwright John, 8, Mexican-terrace, Caledonian-road, London		
Borton John, Mount Sion, Tunbridge-wells, Kent		
Borton Edward, Lincoln's Inn, London		
Borton Arthur, Head Quarters of the 9th Regiment of Infantry		
Butterfant William, Rackheath		
Clarke John, Rackheath		
Elliss William, Blofield		
Fenn John, Strumpshaw		
Lynes Joseph, Blofield		
Mace R., St. Andrew's-terrace, Hastings, Sussex		
Mallett Samuel Robert, Blofield		
Pyle John, Strumpshaw		
Read Richard, Blofield		
Rushmore Anthony, Blofield		
Rushmore William, Sprowston		
Scurll William, Blofield		
Stockings William, Blofield		
Tuck John Henry, Blofield		
Whitbread Rev. Edmund Salter, Strumpshaw		

Bowthorpe.

	S.	C.
Payne John Harvey, clerk, Colney		
	1	0

Bracon Ash.

	S.	C.
Barnard William, Bracon Ash	—	
Butcher William, Theatre-street, Norwich	—	
Berney Rev. Thomas, Bracon Ash	—	
Barnard Edward, Bracon Ash	—	
Cook Rev. Bell, Heigham, Norwich	—	
Gurney Rev. Thomas, Heigham, Norwich	—	
Myhill Charles, Bracon Ash	—	

	S.	C.
Norris Charles, Bracon Ash	—	
Spurgeon Samuel, Bracon Ash	—	
Tillett Robert, Bracon Ash	—	
Williams Rev. Henry, Croxton	—	
	10	1
Kemp Sir William Robert, Gissing		

Bradestone.

Culley John, St. Andrew's, Norwich	—	
Culley Richard, St. Andrew's, Norwich	—	
Gilbert Thomas William, Bradestone	—	
Millard C. William, Bradestone	—	
Nevill H. R., Upper Grosvenor-st., Middlesex	—	
Postle John, Bradestone		
Waters William, Bradestone		

Bramerton.

Blake Joseph John, Palace-street, Norwich	—	
Beaumont Henry, Bramerton	—	
Browne William John Utten, Heigham, Norwich	—	
Forder John, Bramerton	—	
O'Reilly A. James, Penrice-house, Gt. Yarmouth	—	
Rudd Gray Robert, Bramerton	—	
Sexton Joseph Watling, Norwich	—	
Sexton William Watling, Bury St. Edmund's	—	
Todd Joseph, Surrey-street, Norwich	—	
Wilde William, St. Stephen's-street, Norwich	—	
Wilde, W., jun., Post-office-street, Norwich	—	
Wilde Frederic, St. Stephen's-street, Norwich	—	
	5	7
Blade Charles, Brixton-hill, Surrey	—	
Blake the Rev. Edmund, Bramerton	—	
Brightwell Thomas, jun., Norwich		

Brandon Parva.

Atkins Thomas, Kimberley	—	
Briggs James, Brandon Parva	—	
Chaplin Charles, Brandon Parva	—	
Herring Harvey, Fordham, Essex	—	
Howes Jeremiah, Coslany-street, Norwich	—	
Howlet Smith, Barnham Broom	—	
Moll Robert, St. Giles'-street, Norwich	—	
Only Savill Only, Stisted, Essex	—	
Pitcher Daniel, Barnham Broom	—	
Preston Rev. Samuel Tolver, Brandon Parva	—	
Sutton, William, Melton	—	
Sutton William Denny, jun., Brandon Parva	—	
Tice Thomas, Brandon Parva	—	
Turner John Sippins, Brandon Parva	—	
	7	7
Boileau Chas. Lestock, Barnes, Surrey	—	
Leaf Christopher, Wood-street, London	—	
Rose Philip, Heigham, Norwich	—	
Storey John, Wymondham	—	
Wright Robert, Brandon Parva		

Brundall.

Culley George Scott, Witton	—	
Marsh Robert, Epringham	—	
Norton J. Culley, Unthank's-road, Norwich	—	
	2	1

Buckenham.

Beauchamp Thomas, Buckenham	—	
Waters Benjamin, Buckenham	—	
	0	2
Green John, Buckenham		

Burlingham St. Andrew.

	S.	C.
Broughton William, Burlingham St. Andrew	—	
Littlewood Jeremiah, Burlingham St. Andaew	—	
	2	0

Burlingham St. Edmund.

Burton R. Browne, Burlingham St. Edmund	—	
Burroughes Thomas Henry, Lingwood	—	
Green William, Burlingham St. Edmund	—	
Hewitt Samuel, Burlingham St. Edmund	—	
Wilson Robert, Burlingham St. Edmund	—	
	5	0
Read Thomas, Burlingham St. Edmund		

Burlingham St. Peter.

Aldous Robert, Burlingham St. Peter	—	
Burroughes H. Negus, Burlingham St. Peter	—	
Hammond Robert, Burlingham St. Peter	—	
	3	0

Caister St. Edmund's.

Culling Thomas Norman, Caister St. Edmund's	—	
Spurrell John, Caister St. Edmund's	—	
Williamson Thomas, Caister St. Edmund's	—	
Warren William, Bracondale, Norwich	—	
	0	4

Cantley.

Curtis Samuel, Cantley	—	
Crowe Walter, Cantley	—	
Gilbert William Alexander, Cantley	—	
Gowen Isaac, Cantley	—	
Howse, Robert, Cantley	—	
Reynolds Amos, Cantley	—	
Siely William, Cantley	—	
	0	7
Curtis Richard, Martham	—	
England John, Cantley	—	
Gilbert W. Alexander, jun., Cantley	—	
Gilbert Rev. John Denny, Cantley	—	
Hewitt Samuel Smith, Burlingham	—	
Stout William, Cantley		

Carleton Forehoe.

Green Matthew, Carleton Forehoe	—	
Raikes the Rev. Francis, Carleton Forehoe	—	
Spencer William, sen., Heacham hall	—	
Spencer William, jun., Snettisham	—	
Spencer Rev. Henry, Unthank's-road, Norwich	—	
Spencer Edmond, Heacham hall	—	
Spencer John Suckling, Heacham	—	
Twaites John Thurlow, Carleton Forehoe	—	
	5	3

Carleton East.

Browne Robert, East Carleton	—	
Carman Jeremiah, East Carleton	—	
Carman David, East Carleton	—	
Edwards John, East Carleton	—	
Eaton Thomas Damant, Chapel-field, Norwich	—	
Freestone Edwd., St. Peter's Mancroft, Norwich	—	
Fairman James, Cringleford	—	
Francis Rev. Robert John, Beccles	—	
Garthon Jas. Slapp, St. Giles'-street, Norwich	—	
Heard George, East Carleton	—	
Riches Henry, East Carleton	—	
Steward Edward, Eaton, Norwich	—	
Steward Charles, Ipswich	—	
	4	9
Barker Rev. Samuel, East Carleton		

	S.	C.
Hook William, Erpingham		
Huggins William, East Carleton		
Land James, East Carleton		
Steward Rev. John Henry, East Carleton		
Seppings George, Lowestoft, Suffolk		
Smith Matthew, East Carleton		
Thraxton Israel, Wymondham		

Catton.

	S.	C.
Adlam John, Sussex-street, Norwich	—	
Broad John, Catton	—	
Burrell James, junr., St. Saviour's, Norwich	—	
Calver Josiah, St. Clement's, Norwich	—	
Cattermoul Everitt, St. Mary's, Norwich.	—	
Chamberlin Robert, Catton	—	
Clarke William, St. Martin's at Oak, Norwich	—	
Cobb Leggett, St. Augustine's, Norwich	—	
Cook Henry, Catton	—	
Custance Jonathan, St. Saviour's, Norwich	—	
Dann James, Magdalen-street, Norwich	—	
Engall Joseph, St. Augustine's, Norwich	—	
Fox John, Sprowston		
Gilbert W. T., St. George of Colegate, Norwich	—	
Guymer William, Catton-street	—	
Hart Richard, clerk, Catton		
Hinde Ephraim, Catton-lodge		
Hall Charles Henry, Rose-lane, Norwich	—	
Jermy George, St. Augustine's, Norwich	—	
Johnson John Godwin, St. Giles', Norwich	—	
Kemp William, St. Augustine's, Norwich	—	
Kerr John, St. Gregory's, Norwich	—	
Langley John, Hellesdon		
Long Edmund Slingsby, Catton	—	
Millard William Salter, Catton	—	
Minns Samuel, Catton		
Mordaunt Martin Munro, Enfield, Middlesex	—	
North Samuel, St. Martin at Palace, Norwich	—	
Nunn John, St. Augustine's, Norwich	—	
Rushmore William, Sprowston	—	
Stearman Henry, Tombland, Norwich	—	
Springfield Osborne, Catton	—	
Stacey Edward, Orford-hill, Norwich	—	
Steward John, St. George's, Norwich	—	
Sutton H. Merrison, St. Augustine's, Norwich	—	
Waite John Newman, jun., Catton	—	
Walker Robt., St. Michael at Coslany, Norwich		
	14	23
Burrell James, St. Saviour's, Norwich		
Cobb Robert Leggett, St. Saviour's, Norwich		
Jones Charles, Marsham		

Colney.

	S.	C.
Scott Joseph, Colney-hall	—	
Utting John, Colney	—	
	2	0
Postle Rev. Edward, Yelverton		
Webb Edward, Colney		

Colton.

	S.	C.
Beckwith A. A. H., Palace-street, Norwich	—	
Bales Thomes, Colton	—	
Dunnell Henry, Colton	—	
Horstead Henry, Colton	—	
Ives Ferdinand, St. Catherine's-hill, Norwich	—	
Lynn William, Colton	—	
Melton William, Colton	—	
Moor George, Marlingford	—	
Priest George, St. Stephen's-road, Norwich	—	
Whisson Jonathan, Colton	—	
	10	0

	S.	C.
Daveney Chas. Burton, Bethel-street, Norwich		
Daveney Burton Lieut.-Col., the Camp, the Curragh, Ireland		
Girdlestone Rev. Henry, Landford		
Hill John, Norwich		
Hipkin Stephen, Honingham		
Symonds Robt., Colton		

Costessey.

	S.	C.
Bailey Anthony, Heigham, Norwich	—	
Banham William, Costessey	—	
Banham James, Costessey	—	
Barker Robert, Costessey	—	
Culley John, jun., Costessey	—	
Culley Henry Utting, Costessey	—	
Carr John, Costessey	—	
Cole William, Costessey	—	
Edwards W., St. Peter per Mountergate, Norwich	—	
Field Robert, King-street, Norwich	—	
Gunton George, Costessey	—	
Hastings John Edmund, 8, Wapping-wall, Shadwall, London	—	
Hastings Edward, Costessey	—	
Harman Henry, Heigham-field, Norwich	—	
Harman John, Costessey	—	
Howell James, St. Clement's, Norwich	—	
Humphrey Wm., St. Michael Thorn, Norwich	—	
Jerningham Francis Stafford, Costessey	—	
Lynell James, Costessey	—	
Martin Edmond, Costessey	—	
Miller John, St. George's, Norwich	—	
Rising Robert Charles, Costessey	—	
Roulstone Thomas, Birmingham	—	
Taylor John, Costessey	—	
Taylor William, Costessey	—	
Watcham Charles, Costessey	—	
	7	19
Frost William, Bridewell-alley, Norwich		
Gurney John Henry, Catton		
Horne James, Costessey		
Jerningham Hon. H. V. Stafford, Costessey		
Kidd Thomas, Costessey		
Read William, Hempnall		
Spaul Wm. Bartholomew, Close, Norwich		
Taylor J. R., 7, Martlett's-court, London		

Coston.

	S.	C.
Atkins Charles Cadywold, Coston		
Slipper Robert Browne, Hardingham		
	1	1

Cringleford.

	S.	C.
Cannell Abraham, Cringleford		
Cannell Abraham, junr., Cringleford	—	
Candler Horatio, Cringleford		
Drane William, Cringleford		
Edwards John, Cringleford		
Edwards Edward, Mulbarton		
Smyth Rev. William John		
	2	5
Candler Horatio, Cringleford		
George George, Cringleford		
Priest Edward, clerk, Cringleford		
Reynolds John, Cringleford		
Reynolds John, junr., Cringleford		
Tyler William, Cringleford		

Crostwick.

	S.	C.
Bell Edward John, Crostwick		
Bensley John, Scarning		
Bensley Charles Frederick, Crostwick		
Stracey Edward John, Sprowston		
	4	0
Morse Chas., Horstead		
Stracey James William, Sprowston		

Crownthorpe.

	S.	C.
Barker George, Barnham Broom		
Howlett Joseph Gilman, Crownthorpe		
Morris Matthew, Crownthorpe		
Smith John, Crownthorpe		
	0	4
Skoulding William, Wymondham		

Deopham.

	S.	C.
Barker John, Deopham		
Boodle William, Deopham		
Badcock William, Lakenham, Norwich		
Barker Robert, Deopham		
Brunton John, Deopham		
Clarke William, Deopham		
Clarke Thomas Leeder, Deopham		
Clements James Blackburn, Deopham		
Durrant William, Brunswick-square, London		
Eason Robert, Deopham		
Howlett William, Melton Magna		
Jessup William, Deopham		
Jude Charles, Deopham		
Last Philip, Old Buckenham, Norfolk		
Liddelow William, junior, Deopham		
Liddelow William, Deopham		
Lee John Eagling, Deopham		
Mann John, Deopham		
Mann William, Great Ellingham		
Miles William, St. Benedict's-road, Norwich		
Miles Henry, Deopham		
Patrick Robert, Reymerstone		
Phœnix Taylor, senr., Deopham		
Phœnix John, senr., Deopham		
Phœnix John, junr., Deopham		
Phœnix Robert, Deopham		
Pitts Philip, Deopham		
Riches John, Deopham		
Shickle James, Deopham		
Stone Taylor, Hackford		
Taylor William, Hopton, Suffolk		
Turner George Henry, Deopham		
Watling Henry, Deopham		
	6	27
Allen John, Deopham		
Baxter Edward, Acton-green, Middlesex		
Clarke James, Deopham		
Drake Charles, City-road, London		
Goodwin William, Chapel-field, Norwich		
Pitts Phineas, Deopham		
Shaw Henry, Ubbestone-hall, Suffolk		
Taylor Francis Oddin, Winfarthing		
Wingfield John, Deopham		

Drayton.

	S.	C.
Adcock Edmond, Drayton		
Atkins Richard, Bethel-street, Norwich		
Blyth Matthew, Drayton		
Bradshaw Francis Green, Drayton		

	S.	C.
Bunn Samuel, Drayton		
Cannell Peter, Horsford		
Daniels Robert, Trowse		
Evens James William, Drayton		
Fenn Robert, Drayton		
Fitch Robert, Market-place, Norwich		
Gedge John, Drayton		
Hipper Robert, Drayton		
Hipper Thomas, Drayton		
Howard Jeremi, Drayton		
Howell Hindes Rev., the Rectory		
Jarvis Henry, Norwich		
Lacey James Wilkins, Surrey-street, Norwich		
Laton Charles Helveys, Drayton		
Norton Hammond, Drayton		
Pratt Robert, Drayton		
Womack George, Norwich		
	11	10
Blyth William, Drayton		
Cockell Charles, Bridgham		
Moore William, Stoke Holy Cross		

Dunston.

	S.	C.
Fish John, Dunston		
Long Robert Kellett, Dunston-hall		
	1	1

Easton.

	S.	C.
Clarke John, Easton		
Howes John, Crescent, Norwich		
Kelsall Henry, jun., Easton		
Matchett Rev. Jonathon C., Close, Norwich		
Raven William, Easton		
Rix James, Easton		
	6	0
Kilburn Isaac, Easton		
Kilburn Goodwin, Hawkhurst, Kent		

Felthorpe.

	S.	C.
Austin John, Felthorpe		
Brickdale Rev. Richard, Felthorpe		
Brooke William, Felthorpe		
Bloom John Hastead, Felthorpe		
Bowles Benjamin Robert, Felthorpe		
Brewster Philip, Felthorpe		
Furnice John, Felthorpe		
Gilham William, Felthorpe		
Hare Sir Thomas, Stow-hall		
Hill Horace, Pottergate-street, Norwich		
Howe Richard, Felthorpe		
Hastings William, Felthorpe		
Ladbrooke John Barney, St. Andrew's, Norwich		
Larwood William, Tottenham-street, Yarmouth		
Larwood Robert, Felthorpe		
Miller John, Felthorpe		
Pratt James Wortley, Felthorpe		
Rackham Robert M., Surrey-street, Norwich		
Steel Edward, Great Yarmouth		
Sparkes John		
	14	6
Buxton Sir E. N., Bart., Colne-house, Cromer		
Herring Robert, Cromer		
Massingham Henry, Twyford		
Nash Thomas, Felthorpe		
Wade Clarke, Felthorpe		

Flordon.

	S.	C.
Bird John, Flordon		
Brightwell Thomas, Surrey-street, Norwich	—	
Brightwell Barron, Flordon	—	
White Henry, Flordon	—	
Whittaker Gascoigne Frederick, Flordon		
Walpole Frederick, Rainthorpe-hall	0	5

Framingham Earl.

	S.	C.
Barker Thomas, Framingham Earl	—	
Blyth Benjamin, Framingham Earl	—	
Coldham William, Poringland		
Colman Henry, Gaol-hill, Norwich	—	
Colman Barnard, Fordham, Cambridgeshire		
Colman Samuel, Rockland St. Andrew		
Harvard Samuel, Stoke Holy Cross		
Knight George Brown Leak, Framingham Earl	—	
Plummer Charles T., Night-cap-lane, Norwich	—	
Seaman William, Bixley		
	2	8
Cole Henry, Weedon, Northamptonshire		
Colman John, Larkham-rise, Clapham		
Colman Jeremiah, jun., 26, Cannon-st., London		
Goodeve Henry Hurry, Clifton, near Bristol		
Greeves Henry, Norwich		

Framingham Pigot.

	S.	C.
Alexander David, Framingham Pigot		
Beaumont John, Framingham Pigot	—	
Ewing Robert, Framingham Pigot	—	
Gilbert William, Pitt-street, Norwich	—	
Hawkins John, Framingham Pigot	—	
Hawks William, Framingham Pigot	—	
Hawks John, Framingham Pigot	—	
Hilling Frederic, 26, Victoria-street, Norwich	—	
Jecks William, Framingham Pigot	—	
Lawrence William, Framingham Pigot	—	
Mendham Wace Lockett, Norwich	—	
Nunn William, Framingham Pigot	—	
Plume William Henry, Framingham Pigot	—	
Riches Henry, Framingham Pigot	—	
Rigby Edw., New-st., Spring-gardens, London	—	
Robinson William, jun., Norwich	—	
Spink John, Framingham Pigot	—	
Spink John, jun., Framingham Pigot	—	
Thetford William, Trowse Newton	—	
Townshend Zachariah, Mill-st., Lakenham	—	
Winter James, Norwich	—	
Williams I., the younger, Calvert-st., Norwich		
	5	17
Barker Thos., Framingham Pigot		
Christie G. H., Cadogan-place, Chelsea		
Kerrison Roger Matthias, Framingham Pigot		
Paul Francis William, Bracondale, Norwich		
Taylor Adam, Norwich		
Young John, King-street, Norwich		

Freethorpe.

	S.	C.
Bush William, Freethorpe	—	
Crane Thomas, Freethorpe	—	
Gooch Robert, Freethorpe	—	
Key John, Freethorpe	—	
Read Richard, Freethorpe	—	
Smith George, Freethorpe	—	
Turner William, Postwick	—	
Waters Robert, jun., Freethorpe		—

	S.	C.
Walpole R. H. V., Upper Brook-street, London		
Youngs William, Freethorpe		
	7	8
Cannell John, Mundham		
Mallows Stephen, Framlingham, Suffolk		

Frettenham

	S.	C.
Amies John, Frettenham	—	
Hall William, Frettenham	—	
Juby William, Frettenham	—	
Read Robert, Frettenham	—	
Scottow William Wright, Frettenham	—	
Shirley Rev. James, Frettenham		
	1	5

Hackford.

	S.	C.
Brunton William, Hackford	—	
Bush Thomas, Hackford	—	
Cubitt Thomas, Hackford	—	
Darby Martin Baylie, Hingham	—	
Durrant Isaiah, Hackford	—	
Head James, Hackford	—	
Lain James, Hackford	—	
Matthews James Story, Hackford	—	
Smithson John, Hackford	—	
Taylor Joseph, Hackford	—	
Turner Jeremiah, Hackford	—	
Turner William, Hackford	—	
Watts Charles, Hackford		
	4	9
Farrer James, Hackford		
Green Matthew, Carleton Forehoe		
Phœnix William, Hackford		
Taylor Joseph, Bylaugh		
Wade John, Hackford		

Hainford.

	S.	C.
Bowman Henry, Hainford	—	
Burrell James, Magdalen-street, Norwich	—	
Featherstone Thomas, Swardeston	—	
Fitz Roy Hugh, Stratton Strawless	—	
Foster William, Thorpe, Norwich	—	
Fransham Daniel, Hainford	—	
Huson John, Hainford	—	
Keppel William Arnold, Hainford	—	
Keppel Frederick Walpole, East Lexham	—	
Keppel Frederick Charles, Hainford	—	
Lockett James Charles, Hainford	—	
Lockett Samuel, Hainford	—	
Middleton John, Hainford	—	
Pooley Thomas, Northwold	—	
Sexton Richard, Norwich	—	
Sexton William, Hainford	—	
Self Thomas, Lowestoft	—	
Thrower William, Hainford	—	
Woolsey Leonard, Hainford		
	7	12
Birch Wyrley, Wretham		
Clayton William Ray, clerk, St. Giles', Norwich		
Cooper John N. V., St. Stephen's, Norwich		
Cornvil John, Ringfield		
Foulger Francis, Frettenham		
Golding William, Hainford		
Keppel Edward Walpole, East Lexham		
Lovick Thomas, St. Faith's		
Mack Robert, Hainford		
Springfield Thos. Osborne, St. Martin's, Norwich		

Halvergate.

	S.	C.
Batley John, Southtown	—	
Beck James, Halvergate	—	
Crow James, Gorleston, Suffolk	—	
Gaze William, St. Saviour's-lane, Norwich	—	
Gillett Robert, Halvergate	—	
Gilbert Thomas William, Bradistone	—	
Howard Benjamin, Halvergate	—	
Ives Robert, Halvergate	—	
Ives William, Halvergate	—	
Jones Thomas, Halvergate	—	
Mallett John, Halvergate	—	
Ormerod Arthur Stanley, Halvergate	—	
Rumbold Benjamin, Reedham	—	
Read Trivett, Norwich	—	
Warnes Samuel, Halvergate	—	
Wyand Philip Juler, Halvergate	—	
Wyand Alfred, Halvergate	—	
	14	3
Fountaine Andrew, Narford		
Gillett Daniel, Geldestone		
Gillett Richard, Tunstall		
Gooch Robert, Halvergate		
Howard Robert, Halvergate		
Youngs William, Freethorpe		

Hassingham.

	S.	C.
Bessey James Green, Hassingham		
Waters William, Hassingham		
	1	1
Shepard John, Hassingham		

Hellesdon.

	S.	C.
Cross George, Hellesdon Hamlet	—	
Woodcock Henry, St. Giles'-street, Norwich	—	
	0	2
Berners H., Gatcomb Newport, Isle of Wight		
Barnard J. Hilling, All Saints', Norwich		
Barnham Jas. Calthorpe, Lakenham, Norwich		
Gowing George, Hellesdon Hamlet		
Pratt Robert, Town Close, Norwich		

Hemblington.

	S.	C.
Bussey William, Hemblington	—	
Bayes Robert, Hemblington	—	
Benstead Wm., Rose corner, Norwich	—	
Cutton Jeremiah, Hemblington	—	
Evans Edward, Walsham St. Lawrence	—	
Evans William, Blofield	—	
Harris William, Hemblington	—	
Weston Nathaniel, Hemblington	—	
	6	2
Burroughes William, Coltishall		
Gowen Benjamin, Hemblington		
Simmons John, Artillery-lane, London		

Hethel.

	S.	C.
Cook William, Hethel	—	
Claxton James, Hethel	—	
Gardiner Samuel, Hethel	—	
Houlton Bowers Edmund, Hethel	—	
	0	4
Stannard William, Hethel		

Hethersett.

	S.	C.
Appleton Robert, Hethersett	—	
Baker Benjamin, Hethersett	—	
Bush Robert, Hethersett	—	
Betts John, Market-place, Norwich	—	
Browne Henry, St. Peter's Mancroft, Norwich	—	
Browne Edward, Hethersett	—	
Blomfield Miles, Hethersett	—	
Blake Robert Wiffin, Norwich	—	
Buckenham William, Hethersett	—	
Chapman Jas. Denny, King-st., Gt. Yarmouth.	—	
Chittock Timothy, Calvert-street, Norwich.	—	
Collett William Reynolds, Hethersett	—	
Davy John, Hethersett	—	
Faulke J., Victoria-st., St. Stephen's, Norwich	—	
Fish John, Hethersett	—	
Fox James, Hethersett	—	
Guyton Henry Clarke Adcock, Hethersett	—	
Harmer Edward, East Carleton	—	
Hood John, jun., Hethersett	—	
Ireland James, Hethersett	—	
Ireland Robert, Lynch green, Hethersett	—	
Ibrooke Richmond, Heigham, Norwich	—	
Jeffries Henry, Hethersett	—	
Johnson William, Hethersett	—	
Lake William Christmas, Hethersett	—	
Lilly Robert, Hethersett	—	
Ling Edmund, St. Augustine's, Norwich	—	
Lofty Jeremiah, Hethersett	—	
Lofty William, Hethersett	—	
Lofty James, St. George's Colegate, Norwich	—	
Porrett John, Hethersett	—	
Robertson Samuel, Hethersett	—	
Rushmore Robert, Blofield	—	
Seppings Peter, Hethersett	—	
Sewell Samuel, Hethersett	—	
Sewell William, Deopham	—	
Sewell George Drake, Compton-street, London	—	
Stannard William, Hethersett	—	
Smith James, jun., Hethersett	—	
Traxton Richard, Hethersett	—	
	13	27
Andrew Wayte William, Wood-hall, Hethersett		
Bilham James, Saxlingham Nethergate		
Curson Smith, Hethersett		
Denew Manning Robert, Rockland		
Ellis Richard, 75, Mornington-road, Regent's-park, London		
Ellis William, Lancaster-terrace, North Gate, Regent's-park, London		
Fairman James, Cringleford		
Fish John, Hethersett		
Foulsham Thomas, Victoria-street, Norwich		
Harvey John, Hethersett		
Hill J., Manor-street, Old Kent road, London		
Langford George, Hethersett		
Lindley J., 2, St. Mary's-terrace, Paddington, London		
Lofty Charles, Hethersett		
Merrison William, Norwich		
Norgate Benjamin Henry, Bank-street, Norwich		
Norgate Thomas Starling, St. Andrew's		
Richardson John, Hethersett		
Richardson Hardman, Hethersett		
Smith James, sen., Hethersett		
Smith Jonathan, St. Giles'-street, Norwich		
Youngman William, Hethersett		

Hingham.

	S.	C.
Allday John, Griston		
Alexander Daniel, Hingham		
Abram Frederick William, East Dereham		
Bayes John, Hingham		
Bassum Charles, Hingham	—	
Bedford William, Hingham		
Bowles John, Palgrave, Norfolk		
Brasnett William Henry, Hingham		
Bowles William, Hingham		
Brine Richard, Tarrant Abbey, Dorset		
Bullen Benjamin, East Dereham		
Bush John, Hingham		
Drewell William, Hingham	—	
Elsy George, Hingham	—	
Elsy William, Hingham	—	
Emmerson William, Hingham	—	
Feltham James, Hingham		
Feltham George, Hingham		
Gilman Philip Case, Hingham		
Gilman Samuel Heyhoe Le Neve, Hingham		
Gapp James, Hingham		
Griggs Thomas, Hingham	—	
Greave David, Hingham	—	
Gricks John, Hingham	—	
Griston James, Hingham	—	
Holman Robert, Hingham		
Hurnard William Burr, clerk, Hingham	—	
Hardy Charles, East Dereham	—	
Harper John, Wymondham		
Hastings J., Forster's-row, Heigham, Norwich	—	
Harwood George Hardy, Hingham		
Hammond Henry, Hingham	—	
Johnson James, Southburgh		
Lane Frankling, Hingham	—	
Large William, Hingham	—	
Lilly William, Hingham		
Lambert James, jun., Hingham	—	
Lilly Richard, Hingham		
L'Estrange Styleman L'Estrange H., Hingham	—	
Large Robert, Hingham	—	
Langford Samuel Charles, Hingham	—	
Matthews John, Hingham		
Mortlock Joseph, Hingham	—	
Norton Francis, Hingham		
Press Edward, St. George's Tombland, Norwich	—	
Pitts John, Sturston, Norfolk		
Pitts George, Hingham	—	
Pitts Phineas, Hingham	—	
Pottle Thomas, Hingham	—	
Partridge Walter J., clerk, Caston near Watton	—	
Pearce Charles, Hingham	—	
Pigg Charles, Hingham		
Pitts Robert Christopher, Thorpe, Norwich	—	
Ray John, East Dereham		
Rose Thomas, Hingham	—	
Rose Henry, Hingham		
Riddlesworth Francis, Hingham	—	
Riddlesworth Francis Joseph, Hingham	—	
Rushbrooke Reuben, Hingham	—	
Ruddock John Barlow, 2, Terrianna-terrace, Gloucester-place, Kentish town, London		
Sewell William, Hingham		
Sewell William, jun., Hingham	—	
Seaman Charles, Hingham		
Spruce William, Hingham		
Stafford John, Hingham		
Tallent John Thomas, Hingham		
Taylor John Oddin, St. Giles', Norwich	—	
Tingay Thomas Roberson, West Rudham		
Taylor Frederick Garritt Oddin, Thuxton-hall	—	
Turner Frederick Sippins, Hingham	—	
Vince John, Hingham	—	
Vince James, Hingham,	—	
Veal David, Gressinghall		
Wodehouse Hon. Wm., clerk, Hingham	—	
Wayland Richard, 12, John-street, Berkeley-square, London, and Woodrising, Norfolk		
Woodrow John, Hingham		
	49	27
Bayes William, Hingham		
Birch H. W., 49, Welbeck-street, Cavendish-square, London.		
Birch Lawrence, 16, Blandford-street, Portman-square, London		
Birch Peregrine, 49, Welbeck-street, Cavendish-square, London		
Birch Thomas Jacob, West Wretham	—	
Bowles George, Palgrave, near Swaffham		
Chapman Wm. Herbert, clerk, Bassingbourne		
Chamberlin Charles, Hingham		
Dutches John, Hingham		
Fisher, William, Hingham	—	
Fisher Frederick Robert, West Wretham	—	
Feltham Philip, Hingham		
Gapp Charles, Hingham	—	
Hurnard William, Hingham	—	
Hubbard John, Hingham	—	
Hunt John, North Elmham	—	
Hubert Musgrave Samuel H., Brandon, Suffolk	—	
Johnson William, Swaffham	—	
Lock William, Carbrooke		
Matthews Richard Buck, clerk, Hingham		
Pitts Philip, Deopham	—	
Partridge Henry Samuel, Great Hockham		
Partridge C. F., clerk, Irchester, Northamptonshire		
Partridge Frederick Robert, Littleport-street, King's Lynn		
Peck James, Swaffham		
Riches James, Hingham	—	
Scott Thomas Edward, Carbrooke		
Thorne Robert Samuel, Horstead		
Vince Edward, Barton Bendish	—	
Wrightup Thomas, Ashill	—	

Holveston.

	S.	C.
Andrews Jesse, Holveston		
Marcon John, Marham-hall		
	2	0

Honingham.

	S.	C.
Balls Thomas, Honingham		
Gooch Stephen, Honingham		
Hipkin Stephen, Honingham		
Hipkin Thomas, Honingham		
Neeve Robert J., Honingham		
Thurston James, Honingham		
Young James, Honingham		
	7	0

Horsford.

	S.	C.
Andrews Robert, Horsford	—	
Andrews Benjamin, Horsford	—	
Allen Henry, Norwich	—	
Booty Benjamin, Blakeney	—	
Blyth Philip, Horsford	—	
Baker John, Horsford	—	
Birkbeck William, Keswick	—	

	S.	C.
Bunn John, Drayton		
Canham John, Horsford	—	
Crome Samuel, Horsford	—	
Cunnell John, Horsford		—
Dalrymple Donald, Norwich	—	
Day James, Horsford	—	
Dunnan Coppin Robert, Norwich	—	
Gage William, Witchingham	—	
Greeves Thomas, Horsford	—	
Greeves James, Horsford	—	
March James, Horsford		—
North Thomas, Ber-street, Thorn, Norwich	—	
Pratt William, Horsford		—
Punt Elijah, Attlebridge	—	
Pye Theophilus, Horsford	—	
Sadd William, Norwich	—	
Sadd William, jun., Coslany-street, Norwich	—	
Savage Robert, Horsford	—	
Steward Timothy, Norwich	—	
Springfield Edmund, Norwich	—	
Springfield Edmund, jun., Norwich	—	
Wortley Robert, Horsford	—	
Wade John, Horsford	—	
Whitear John, Bank-street, Norwich	—	
Winter Thomas, Ber-street, Norwich	—	
	15	**17**
Punt Abraham, Horsford		
Springfield Thomas Osborn, Norwich		

Horsham St. Faith's and Newton St. Faith's.

	S.	C.
Bullard Robert, jun., Horsham St. Faith's	—	
Bullard Robert, sen., Horsham St. Faith's	—	
Bagge Richard, Gaywood	—	
Barker Thomas, St. Mary's, Norwich	—	
Cossey John, Middle-street, Colegate, Norwich	—	
Cook James, Newton St. Faith's	—	
Cook W. Warner, Horsham St. Faith's	—	
Eglington Richard, Horsham St. Faith's	—	
Gunton T., jun., St. Martin's at Oak, Norwich		—
Holl George, New Buckenham	—	
Horne Robert, Cross-street, Heigham	—	
Jex Blake Robert Ferrier, clerk, Great Dunham, Norfolk	—	
King Francis, Smallburgh	—	
Laflin Joseph, Heigham, Norwich	—	
Lovick Thomas, Horsham St. Faith's	—	
Lovick John, Horsham St. Faith's	—	
Newton William, Newton St. Faith's	—	
Newton Richard, Newton St. Faith's	—	
Palmer Benjamin, Newton St. Faith's	—	
Pearse John, Horsham St. Faith's	—	
Pointer George Edmund, Newton St. Faith's		—
Ranelagh Thos. Heron Jones, Viscount, 4, Park-place, St. James', Westminster	—	
Risebrooke John, Horsham St. Faith's	—	
Rackham Matthew, Thorpe, Norwich	—	
Reynolds Samuel, Horsham St. Faith's	—	
Reynolds Edward, Horsham St. Faith's	—	
Reynolds Joshua, Newton St. Faith's	—	
Skipper John, Thorpe, Norwich	—	
Smith Washington, Smallburgh, Norfolk	—	
Scarnett John, Horsham St. Faith's	—	
Tillett William, St. Augustine's-street		—
Turner Edward, Horsham St. Faith's	—	
West John, jun., Horsham St. Faith's	—	
Woodcock Joseph, Newton St. Faith's	—	
Webb Benjamin, Horsham St. Faith's	—	
Watering John, St. Stephen's, Norwich	—	
	24	**12**

	S.	C.
Booty James, Beverley, Yorkshire		
Bilby Walter, St. Clement's, near New Catton Church		'
Brunning James, St. Augustine's-street		
Carman Philip Lincoln, Horsham St. Faith's		
Lemon Benjamin, Aylsham		
Lovick Samuel, Horsham St. Faith's		
Middleton John, Surrey-street, Norwich		
Rice James, Horsham St. Faith's		
Roofe William, Spitalfields, Thorpe Hamlet, Norwich		
Wright Robert, St. Gregory's, Norwich		
Wolsey Cardinal, Hall-lane, Lakenham, Norwich		

Horstead.

	S.	C.
Blake Thomas, LL.D., Doctors Commons, London		
Baldwin John, Horstead		
Bagshaw George, Catton Ward, St. Clement's, Norwich		
Bignold Sir Samuel, Surrey-street, Norwich	—	
Collins John, Horstead		
Cook John, Horstead		
Carman Samuel John, Horstead		
Dawes Willimot Chas., Union-place, Norwich		
Gostling William, jun., Horstead		
Gostling Wm., West Hay, Northamptonshire		
Howlett Horatio, Horstead		
Knott Taylor G., Eye-park, Suffolk		
Kitton John, Ber-street, Norwich		
Lee John, Horstead		—
Morse Charles, Horstead		
Minns Jacob Spence, Horstead		
Postle Robert, Horstead		
Pratt John, Horstead		
Renacre Richard, Horstead		
Thackeray Joseph, Horstead		
Thorne Robert Samuel, Horstead		
Utting John, Stanninghall		
Warman James, Horstead		
Wright James, Horstead		
	17	**7**
Cooke Samuel Cubitt, Horstead		
Gambling John, Buxton Mills		
Lyon E. H., Vaenor Park, Montgomeryshire		
Williamson Thomas, Horstead		

Intwood.

	S.	C.
Allden William Spratt, Intwood		
Muskett Joseph Salisbury, Eaton		
Unthank Clement William, Intwood Hall		

Keswick.

	S.	C.
Blomfield Miles, Keswick		—
Gurney Hudson, Esq., Keswick		
	1	**1**

Ketteringham.

	S.	C.
Blomfield William, Kettering		
Boileau Sir John Peter, Bart., Ketteringham		
Cook John Sewell, Ketteringham		—
Houlton Matthias, Ketteringham		—
	0	**4**
Andrew William Waite, clerk, Hethersett		
Gore Robert, Ketteringham		

Kimberley.

	S.	C.
Cunningham James, Kimberley	—	
Smith Richard, Kimberley	—	
Shingles James, Wicklewood	—	
	0	3

Kirby Bedon.

	S.	C.
Bird William, Kirby Bedon	—	
Day Rev. Edward, Kirby Bedon	—	
Florence William, Ber-street, Norwich	—	
Goose Agas, Theatre-street, Norwich	—	
Harvey William, Mulbarton	—	
Mendham Richard, Kirby Bedon	—	
Money William Frederic, Kirby Bedon	—	
Tomlinson Robert Stewart, St Peter's, Norwich	—	
Turner Charles, Crescent, Norwich	—	
Varvill James, Kirby Bedon	—	
Walley George, Hamlet of Thorpe, Norwich	—	
	9	2
Clare Charles, jun., Kirby Bedon		
Johnson John Godwin, St. Giles', Norwich		
Millett William, Billingford		
Pilgrim John, Chapel-field, Norwich		

Limpenhoe.

	S.	C.
Ayden Benjamin, Limpenhoe	—	
Collins Daniel, Limpenhoe	—	
Douglas Michael, jun., Limpenhoe	—	
Douglas Michael, Limpenhoe	—	
Drake Francis, Limpenhoe	—	
Everitt Isaac, Limpenhoe	—	
Everitt Isaac, jun., Limpenhoe	—	
England John, Limpenhoe	—	
Gray Robert, Limpenhoe	—	
Jermyn William, Limpenhoe	—	
Playford Daniel, Limpenhoe	—	
Wymer William, Southwood	—	
	3	9
Browning Henry, Limpenhoe		
England William, Norwich		

Lingwood.

	S.	C.
Aldous James, Lingwood	—	
Beckett Robert, Lingwood	—	
Burroughes Rev. Jeremiah, Lingwood	—	
Edrich Henry, Blofield	—	
Hinds Thomas, Caister	—	
Mingay William, Lingwood	—	
Mingay William, Herringfleet, Suffolk	—	
Moore John, jun., Thorpe-hamlet	—	
Mitchell William, Lingwood	—	
Pryke James, Lingwood	—	
Read Thomas, sen., Lingwood	—	
Steward Philip, Lingwood	—	
Symonds William, Lingwood	—	
Wright John, Lingwood	—	
Ward William, Lingwood	—	
	13	2
Burroughes William, Coltishall		
Crane Jacob, Reedham		
Howes Thomas, Lingwood		
Read Robert, Norton Subcourse		

Marlingford.

	S.	C.
Carman John, Hardingham	—	
Coggle John, Marlingford	—	
Cooper Rev. John Nelson, Marlingford	—	

	S.	C.
Ewen Thomas L'Estrange, Dedham, Essex	—	
Riches Robert, Marlingford	—	
Riches Henry Bacon, Marlingford	—	
Reeve John, Marlingford	—	
Tooley Jeremiah, Marlingford	—	
	7	1
Cater John, Ipswich-road, Norwich		
Wright Robert, Brandon Parva		

Melton Magna.

	S.	C.
Burrell John Limmer, Melton Magna	—	
Darby James, Marlingford	—	
Eyers Charles, Melton Magna	—	
Pearson George, Melton Magna	—	
Pearson James, Melton Magna	—	
Reynolds John, Melton Magna	—	
Rose Philip, Melton Magna	—	
	1	6
Bloom Thomas, Melton Magna		
Dodd Robert, Melton Magna		
Lombe Charles, Berners-street, Oxford-street, Middlesex		
Rose Thomas, Melton Magna		
Sutton William, Melton Magna		

Melton Parva.

	S.	C.
Aldred Thomas Dove, Melton Parva	—	
Bailey Isaac, West Pottergate-street, Norwich	—	
Barkley Rev. J. C., Melton Parva	—	
Cooper William, Heigham, Norwich	—	
Davey Thomas, Hethersett	—	
Foster Thomas, Melton Parva	—	
Hipperson Samuel, Melton Parva	—	
Long James, Melton Parva	—	
Lovett Robert, Attleborough	—	
Ringer Daniel, Melton Parva	—	
Reynolds John, Melton Magna	—	
	4	7
Tompson James, Melton Parva		
Wright Robert, Union-place, Norwich		

Morley St. Botolph.

	S.	C.
Blazer Robert, Morley St. Botolph	—	
Cooper the Rev. C. B., Morley St. Botolph	—	
Haythorpe William, Morley St. Botolph	—	
Long Berney, Morley St. Botolph	—	
Matthews Thomas, Merton	—	
Peacock George, Morley St. Botolph	—	
Rowing Archibald, Wicklewood	—	
Sutton Thomas, Morley St. Botolph	—	
	7	1
Potter Thomas, Wattlefield, Wymondham		

Morley St. Peter.

	S.	C.
Ayton Noah, Morley St. Peter	—	
Anthony Edward, Morley St. Peter	—	
Browne, J. T. G., Morley St. Peter	—	
Barker George, Morley St. Peter	—	
Clarke Robert, Morley St. Peter	—	
Howell Richardson, Morley St. Peter	—	
Matthews John, Morley St. Peter	—	
Tubby William, White Cottage, Scotland-green, Tottenham, Middlesex	—	
Wright Murrell, Morley St. Peter	—	
	8	1

Moulton.

	S.	C.
Bellman Augustus Frederick, Moulton		
Boult Edward, Moulton		
Broom John, Moulton		
Fane Christopher, Moulton	—	
Woods George James, Moulton		
Wright Adam, Moulton		
Wright Samuel, Moulton		
	6	1
Howard Robert, Halvergate		

Mulbarton.

	S.	C.
Castle Wm., St. Peter's Mancroft, Norwich	—	
Claxton George, Mulbarton	—	
Cremer Charles, Mulbarton	—	
Gaze Thomas, Hingham		
High Samuel, Stoke Holy Cross		
King Sam, 3, Chapel Field-road, Norwich	—	
Lucas, Rev. R. G., Mulbarton	—	
Squires Paul, Mulbarton		
Todd William, Mulbarton	—	
Turner John, Mulbarton		
Titlow Rev. Samuel, Crescent, Norwich	—	
Youngs John, King-street, Norwich	—	
	7	5
Bellairs Sir Wm., Oakley-square		
Brookes Christmas, East Harling		
Blake John, Mulbarton		
Branch Benjamin, Swainsthorpe		
Brett Davy John, Mulbarton		
Brown John, Bagnigge Wells-road		
Cooper John V. N., No. 3. Crescent, Norwich		
Davy John, Mulbarton		
Lain John, Mulbarton		
Sewell, Rev. Thomas, Brooke		
Sexton Richard, Gaywood Hall		

Newton Flotman.

	S.	C.
Garrard James, Newton Flotman	—	
Harvey Charles, Newton Flotman		
Long H. Churchman, clerk, Newton Flotman		
	2	1
Fellowes R., jun., Betteswell Hall, Leicestershire		
Muskett James, Newton Flotman		
Muskett James, Surlingham		
Mutimer George, Newton Flotman		
Thorpe William Smyth, Shropham		

Plumstead Great.

	S.	C.
Bacey Robert, Hellesdon		
Brown Robert, Great Plumstead		
Cole Edward Rev., Great Plumstead	—	
Foster Francis, Great Plumstead	—	
Goose William, Great Plumstead	—	
Haggata Isaac, Great Plumstead	—	
King Randell, Great Plumstead	—	
Newman Robert, Great Plumstead	—	
Scott Jonathan, Great Plumstead	—	
Tills John, Great Plumstead	—	
Tuck J. J., clerk, Stevenage, Little Wymondley, Hertfordshire		
	8	8
Campbell A. Francis, Great Plumstead		
George John, Great Plumstead		
Muskett Joseph Salisbury, Eaton		
Maidstone Robert, Great Plumstead		

Plumstead Little.

	S.	C.
Boast Moses, Little Plumstead	—	
Crowe John, St. Stephen's-street, Norwich	—	
Crowe Robert, Little Plumstead		
Gaze Charles, Little Plumstead	—	
Jarmy Daniel, Little Plumstead		
Newman James, Little Plumstead		
Nicholls John, Little Plumstead		
Nicholls George, Little Plumstead		
Tubby John, Little Plumstead	—	
Waters John, Little Plumstead		
	7	3
Boughton John, Little Plumstead		
Letherdale John, Little Plumstead		
Read George, Little Plumstead		

Poringland.

	S.	C.
Beverly Michael, Brooke	—	
Beverly Tobias, Great Poringland		
Beverly Thomas, Poringland		
Cooper John Norton Valentine, St. Stephen's, Norwich		
Critoph Joseph, Great Poringland		
Clarke Edward, 3, Lyall-place, Belgrave-square, London		
Ellwood Henry, St. John's Timberhill, Norwich	—	
Fox John, Heigham, Norwich		
Harvey Edward Kerrison, Mousehold		
High Isaac, Lakenham, Norwich		
Jones Peter, St. Margaret's, Norwich		
King Charles, Poringland		
King James, junr., St. Benedict's, Norwich		
Matthews Norman, Poringland		
Parker John, Great Poringland		
Seago Thomas, West Poringland		
Taylor Joseph, Great Poringland		
Thetford Robert, Great Poringland		
Utting Henry, Great Poringland		
Wright Jonathan, Great Poringland		
Wright Joseph, Great Poringland		
	12	9
Baily Rishton Roberson, Tower, London		
Black William, Dawlish, Devon		
Brereton Rev. Shovel, Briningham		
Culling James, Belaugh		
Fiske Rev. John Hammond, East Cliff-house, Hastings, Sussex		
Harvey John, Mousehold House, Thorpe		
Haward John, East Tuddenham		
Johnson John Lovick, Swaff ham		
Pilch Anthony, Yarmouth		
Utting Henry, Rackheath		
Utting John Colney		

Postwick.

	S.	C.
Attoe William, jun., Postwick	—	
Fox Thomas Colman, Norwich	—	
Fox Richard, Blofield		
Fox Frederick, Surrey-street, Norwich	—	
Gillet Cyrus, Postwick-hall	—	
Goose William Norman, Postwick	—	
Seeley John, Postwick		
	1	6
Attoe George, Postwick		
Ford Rev. Charles, Postwick Rectory		
Herring Rev. Armine, Thorpe		
Parker John William, Postwick		
Parker James, Postwick		

	S.	C.

Rackheath.

Barnes George, Rackheath —
Clarke John, Rackheath —
Etheridge Thomas, Rackheath —
Hodgson Francis Henry Stone, Rackheath —
Stracey Henry Josias, Rackheath-hall —
Utting Henry, Rackheath —
Watts Robert, Rackheath —

Pilgrim John, Chapel Field, Norwich —
Tuck John, Rackheath —

7 | 0

Ranworth with Panxworth.

Cutton William, South Walsham St. Mary —
Cutton Jeremiah, Ranworth —
Drake John, Ranworth —
Greaves John William, Ranworth —
Kerrison Roger, St. George's Tombland, Norwich —
Kerrison John, Ranworth —
Palmer Frederick, Panxworth —
Rose William, Panxworth —
Rix Matthew, Panxworth —
Saunders Thomas, Ranworth —
Thurtle Robert, Panxworth —
Thurtle Robert, Ranworth —

Base John, Westhall, Suffolk —
Elliott Edward, Ranworth —
Riches John, Panxworth —

11 | 1

Reedham.

Browne Robert, Reedham —
Bee Robert, Reedham —
Barnes William, Reedham —
Barton William, Reedham —
Boult George, Reedham —
Crane Jacob, Reedham —
Duffield John, Reedham —
Gilbert Horace, Reedham —
Goffin James, Reedham —
Gowing William, Reedham —
Hudson George, Reedham —
Hindle William, Lowestoft —
Jackson John, Limpenhoe —
Jones Samuel, Reedham —
Knights James, Berney Arms, Reedham —
Mallett John Browning, Wicklewood —
Nichols Jonathan, Reedham —
Rose John, Shoreditch, London —
Sales John, Reedham —
Smith Samuel, Reedham —
Stone Benjamin, Reedham —
Ward James, Reedham —

18 | 4

Barnes James, Reedham —
Cockerill Ezekiel, Reedham —
Chester Francis, Reedham —
Hindle Nathaniel, Reedham —
Shephard Stephen, Norton —

Rockland St. Mary.

Blake George, Eaton, Norwich —
Blake Joseph, City-road, Lakenham, Norwich —
Browne James, Mutford-hall, Suffolk —
Blake William, Rockland St. Mary —

	S.	C.

Dewe Rev. Joseph, Rockland —
Edwards John, Rockland St. Mary —
Forder Robert, Rockland —
George George, Rockland —
King James, Caister, near Norwich —
Nobbs John, Bramerton —
Parker John, Rockland St. Mary —
Steward Robert, Rockland —

4 | 8

Blake Robert, Rockland St. Mary —
Goodram Richard, Rockland —
Goodram William, Ashby —
Goose Robert, Union-place, Norwich —
Gilbert Robert, jun., Ashby-hall —
Moore Julian, Rockland —
Nobbs Samuel, Rockland —
Roberts James, Rockland St. Mary —
Thurston Robert, Rockland St. Mary —
Wall John, Rockland —

Runhall.

Atkins Henry, Runhall —
Breeze William, Runhall —
Brown Murrell, Runhall —
Brown William, Runhall —
Cobb Richard, Runhall —
Coleman John, Runhall —
Hardy Charles, Runhall —
Murrell Charles, Runhall —
Neve John, Runhall —
Neve William, Runhall —
Rose Philip William, Norwich —
Smith Jeremiah, Runhall —
Smith George, Hingham —
Thurling Peter, Carleton Forehoe —

8 | 11

Thurling Robert, Runhall —

Salhouse.

Barber Benjamin J., Salhouse —
Browne Samuel, Salhouse —
Browne S., jun., St. Martin's-at-palace, Norwich —
Bateman William, Shottisham —
Bussey Charles, Salhouse —
Campling John, jun., Salhouse —
Colman James Jeremiah, Stoke Holy Cross —
Fox Edward, Sprowston —
Farman William, Salhouse —
Farman Bartholomew, Salhouse —
Farman Henry, St. Martin at Oak, Norwich —
Flowerday Joshua, Salhouse —
Hargrave William, Salhouse —
Hargrave Hezekiah, Salhouse —
Hall William, Salhouse —
Hales Baseley, Salhouse —
Holsworth Robert, Union-street, Boston-street, Hackney-road, London —
Howlett Harcourt, Salhouse —
Jones John, Salhouse —
Leist William, Salhouse —
Leeder William, Salhouse —
Nicholson Jesse, Salhouse —
Plowman Robert, Old Catton —
Sutton Robert, Salhouse —
Sutton John, Salhouse —
Sutton Edward, Salhouse —
Trower William, Salhouse —

	S.	C.
Von Halle John Henry, Oulton	—	
Ward Richard, Salhouse	—	
Winter Thomas, Salhouse	—	
	24	6
Campling John, Salhouse		
Crowe Robert, Horning Ferry		
Hawse William, Lakenham		
Wilkin John, St. Augustine, Norwich		
Woodcock William, Salhouse		

Southwood.

	S.	C.
Case William, Southwood	—	
Tuthill John, Southwood	—	
	2	0
Emeris Rev. John, Barton-street, Gloucester		
Leathes Henry Carteret, Limpenhoe		

Spixworth.

	S.	C.
Eaton George, Spixworth	—	
Howes Henry, clerk, Spixworth	—	
	2	0
Holmes Benjamin, St. Clement's-hill, Norwich		
Holmes Benjamin, jun., Spixworth		
Longe John, Spixworth		

Sprowston.

	S.	C.
Atkinson Robert, Sprowston	—	
Aldridge John, Sprowston	—	
Anderson William, Sprowston	—	
Barnes George, Sprowston	—	
Bailey Elijah C., the Shrubbery, Norwich	—	
Bailey Anthony Winter, clerk, Mount-street, Everton, Liverpool	—	
Banfather Henry William, Sprowston	—	
Buckenham John Charles, Tombland, Norwich	—	
Burrows William, St. Saviour's, Norwich	—	
Burrows Peter, Sprowston	—	
Burrows Thos. Yeomans, Pockthorpe, Norwich	—	
Burrows John, Sprowston	—	
Burrows Thomas, Sprowston	—	
Bream J., 4, Jamaica-place, Kennington, Surrey	—	
Bream Charles John, Upper-market, Norwich	—	
Bunting John, St. Giles'-gates, Norwich	—	
Brooks Thomas, St. Andrew's, Norwich	—	
Baxter William, St. Julian, Norwich	—	
Baxter Henry, East Dereham	—	
Barnard John Cuthbert, St. Swithin's, Norwich	—	
Bugden Thomas, St. Mary's, Norwich	—	
Bugg Isaac, Surrey-street, Norwich	—	
Bridges Benj., Constitution-place, Sprowston	—	
Clarkson Frederick, Sprowston		
Chambers John William, Sprowston		
Coaks Richard, Golden Dog-lane, St. Saviour's Norwich	—	
Cozens James, St. Swithin's, Norwich		
Copeman J., jun., St. Peter's Mancroft, Norwich	—	
Copeman Wm., St. Peter's Mancroft, Norwich	—	
Campbell Charles, Weasenham, Norfolk	—	
Copeman Davy J., Fish-street-hill, London		
Crawshay Charles, Bracondale, Norwich		
Cutler John, Sprowston		
Copeman P. T., St. Peter's Mancroft, Norwich	—	
Decaux William, Dereham-road, Norwich	—	
Delph William, St. Augustine's, Norwich	—	
Edwards William, Sprowston		
Fitt John, Sprowston		
Fickling Robert, Elm-hill, Norwich	—	
Francis Thomas, Newmarket-road, Norwich	—	

	S.	C.
Gale William, Sprowston	—	
George William, Sprowston	—	
Goose Robert, Union-place, Norwich	—	
Hammond George, Ber-street, Norwich	—	
Hicklenton T., Julian-place, Heigham, Norwich	—	
Hicklenton William, London-street, Norwich	—	
Harrison Edmund, Sprowston	—	
Hardy Henry, Beccles	—	
Hicklenton George, St. Faith's lane, Norwich	—	
Hardy William Hardy Cozens, Letheringsett	—	
Hastings John, West Pottergate-st., Norwich	—	
Hastings Edmund, Sprowston	—	
Ives Richard Newton, King-street, Norwich	—	
Lingwood Jeremiah, Sprowston	—	
Loose Charles, Sprowston	—	
Mason John, Constitution-place, Sprowston	—	
Mann Samuel, Magdalen-street, Norwich	—	
Millard Chas. Wm., St. George of Tombland	—	
Meachen Edward, Dereham, Norfolk	—	
Methold John William, Wighton, Norfolk	—	
Middleton George, the Grove, Lakenham	—	
Mitson Samuel, Norwich	—	
Palmer William, St. Augustine's, Norwich	—	
Pilgrim Robert, Thetford	—	
Pratt William, Sprowston	—	
Robertson George Rockhill, Sprowston	—	
Robertson Robert William, Oulton, Suffolk	—	
Smith John, St. Augustine's, Norwich	—	
Smith David, St. Clement's, Norwich	—	
Stracey John, Sprowston	—	
Scott Samuel, Sprowston	—	
Slade Daniel Davis, Sprowston	—	
Smith Joseph De Carle, Magdalen-st., Norwich	—	
Stamp William, Norwich	—	
Sexton R. W., St. George's Colegate, Norwich	—	
Sexton W. H., St. Swithin's, Norwich	—	
Sexton R. A. W., Calvert-street, Norwich	—	
Soman D., St. George's Colegate, Norwich	—	
Stafford Thomas, Crook's-place, Norwich	—	
Sadler John, Ludham	—	
Steward Isaac, Rose-cottage, Sprowston	—	
Spinks Samuel, Calvert-street, Norwich	—	
Towler Michael, Spitalfield's, Norwich	—	
Towler Abel, Unthank's-road, Norwich	—	
Tillett Henry Jacob, St. Andrew's-st., Norwich	—	
Thorn William, Sprowston	—	
Wilson William, Scarning, Norfolk	—	
Watts Thomas, St. Augustine's, Norwich	—	
White William, Pearce's field, Sprowston	—	
Widdows John, Sprowston	—	
Wiseman Purland R., Muspole-street, Norwich	—	
Yallop William, Sprowston	—	
Yellop Henry, Sprowston	—	
	38	55
Acocks David G. D., 16, Sussex-gardens, London		
Allen John D. H., Sprowston		
Andrews Frederick, Sprowston		
Blake Joseph, City-road, Lakenham, Norwich		
Bacon Robert, Fring		
Brown William, St. Margaret's, Norwich		
Brown William, Calvert-street, Norwich		
Batchelor Thomas, Bracondale, Norwich		
Baxter William, St. Julian, Norwich		
Berney Hanson, Bart., Sheepy, Warwickshire		
Barnard James Michael, Old Bailey, London		
Browne Edmund, Ten Bell-lane, Norwich		
Browne Edmund, Fleet-street, London		
Clark John, St. Paul's, Norwich		
Chambers William, Thorpe Hamlet		
Denny Thomas, Hardingham, Norfolk		
Edwards Edward M., London-street, Norwich		

S. | C.

Edwards Thomas Paul, Sprowston
Hall William, King-street, Norwich
Head George Head, Carlisle
Ketton John, Sprowston Grange
Mears Thomas, Whitechapel-road, Middlesex
Martineau P., Brixton-hill, Streatham, London
Middleton George, Eaton, Norwich
Rolfe Chas. E. N. S., clerk, Heacham, Norfolk
Rolfe Edmund Nelson, clerk, Morningthorpe
Smart Henry, St. Saviour's-lane, Norwich
Stracey Sir Henry Josias, Rackheath-hall
Sadler Samuel, North Walsham
Tilt William, Claremont-square, London
Thurlow Charles Augustus, Malpas, Cheshire
Wethers John, Hellesdon, Norwich
Wilson King Samuel, 25, Mincing-lane, London
Withers Peter, St. Clement's, Norwich
Wilde Wm., St. John's Maddermarket, Norwich
Widdows Jonathan, Norwich
Widdows Philip, Heigham, Norwich

Stoke Holy Cross.

Bailey Rev. John, Stoke Holy Cross
Birkbeck Henry, Stoke Holy Cross
Castleton Elijah, Stoke Holy Cross
Claxton William, Stoke Holy Cross
Colman Edward, Cannon-street, London
Drake John, Stoke Holy Cross
Gunn Daniel, Stoke Holy Cross
Harvey Sir R. J., Mousehold-house, Norwich
Harmer Frederic William, Heigham, Norwich
Harmer Thomas, Heigham-road, Norwich
Hearn Matthew, Stoke Holy Cross
Pearce Robert, Stoke Holy Cross
Tillett John, Stoke Holy Cross
Underwood John, King-street, Norwich
Womersley Joshua, Stoke Holy Cross
Westrup Philip, Stoke Holy Cross

9 | 7

Burrows George Crisp, Palace-plain, Norwich
Colman Jeremiah James, Stoke Holy Cross
Colman Robert, Newmarket-terrace, Norwich
Dix Thomas, Stoke Holy Cross
Edwards Samuel, Surlingham
Horne William, Stoke Holy Cross
Kerrison Roger, Tombland, Norwich
Stevens John Thomas, Castle-ditches, Norwich
Seago Jeremiah, Stoke Holy Cross

Strumpshaw.

Atkins Thomas, Strumpshaw
Burton Robert, Strumpshaw
Denton James, Strumpshaw
Goffin Alexander, Strumpshaw
Hylton John, Strumpshaw
Josselyn John, Sproughton, Ipswich
Moore John, Plumstead-road, Thorpe
Plow Christopher, Strumpshaw
Pyle Thomas, Burlingham St. Andrew
Simmons Thomas, Strumpshaw
Thurkettle William, Cantley
Whitbread Edward Salter, Strumpshaw

7 | 5

Barnes John Tuck, Strumpshaw
Fox Thomas Colman, St. Stephen's, Norwich
Spooner John, sen., Strumpshaw
Spooner John, jun., Strumpshaw
Thompson James, Hassingham

S. | C.

Tuck Thomas Gilbert, Strumpshaw
Waters John, Strumpshaw
Wells William, Strumpshaw

Surlingham.

Barnes Samuel, Surlingham
Bignold William Atkins, Wymondham
Fisk Henry, Surlingham
Florence William Daniel, Norwich
Freeman James, Norwich
Frosdick Henry, Surlingham
Gowen Thomas, Trowse Newton
Julians John Read, Surlingham
Murrell Gibbs Howes, Surlingham
Muskett James, jun., Surlingham
Morgan John Brandram, Norwich
Nickolds Stephen, Surlingham
Pottle Robert, Surlingham
Parker Samuel, Surlingham
Parker Walter, Surlingham
Quadling William, Surlingham
Rich James, Surlingham
Rudd John Martin, Surlingham
Scott John, clerk, Surlingham
Skipper Thomas, Surlingham
Tuck Charles Edward, St. Giles'-street, Norwich

10 | 11

Brightwell Thomas, jun., Norwich
Collett Rev. William, Thetford St. Mary
Edwards Samuel, Surlingham
Florence Richard Robert, Yarmouth
Glendening John Browne, Norwich
Osborn Richard, Surlingham
Primrose Archibald Dalmany, Dalmeney-park
Tuck Rev. William Gilbert, Moulton
Westgate Robert Bond, Surlingham

Swainsthorpe.

Cannell Jacob, Swainsthorpe
Gooch George Sutton, Swainsthorpe
Mutimer George, Swainsthorpe
Raven Benjamin, Swainsthorpe

2 | 2

Carpenter Robert, Swainsthorpe
Long Henry Churchman, Newton Flotman
Raven John, Swainsthorpe

Swardeston.

Bond Robert, Swardeston
Bullard Richard, St. Giles'-street, Norwich
Cannell Henry, Swardeston
Cannell H., Nightingale-lane, Clapham, Surrey
Cannell Isaac Webster, New Lakenham
Cannell Charles, Trowse
Hubbard John, Swardeston
Hall James, Swardeston
Hall James, jun., Swardeston
Jeffries Samuel, Lakenham
King Robert, Swardeston
Kemp Robert Palmer, Coltishall
Parr Ezra, Swardeston
Raven Benjamin, Swardeston
Wenn James William, Swardeston

2 | 13

Bailey Edmund, Swardeston
Cunningham William, Swardeston
Davy Robert, Hethersett
Featherstone Thomas, Swardeston

	S.	C.
Hall James, Swardeston		
Shimmon Robert Hy., Scoles'-green, Norwich		
Twiss Christopher, Swardeston		

Taverham.

	S.	C.
Burton Rev. Robert Clerke, Taverham	—	
Cross John, Taverham	—	
Micklethwait Rev. John Nathnl., Taverham-hall	—	
Mumford William, Taverham	4	0
Delane William, Hellesdon		
Walter Henry F., 17, Taviton-street, Gordon-square, London		

Thorpe St. Andrew.

	S.	C.
Albin Daniel, Thorpe	—	
Belding William, St. Clement's-hill, Norwich	—	
Bolingbroke Augustus Frederick Cooke, Thorpe	—	
Bracey Robert, Thorpe	—	
Brightwin John, Thorpe	—	
Bright John, Thorpe	—	
Clabburn William Houghton, Thorpe	—	
Dale James, Thorpe	—	
Dale James, jun., Euston-square, London	—	
Dale Robert, Thorpe	—	
Dale William, Framingham Pigot	—	
Dye George Arthur, St. Andrew's Broad-street	—	
Frost Rev. William, Thorpe-lodge	—	
Goldsmith Thomas, Thorpe	—	
Gurney Francis Hay, Thorpe	—	
Herring Rev. Armine, Thorpe	—	
Jay George, Thorpe	—	
Jecks Charles, Thorpe-grove	—	
Jecks Isaac, Trowse Newton	—	
Matthews John, Thorpe	—	
Moore Stephen, Thorpe St. Andrew	—	
Moll Abraham, Thorpe	—	
Palmer Thomas Hitchen, Thorpe	—	
Patteson Henry Staniforth, Thorpe	—	
Rayner John, Thorpe	—	
Starling William, Thorpe	—	
Starling Samuel Gibson, Thorpe	—	
Weston Charles, Thorpe	—	
Wright John, Norwich	—	
Whittaker Samuel, Thorpe	—	
	15	15
Albin Samuel, Thorpe		
Davey Joseph, Thorpe		
Harvey Kerrison, Boulogne, in France		
Hawkins John, Trowse Millgate		
Jecks Charles, jun., Thorpe		
Jecks William, jun., Thorpe		
King Robert, Thorpe		
Leathes Henry M., Herringfleet, Suffolk		
More John, Thorpe Hamlet		
Rump Robert, St. Clement's, Norwich		
Sabberton Thomas, Thorpe		
Shardelow Benjamin, Thorpe		
Steward William, Richmond-place, Bracondale, Norwich		
Wright Robert John, Thorpe		

Trowse Newton.

	S.	C.
Alborough Thomas, Trowse Newton	—	
Gowing George L., Trowse Newton	—	
Gowen John, Trowse Newton	—	

	S.	C.
Plant James, Trowse Newton	—	
Read Thomas William, Trowse Milgate	—	
Spencer Christopher J. M., King-st., Norwich	—	
Turner John, Trowse Newton	—	
	4	3
Bayliss Henry, Pottergate-street, Norwich		
Carter Rev. Geo., Church Close, Norwich		
Goose Robert, Trowse Newton		
Lock Henry, St. Catherine's-terrace, St. John's Sepulchre, Norwich		
Money Archibald General, Crown-point, Trowse Newton		
Morgan Jno. Brandram, King-street, Norwich		
Sparke Alfred, Trowse Newton		

Tunstall.

	S.	C.
Boult Edward Robert, Tunstall	—	
Gillett John, Halvergate	—	
Gillett George, Brooke	—	
Skinner James, Tunstall	—	
	4	0
Gillett William, Martham		
Haddon Rev. Thomas Comfield, Freethorpe		

Upton with Fishley.

	S.	C.
Adams Benjamin, Upton	—	
Agus Robert, Upton	—	
Brown William Henry, Upton	—	
Cater John, South Walsham St. Mary	—	
Capon Robert, Upton	—	
Farman Samuel, Upton	—	
Hood James, Upton	—	
Maddle John, Aldeby	—	
Potter Rev. Joseph, Lingwood	—	
Stout Joseph, Upton	—	
Squire John, Fishley	—	
Turner John, Upton	—	
Turner William, Upton	—	
Waters John, Upton	—	
Waters Adam, Upton	—	
Willgrass John Daniels, Upton	—	
Willgrass Benjamin, Upton	—	
Wright George, Upton	—	
	17	1
Allen Robert Stout, Upton		
Brown E., St. Mary, Cardiff, Glamorganshire		
George Thomas, Upton		
Greaves Rev. John William, Ranworth		
Ireland Thomas, Sall		
Marsham Rev. Edward, Sculthorpe		
Meadows T., 98, Crawford-st., Bryanstone-square		
Mumford Benjamin, Upton		
Paxman John, Upton		
Stout James, Brentford		
Taylor William Huke, Upton		
Whaites Edward, Langley		
Wright James, Caister West-end		

Walsham South Saint Lawrence.

	S.	C.
Cater John, Ipswich-road, Norwich	—	
Fowler Read R., South Walsham St. Lawrence	—	
Harbord Richard B., South Walsham St. Mary	—	
Harbord Robert, South Walsham St. Mary	—	
Littlewood Wm., South Walsham St. Lawrence	—	
Sibel Thomas, South Walsham St. Lawrence	—	
Westgate Wm., South Walsham St. Lawrence	—	
	6	1

	S.	C.
Broom Samuel, Upton		
Cater Enoch, South Walsham St. Lawrence		
Heath William, Ludham		
Hewitt Edward, South Walsham St. Lawrence		
Millard William Salter, Catton		
Pearce William, Aldeby		
Toplis Rev. John, South Walsham St. Lawrence		

Walsham South St. Mary.

	S.	C.
Benns John, South Walsham St. Mary		
Burton Luke John, South Walsham St. Mary	—	
Bugg James, South Walsham St. Mary	—	
Edrich Robert, South Walsham St. Mary	—	
Jary Wm. Heath, South Walsham St. Mary	—	
Juby Joseph, South Walsham St. Mary	—	
Roberson George, South Walsham St. Mary	—	
Spanton James, South Walsham St. Mary	—	
	8	0

Welborne.

	S.	C.
Colls John, Welborne		
Donne W. Bodham, 12, St. James'-sq., London	—	
Gooch J. Kerr, East Tuddenham	—	
Green Charles, Welborne	—	
Howe Thomas, Welborne	—	
Hatton Jonathan, Mattishall	—	
Holland Robert, Welborne	—	
Norton Leonard, Welborne	—	
Porrett Richard, Welborne	—	
Porrett William, Hellesdon, Norwich	—	
Sands Nicholas, Welborne	—	
Vassar William, East Tuddenham	—	
Vassar George, Mattishall	—	
Vassar George, East Tuddenham	—	
Wilkinson John, Welborne	—	
	4	11
Crawshay Richard, Ottershaw-park, Surrey		
Child David, Bawburgh		
Doy William, Loddon		
Edwards Timothy, Pentney		
Johnson J. Barham, Welborne		
Porrett James, Welborne		
Taylor George, Mattishall		

Whitlingham.

	S.	C.
Taylor Samuel, Whitlingham	—	
Lombe Chas., Berner's-st., Oxford-st., Middlesex	0	1

Wickhampton.

	S.	C.
Bullman Robert, Wickhampton	—	
High John, Wickhampton	—	
Leathes Rev. Frederick, Reedham	—	
Waters William, Freethorpe	—	
Wiffen Josiah, Wickhampton	—	
Youngs James, Wickhampton	—	
	4	2

Wicklewood.

	S.	C.
Acton William, Wicklewood	—	
Bacon James, Wicklewood	—	
Barker William, Wicklewood-hall	—	
Barker William, Wicklewood	—	
Barker William, Hingham	—	
Barnard William, Wicklewood	—	
Boardman James Theobald, Eaton, Norwich	—	

	S.	C.
Cann James Cooper, St. Benedict's, Norwich	—	
Collison Rev. Henry, East Bilney	—	
Culpit Samuel, Wicklewood	—	
Cann James, Wicklewood	—	
Colman Thomas, Norwich	—	
Colman Thomas Edward T., Wymondham	—	
Duffield John, Wicklewood	—	
Darby William, clerk, Riddlesworth, Norfolk	—	
Day George, Ber-street, Norwich	—	
Garth John, Wicklewood	—	
Head Robert, Wicklewood	—	
Head William, jun., Wicklewood	—	
Kirk James, Wicklewood	—	
Miller George, Wicklewood	—	
Mann Richard, Wicklewood	—	
Mann John, Wicklewood	—	
Patterson Frederick William, Norwich	—	
Plowman John, Wicklewood	—	
Roe Simon, Wicklewood	—	
Sultzer John, St. Augustine, Norwich	—	
Turner Joseph, Hackford	—	
Tuttle William, Wicklewood	—	
Wade Christmas, Wicklewood	—	
Wrigglesworth John, Barnham Broom	—	
	15	16
Boardman Alfred, Upper Surrey-st., Norwich		
Cann Samuel, Wymondham		
Foulsham Ambrose, Wicklewood		
Hubbard Henry, Wicklewood		
Rix William, Wicklewood		
Rivett James, Gorleston		
Rowing Archibald, Wicklewood		
Scott William, Wicklewood		
Webster John, Wicklewood		
Weston Godfrey, Wicklewood		
Wrigglesworth William, Wicklewood		

Witton.

	S.	C.
Culley George Buddry, Witton		
Green James Spurgeon, Witton		
Green Henry Prescott, Witton		
Penrice John, Witton		
Ward Joseph, Witton		
	5	0
Penrice Thomas, Kilborough-house, Swansea, Glamorganshire		
Whaites Charles, Rougham		

Woodbastwick.

	S.	C.
Cator Albemarle, Woodbastwick	—	
Dunster Rev. Henry Peter, Woodbastwick	—	
Goulder Samuel, Woodbastwick	—	
Goulder John, Woodbastwick	—	
Long Charles, Woodbastwick	—	
	5	0
Cator John, Woodbastwick		
Sutton Robert, Woodbastwick		

Wramplingham.

	S.	C.
Bretton Robert, Wramplingham	—	
Cann John Stephenson, Wramplingham	—	
Cullyer George, Wramplingham	—	
Cullyer William, Wramplingham	—	
Fisher Joseph, Wramplingham	—	
Fisher George, Wramplingham	—	

	S.	C.
Marsham Rev. Thos. John G., Wramplingham	—	
Matthews Thomas, Wymondham	—	
Ringer William, Wramplingham	—	
Sayer Shadrach, Wramplingham	—	
	5	5
Fisher Clear, Wramplingham		
Fisher Thomas, Wramplingham		
Leeder Ambrose Goldsmith, East Dereham		

Wreningham.

	S.	C.
Alexander John, Wreningham		
Day James, Wreningham		
Day Matthew, jun., Carleton Rode	—	
Jermyn Vincent, Wreningham	—	
Kersey James, Wreningham		
Nicholds Peter, Wreningham	—	
Pigg James William, Thorpe-road, Norwich	—	
Rushbrooke Thomas Allen, Wreningham	—	
Upcher Arthur Wilson, Wreningham		
	5	4
Atthill Lombe, clerk, Halesworth		
Day Robert, Wreningham		
Jeffers Samuel, Norwich		
Long Berney, Morley		
Parker James, Wymondham		
Saint Samuel, Norwich		

Wroxham.

	S.	C.
Crowe William, Wroxham		
Dyball Daniel, Wroxham	—	
Green James, Wroxham	—	
Green William Frederic, Wroxham	—	
Humfrey Robert Blake, Wroxham	—	
Hayward Nelson Hylton, Wroxham	—	
Hylton Henry Hayward, Wroxham	—	
Nuthall Nevil, Wroxham	—	
Pile Robert, Wroxham	—	
Trafford Edward William, Wroxham	—	
Trafford William Henry, Wroxham	—	
Utting Charles, Wroxham		
	11	1
Green Henry Prescott, Witton		
Platten John, Magdalen-street, Norwich		

Wymondham.

	S.	C.
Able William, Wymondham		
Adams Samuel, Wymondham		
Ayton Charles, Wymondham		
Ayton James, Wymondham	—	
Anderson John, Wymondham		
Aves Richard, Spooner-row		
Allen Bryant, Scole's-green, Norwich		
Barnard George, Wymondham		
Bale William, Wymondham		
Banham William, Wymondham		
Barker William, Wymondham		
Betts John, West Pottergate-street, Norwich	—	
Betts Thomas, Wymondham		
Bedford Philip, Thorpe hamlet, Norwich	—	
Bell Robert, Davey-place, Norwich	—	
Bolingbrooke George E., St. Giles', Norwich	—	
Blazey James, Wymondham		
Boileau Francis George M., Ketteringham		
Boileau John Elliot, Ketteringham		
Bolton Esau, Wymondham		
Browne Charles, Wymondham	—	
Browne Thos., Wattlefield division, Wymondham	—	
Bunn Austin, Wymondham	—	

	S.	C
Bunn John, Wymondham	—	
Bunn John, Wymondham	—	
Burcham John, Wymondham	—	
Buttolph John, Wymondham	—	
Buttolph William, Wymondham	—	
Bignold John Henry, Surrey-street, Norwich	—	
Bignold Chas. Edward, Surrey-street, Norwich	—	
Blazey Lazarus, Wymondham	—	
Bunn Anthony, Wymondham	—	
Banham Robert, Wymondham	—	
Burgiss Robert, Wymondham		
Burrell William, Wymondham	—	
Cann Thomas Frederic, Wymondham	—	
Cann John, Wymondham		
Cann Samuel, Wymondham		
Cann William Robert, Wymondham	—	
Cann William, Wymondham		
Cann William, Wymondham		
Cann John Stephenson, Wymondham		
Carpenter Joseph, Wymondham		
Clarke Cardell, Wymondham	—	
Clarke William Robert, Wymondham		
Clarke John Welham, Bracondale, Norwich		
Clarke William Batson, Wymondham		
Clarke Alfred John, Wymondham		
Colsey Francis, King-street, Norwich		
Coleman Dennis, Wymondham		
Colman James Roger, Wymondham		
Cooper Charles, Wymondham		
Cooper James, jun., Wymondham		
Cooper Robert, Wymondham		
Cooper James, sen., Wymondham		
Cowell William, Wymondham		
Cowell Henry, Wymondham		
Crane Charles, Wymondham		
Cranness William, Wymondham		
Culpit John, Wymondham		
Daniel James, jun., Wymondham		
Daniel William Dack, clerk, Wymondham		
Dannock William, Wymondham		
Davy John, Wymondham		
Davy Joseph, Thorpe, Norfolk		
Eagling Joseph, Wymondham		
Emms Thomas, Thorpe St. Andrew's		
Eden Robert, Wymondham		
Ellis William, Wymondham		
Foulsham James, Wymondham		
Foulsham Richard, Wymondham		
Frost Thomas, Fishgate-street, Norwich	—	
Fryer William Goodwin, Wymondham	—	
Gay Jonathan, Wymondham	—	
Gibbs Edward Charles, Exmouth, Devonshire	—	
Gleeds Ellis Leathes, Hoe Hall, Suffolk	—	
Goodman Robert, Wymondham	—	
Gowing James, Mattishall	—	
Grisdale Joseph, Wymondham	—	
Halls Robert Coggle, Wymondham	—	
Hardiment Thomas Mace, Carbrooke	—	
Hardiment Joseph Mace, Wymondham	—	
Hardiment John Mace, Wymondham	—	
Harper Samuel, Watton	—	
Hare Richard, St. Gregory's, Norwich	—	
Hart Charles, St Giles'-street, Norwich	—	
Hare John, Wymondham	—	
Harvey William, Wymondham	—	
Haylett John, Suton-street, Wymondham	—	
Hewison Joseph, Rose-lane, Norwich	—	
Hill Samuel Secker, Mile-end-lane, Eaton	—	
Hill Samuel, St. Augustine, Norwich	—	
Hobart Charles Robert, Bramerton	—	
Holman Edward, St. Benedict's, Norwich	—	

D

	S.	C.
Hubbard John, Wymondham		
Hutt James, Great Russell street, Bloomsbury, Middlesex	—	
Ives George, No. 8, Belgrave Terrace, Great College-street, Camden Town, London	—	
Kemp Richard, Wymondham	—	
Kemp Jonathan, Swanton Morley	—	
Kemp Henry John, Wymondham	—	
Kemp John, Wattlefield, Wymondham	—	
Kerrison James, Norwich	—	
Kett William, Wymondham	—	
Knight George Custance Leak, Wymondham	—	
Knights James, St. Gregory's, Norwich	—	
Lain Bartholomew, Wymondham	—	
Lain William, Wymondham	—	
Lewis Lewis, Wymondham	—	
Lee Edward, Sparham	—	
Leeder James, Wymondham	—	
Long David, Wymondham	—	
Long Robert, Wymondham	—	
Long Robert, Besthorpe,	—	
Lucas Chas. T., Sister-house, Clapham, Surrey	—	
Mays Thomas, Wymondham	—	
Massingham Henry Alpe, St. Catherine's-plain, Norwich	—	
Mare Robert, St. Augustine, Norwich	—	
Miller John, Wymondham	—	
Mitchell John, Wymondham	—	
Morris Noah, Wymondham	—	
Mayhew George, Heigham, Norwich	—	
Minns William M. J., St. Gregory's, Norwich	—	
Neave Jonathan, Wymondham	—	
Ockley Simon, Wymondham	—	
Parker James, Wymondham	—	
Parker John, Hockering	—	
Paul William Francis, Bracondale, Norwich	—	
Peto Sir Samuel Morton, Bart., Somerleyton-hall	—	
Peel Edmund, Crook's-place, Norwich	—	
Pigg Joseph, Hellesdon-road, Norwich	—	
Poll David, Wymondham	—	
Poll John Cooper, Wymondham	—	
Poll Samuel, St. Saviour's, Norwich	—	
Poll Jeremiah, Wymondham	—	
Potter Thomas, Wymondham	—	
Plowman Samuel, Wymondham	—	
Race John, Wymondham	—	
Race Miller, Wymondham	—	
Race William, Wymondham	—	
Race William, Wymondham	—	
Ray Henry, clerk, Hunston, Suffolk	—	
Reynolds Zaccheus, Wymondham	—	
Rix Thomas Colman, Wymondham	—	
Rolfe James, Wymondham	—	
Roper Samuel, Croxton	—	
Rudling Edward, Wymondham	—	
Rudling John, Wymondham	—	
Runacres Wm., Oxford-st., Heigham, Norwich	—	
Secker Robert, Wymondham	—	
Smith Robert, Wymondham	—	
Skippon James, Market-place, Norwich	—	
Skippon James, jun., Mancroft, Norwich	—	
Sparkhall John Hovell, Attleborough	—	
Spalding John, Wymondham	—	
Spinks Thomas Gardiner, Wymondham	—	
Spruce Robert, Carleton Forehoe	—	
Standforth Saul, Wymondham	—	
Standley John, Wymondham	—	
Standley William, Wymondham	—	
Story Jehu, Wymondham	—	
Stanforth Stephen, Wymondham	—	

	S.	C.
Stammers Robert, Wymondham	—	
Swann Joshua, Pottergate-street, Norwich	—	
Taylor Thomas, Wymondham	—	
Taylor William, Wymondham	—	
Thurston John, Wymondham	—	
Thurston Jonathan, Wymondham	—	
Tipple Jasper Howes, Wymondham	—	
Tipple George, Wymondham	—	
Turrell William, Wymondham	—	
Thurling Benjamin, Wymondham	—	
Townshend Timothy, St. Clement's, Norwich	—	
Trixon Frederic, Wymondham	—	
Ward Randall, Wymondham	—	
Warman James, Castle Meadow, Norwich	—	
Watson Henry Spore, Wymondham	—	
Watts William Harvey, Wymondham	—	
Weston Godfrey, Wymondham	—	
Wilkinson Benjamin, Town-close, Norwich	—	
Wilden John, East Dereham	—	
Willett Edward, Eaton, Norwich	—	
Wodehouse G. F. Queen's-road, Yarmouth	—	
Wodehouse Edward, Witton-hall	—	
Woodbine John, Wymondham	—	
Wright Robert, Wymondham	—	
	61	123
Barker Edmd., Duke-street, Norwich	—	
Barnard Richard, Wymondham	—	
Beeston John, Wymondham	—	
Beevor Charles, Chelsea, London	—	
Bidder G. P., Great George-street, Westminster	—	
Bolingbrook A. F. C., Thorpe next Norwich	—	
Boileau Sir John Peter, Ketteringham	—	
Bowgen Philip, Wymondham	—	
Browne Thomas, Wymondham	—	
Browne Charles, Wymondham	—	
Bunn Thomas, Southtown, Great Yarmouth	—	
Bignold Samuel Frederick, clerk, Tivetshall	—	
Buck Zachariah, Upper Close, Norwich	—	
Blyth Samuel, Wymondham	—	
Camp William alias Jermyn, Wymondham	—	
Cann John Stephenson, Wymondham	—	
Carver James, 28, Finsbury Circus, London	—	
Chapman John, Diss	—	
Chapman John, Diss	—	
Clarke Edward Palmer, Wymondham	—	
Clint George, Bedford square, London	—	
Cowell Robert, Wreningham	—	
Cowell William, Brixton, Surrey	—	
Cowell George, Pimlico, London	—	
Cook John, Wacton	—	
Cross James, Victoria-street, Norwich	—	
Davy Walter, Barnham Broom	—	
Donthorne W. J., Hanover-square, London	—	
Emma Thomas, Thorpe St. Andrew's	—	
Edwards John, Cambridge	—	
Edwards Henry, Cambridge	—	
Fickling Robert, Hungate, Norwich	—	
Flower Samuel, Wymondham	—	
Foyson Robert, Norwich	—	
Fulcher Edward, Wymondham	—	
Geldart Thomas, 51, Piccadilly, Manchester	—	
Gray George, Wymondham	—	
Grimes John, Norwich	—	
Hall John, Wymondham	—	
Hippesley John S., Stratton,-street, Middlesex	—	
Hood John, Sussex-street, Norwich	—	
Jermyn William, Wymondham	—	
Johnson Samuel, Lowestoft	—	
Kippon Joseph, Ber-street, Norwich	—	
Kuivett William, Wymondham	—	
Knivett William, jun., Wymondham	—	

	S.	C.
Knight George Brown Leak, Framingham Earl		
Knowles Matthew, Runeton		
Lain Edward, Wymondham		
Laskey William, Goat-lane, Norwich		
Leatherdale John, Wymondham		
Lincoln James, King-street, Norwich		
Long James, Wymondham		
Lofty Charles, Hethersett		
Lucas Thomas, Roehampton, Surrey		
Mace John, Coltishall		
Marshall John, Horsforth-hall, Leeds		
Matthews Robert, Wymondham		
Mendham Thomas, Yarmouth		
Moore Foster Grand, Norwich		
Mottram James, Bank-street, Norwich		
Newhouse Robert, Coltishall		
Ninham Henry, Thorpe Hamlet, Norwich		
Page Samuel, Black Horse-road, Norwich		
Page Samuel, Thorpe, Norwich		
Peacock George, Wymondham		
Pigg Joseph, St. George's Colegate, Norwich		
Pigg Joseph Gage, Wymondham		
Poll Joshua, Nazing, Essex		
Postle Samuel Tolver, Wymondham		
Preston Frederick, East India-road, London		
Rackham Thomas, St. Peter Hungate, Norwich		
Race William, Wymondham		
Reynolds Noah, Blofield		
Richardson John James, Rose Cottage, Suffolk-street, Forest-gate, West Ham, Essex		
Ridgeway Thomas, 5, King William-st., London		
Rogers Nathaniel, senr., 15, Pearl-st., Spital-fields, London		
Rudledge William, Carleton Forehoe		
Sexton Benjamin, Wymondham		
Skoulding Charles, Wymondham		
Sparkhall James Limmer, Wymondham		
Springfield Thos. Osborn, St. Mary's, Norwich		
Standley John, jun., Wymondham		
Stoughton Clarke, Sparham		
Stammers John, Wymondham		
Stubbs James, Wymondham		
Tipple Jasper Howes, Wymondham		
Tipple William Howes, Wymondham		
Tipple William Howes, Brochand House, Lower Meudon, near Paris		
Tipple Cornelius, Oldfield-road, Salford, Lancashire		
Tunaley Robert James, Wymondham		
Turner Edward, Norwich		
Traxton Israel, Wymondham		
Tillott Samuel, New Buckenham		
Warner William Wilson Lee, East Dereham		
Wicks William Watts, Thetford		
Wild William, Post Office-street, Norwich		
Wiseman Isaac, Norwich		
Wodehouse Berkeley, Kimberley-hall		
Wood Starr, Suffolk-street, Pentonville		
Woods Henry, Wymondham		
Wright Daniel Bishop, Besthorpe		
Youngman John Turner, Wymondham		

Norwich Outvoters.

	S.	C.
Abbs Zachariah, St. Giles'-hill, Norwich	—	
Alexander Francis, Gatesend near Fakenham	—	
Addison Thomas, Tombland, Norwich	—	
Barnard Dennis, Bracondale, Norwich	—	
Barwell John, jun., Surrey-street, Norwich	—	
Barber John, Chalk-farm, Norwich	—	
Barber Alfred Willsea, Norwich	—	

	S.	C.
Barber John Lee, Norwich		—
Beare Samuel Shalders, Town-close, Norwich		—
Benyon Richard, 84, Grosvenor-square, London	—	
Benyon John Fowler, Lower-close, Norwich		—
Bolingbroke Charles Nathl., St. Giles', Norwich		—
Bower Garton J., Golden Dog-lane, Norwich		—
Brown Philip Utton, Hellesdon		
Bright John, Earlham, near Norwich		
Cavell Robert Corry, St. Swithin's, Norwich		—
Coldham Rev. John, Snettisham		
Collyer, William, Tombland, Norwich		—
Cooper Fletcher John, Lakenham		
Coppin Edward, 4, Crescent-place, Norwich		—
Copeman Edward, Bethel-street, Norwich		.
Cooke William Harris, the Close, Norwich		—
Darkens Canuel, St. Stephen's-road, Norwich		—
Day Peter, Heigham, Norwich		—
Day William, Hamlet of Trowse, Norwich		—
Decaux Arthur, Norwich		—
Durdin Alexander Warham, Heigham, Norwich		—
Elmer John, St. John's Sepulchre, Norwich		—
Emery George, Norwich		—
England William, M.D., Ipswich		—
Field John, Coltishall		
Forrester George, St. Andrew's, Norwich		—
Fox William, St. Stephen's, Norwich		—
Ford Foyster W. N., Calvert-street, Norwich		—
Ford Robert, St. George's-plain, Norwich		—
Francis John, No. 1, New Boswell-street, Lincoln's Inn, Middlesex		
Francklin George Fairfax, Attleburgh		
Francklin Frederic Fairfax, Attleburgh		
Francklin John Fairfax, West Newton		
Grimmer Frederic, Crescent, Norwich		—
Gostling F., Bedford-street, Heigham, Norwich		—
Grout George, Magdalen-street, Norwich		—
Hart Edward Fair, 1, South-street, New North-road, London		
Hall William, Town-close, Norwich		—
Hill James F., St. Giles'-terrace, Norwich		—
Hotblack John, Orford-hill, Norwich		—
Hurry Thomas, St. Peter's Mancroft, Norwich		—
Jarrold W. Pightling, Newmarket-road, Norwich		—
Jarrold Samuel, Bracondale, Norwich		
Jarrold Thomas, Thorpe next Norwich		
Johnson Jacob, London-street, Norwich		
Kerrison John, Norwich		
Kemp Isaac, Heigham, Norwich		
Ledger Nassan William, Ipswich		—
Minns George William, Tombland, Norwich		—
Mills James, Castle-meadow, Norwich		
Mottram James Nasmith, Bank-street, Norwich		
Neal William Valentine, Hamilton-place, St. Pancras, London		
Nichols William Peter, Surrey-street, Norwich		—
Noverre Frank, near Theatre, Norwich		
Page Samuel, Starling-place, Norwich		
Page Jeremiah, Chapel-field-road, Norwich		
Page Robt., King-street, St. Etheldred, Norwich		
Page William, Rupert-st., Union-place, Norwich		
Palmer Nathaniel, Thorpe, Norwich		
Parker William Hooper, Saham, Norfolk		
Paddon Rev. Thomas, Mattishall		
Parr William Burrell, St. Giles', Norwich		—
Pellew George, clerk, Lower-close, Norwich		
Phillippo Matthias, Newmarket-road, Norwich		—
Pratt William, Lowestoft		
Preston Arthur, Bank-street, Norwich		
Postle William, Chapel-field, Norwich		
Rackham Thomas, Elm-hill, Norwich		
Rackham Robert A., clerk, Whatfield, Suffolk		—

	S.	C.
Restieaux Joseph, Lady's-lane, Norwich	—	
Ross John, near the Barrack, Norwich	—	
Rust Rev. Cyprian T., The Crescent, Norwich	—	
Sharman John, Pottergate-street, Norwich	—	
Sothern Samuel, Norwich	—	
Starr Thomas, Union-place, Norwich	—	
Sharp W. Robert, Chapel-field, Norwich	—	
Theobald Thomas, London-street, Norwich	—	
Unthank Clement William, Intwood-hall	—	
Watson George, Fakenham	—	
Webster Wm., Mousehold-house, Thorpe Hamlet	—	
Webster Benj., Grove-place, Lakenham, Norwich	—	
Wells Robert, Thorpe, Norwich	—	
Wright Thomas Lane, East Dereham	—	
	39	49
Barker George, jun., Close, Norwich		
Bircham Francis Thomas, Burhill-house, Walton-on-Thames, Surrey		
Blake Charles Jex, the Close, Norwich		
Browne Ebenezer, Earlham		
Bradell Alexander, Castle Meadow, Norwich		
Buxton Edward Charles Henning, Chigwell, Essex		
Cater John, Ipswich-road, Norwich		
Calvert Thomas, All Saints', Norwich		
Chittock Timothy, Calvert-street, Norwich		
Clowes Francis, St. Andrew's, Norwich		
Clowes Thomas, Ashbocking, Suffolk		
Clark Alfred, Wymondham		
Cole Edward, Great Plumstead		
Coalman George Rising, St. Peter per Mountergate, Norwich		
Cross James, Victoria-street, Norwich		
Dalrymple Donald, Norwich		
Eade Hartt, Norwich		
Elwin Hastings, Thorpe		

	S.	C.
Francis Benjamin, Twyford		
Garnham Richard, Creeting		
Grout George, St. Saviour's, Norwich		
Houghton Richard, St. Faith's-lane, Norwich		
Hudson Anthony, Norwich		
Kent Edmund, Fakenham		
King John, Lynn		
Laws John Porter, 5, St. George's Terrace, Yarmouth		
Lown Thompson, St. Stephen's-road, Norwich		
Mendham Lockett Wace, Norwich		
Miller Henry, Norwich		
Minns Isaac, Crook's-place, Norwich		
Morse Charles, Thorpe, Norwich		
Nichols James, 13, Smith-row, Burlington Gardens, London		
Page Robert, senr., Bawburgh		
Page Robert, jun., Toll's-court, St. Stephen's, Norwich		
Page Robert, jun., Bawburgh		
Page Timothy, Rupert-st., Union-place, Norwich		
Riches Daniel William, London-st., Norwich		
Rigg Richard, Bethel-street, Norwich		
Rix Henry, Golden Ball-street, Norwich		
Rump James Smith, Booton		
Smart William, King-street, Norwich		
Smith Robt., Crawford-st., Marylebone, London		
Smith Samuel, 8, Star-st., Paddington, London		
Specer William, Heacham		
Spink Henry, Eaton, Yorkshire		
Steward Timothy, Heigham, Norwich		
Taylor George, 13, Upper St. Giles'-st., Norwich		
Titlow Samuel, Crescent, Norwich		
Tomlinson Robt. Stewart, Davey-place, Norwich		
Turner Charles, Crescent, Norwich		
Wade John, Bank-street, Norwich		
Woolsey John, Heigham, Norwich		

LODDON DISTRICT,

COMPRISING THE PARISHES OF

	S.	C.
Aldeby.		
Beckett Robert, Aldeby		
Carpenter Philip Samuel, Norwich	—	
Chandler John, Aldeby	—	
Godbolt William, Blundeston, Suffolk	—	
Gowing James Warden, Aldeby		—
Grimmer James, Aldeby		—
Hunt Robert, Aldeby		—
Lurkins James, Aldeby		—
Powles Isaac, Aldeby		—
Spratt Samuel, Burgh St. Peter		—
Woodroffe Thomas, Beccles, Suffolk		—
Youngs William, Aldeby		
	4	8
Carpenter Thomas, Ronde, Devizes		
Colman Edward Hovell, Toft Monks		
Pearce William, Aldeby		
Read Henry, Beccles		
Sutton William Merrison, Aldeby		
Weavers William, Aldeby		
Alpington.		
Andrews Samuel, Alpington		—
Minister James, Alpington		—
Reeder Charles, Alpington		—
Ward Randall, Alpington		—
	0	4
Nichols William Peter, Norwich		
Postle Rev. Edward, Yelverton		
Seago Thomas, Poringland		
Trafford William Edward, Wroxham		
Utting Samuel, Brooke		
Ashby.		
Basey George, Ashby		—
Berry William, Ashby		—
Elden Richard, Ashby		—
Folkes Sir Wm. John Henry B., Hillington Hall		—
Goodram William, Ashby		—
Gilbert Robert, Ashby		—
Mansfield Daniel, Ashby		—
Pegg David, Ashby		—
Smith John, Ashby		—
Starling James, Claxton		—
Starling James, jun., Ashby		—
	0	11
Goodram Richard, Rockland		
Webster Thomas, St. Stephen's, Norwich		
Bergh Apton.		
Batchelder Jeremiah, Claxton		—
Broad John, Bergh Apton		—
Clarke Samuel, Bergh Apton		—
Cook Robert William, Bergh Apton		—
Freestone James, Alpington		—
Freestone George, Alpington		—
Goff George, Bergh Apton		—

	S.	C.
Madden Wyndham Carlyon, Bergh Apton		—
Peake John, Bergh Apton		—
Pearston Thomas, Bergh Apton		—
Smith William, Bergh Apton		—
Seago William, Bergh Apton		—
Smith John, Bergh Apton		—
Strowger Samuel, Bergh Apton		—
Tompson Henry Kett, Great Witchingham		—
Utting Samuel, Mundham		—
Utting James, Bergh Apton		—
Wall Thomas, Bergh Apton		—
Youngs William, Rockland		—
Youngs James, Rockland		
	8	12
Batchelder Samuel, Bergh Apton		
Cook Thomas, Swanington		
Clarke Thomas, Bergh Apton		
Carr Freeman, Bergh Apton		
Collison Rev. Henry, East Bilney		
Dunham James, Bergh Apton		
Holmes Rev. John, Brooke		
Mayes James, Ashby		
Brooke.		
Albrough Charles, Brooke		—
Barling Rev. Charles Harris, Brooke		—
Bridges James, Brooke		—
Beal Rev. William, L.L.D., Brooke		—
Brown Joseph, Brooke		—
Daniels John Cater, Brooke		—
Horne Robert, jun., Heigham, Norwich		—
Holmes George John, Brooke		—
Harwin Benjamin, Brooke		—
Maggs John, Brooke		—
Tidnam James, Brooke		—
Utting Geo., St. Andrew's, Ilketshall, Suffolk		
	7	5
Bridges Henry James, Brooke		
Brigham John, St. Catherine's-plain, Norwich		
Critoph John, Brooke		
Fisher Francis, Brooke		
Gillett George, Brooke		
Harvey George, Brooke		
Holmes Rev. John, Brooke-hall		
Hurring Simon, Brooke		
Kett George Samuel, Brooke-house		
Scadding William, Brooke		
Stanton Robert, Rendham, Suffolk		
Tibbenham Charles, Brooke		
Tidnam James, jun., Brooke		
Broome.		
Aldus Charles, Broome		—
Boatwright Ambrose, Bungay		—
Chase Robert, Bungay		—
Crowfoot William, Broome		—
Copeman Job, Ashley-crescent, City-road, London		—
Darby Robert, Bungay		—

	S.	C.
Harper William James, Broome		
Long James Ford, Broome	—	
Lawn John, Broome	—	
Lawn Thomas, Broome	—	
Mann William, Ditchingham	—	
Meade John, Broome	—	
Palmer John, Broome	—	
Palmer Jonathan, Broome	—	
Scott Samuel, Bungay	—	
Spilling Benjamin, Broome	—	
Smith Thomas, Bungay	—	
Wills Charles, Bungay	—	
	9	9
Chenery Frederick, Bungay St. Mary		
Colvile William, Baylham		
Copeman Job, Lowestoft		
Elden James, Broome		
Gamble Geo. S., 11, St. James'-square, London		
Harper William James, Broome		
Hogg Robert, Bungay		
Johnson Charles Thos., jun., Rowland's Castle, Haveant, Hants		
Kitton William M., Palace-street, Norwich		
Lawn James, Great Yarmouth		
Lawne John, St. Nicholas, Southtown, Suffolk		
Mann Richard, Ditchingham		
Spalding Benjamin, Broome		

Burgh St. Peter.

	S.	C.
Barber James, Gorleston		
Beare Robert, Aldeby		
Boon George William, Burgh St Peter		
Boon William, Burgh St. Peter		
Cooper Robert, Burgh St. Peter		
Ellis Thomas, Burgh St Peter		
Flaxman Benjamin, Burgh St. Peter		
Grimmer Marcus John, Haddiscoe		
Hammond John, Gorleston, Suffolk		
Hammond George, Burgh St. Peter		
Jones Samuel Simpson, Beccles, Suffolk		
Love Rev. Edward Messenden, Somerleyton		
Larkman Robert, Somerleyton		
Reeve Richard Henry, Lowestoft		
Sayer John, Burgh St. Peter		
Tibbenham Thomas, Burgh St. Peter		
Tripp Edward, Burgh St. Peter		
Woolterton James, Burgh St. Peter		
Yallop Robert, Burgh St. Peter		
	10	9
Boycott Rev. William, Burgh St. Peter		
Boon Charles, Hedenham	·	
Cottingham Edmond, Cove Hithe, Suffolk		
Daniels Thomas, Burgh St. Peter		
Durrant James, Burgh St. Peter		
Parker John, Lowestoft		
Parker William, Burgh St. Peter		

Carleton St. Peter.

	S.	C.
Beauchamp George, Birch-hill, near Reading	—	
Fish John, Carleton	—	
Hylton Edmund Perkins, Carleton	—	
	1	2

Chedgrave.

	S.	C.
Armsby Joseph, Chedgrave	—	
Barrett Rev. Henry Alfred, Chedgrave	—	
Burton William, Thurton		
Branch Robert, Chedgrave	—	
Gilbert Rev. John, Chedgrave		
Gilbert Edward, Chedgrave	—	
Hoddy Edgar, Chedgrave	—	
Webster John Crisp, Beccles		
Watson James, Chedgrave	—	
	0	9
Amy William, Thorpe		
Beaumont John, Mendham		
Crisp John, travelling abroad		
Tuck Rev. George, Wollington, Herts		

Claxton.

	S.	C.
Chapman Jeremiah, Claxton	—	
Gilbert George, Claxton	—	
High William, Shottesham	—	
Martin Robert, Claxton	—	
	2	2
Batchelder Jeremiah, Claxton		
Chapman Benedict Lawrence, Stone Buildings, Lincoln's Inn, London		

Ditchingham.

	S.	C.
Alborough John, Bungay	—	
Barrett Benjamin, Ditchingham	—	
Bedingfield.John Longueville, Ditchingham	—	
Brock Jeremiah, Ditchingham	—	
Browne George, Ditchingham	—	
Brown Gilbertson Matthias, Ditchingham	—	
Bull Isaac, Bungay	—	
Chapman James, 29, Bethel-street, Norwich	—	
Cudden William, sen., Ditchingham	—	
Davy Robert, Ditchingham	—	
Dutt William, Ditchingham	—	
Gordon Alexander, Ellingham	—	
Harris Absolom, Ditchingham	—	
King Michael, Ditchingham	—	
Mann Richard, Ditchingham	—	
Minns James, Broome	—	
Minns John, Ditchingham	—	
Millard Philip Salter, Ditchingham	—	
Moore John, 2, St. James'-terrace, Camden-town, London	—	
Ninham James, Ditchingham	—	
Pipe John Watson, Ditchingham	—	
Raven Mark, Ditchingham	—	
Sayer Manning, Bungay Trinity	—	
Scudamore William Edward, Ditchingham	—	
Smith Frederic, Bungay	—	
Sutton Robert, Broome	—	
Tibnam Samuel, Ditchingham	—	
Titshall William, Beccles	—	
Tyrrell Mark, Ditchingham	—	
Utting Thomas, Ditchingham	—	
Walker William, Ditchingham	—	
Woodrow Robert, Bungay	·	
	18	19
Brown John, Gorleston, Suffolk		
Cuddon William, Ditchingham		
Earl Richard, Bungay		
Margitson John, Ditchingham		
Minns James, Ditchingham		
Minns Jacob Spence, Horstead		
Pulford Robert, 65, St. James'-street, London		
Smith Robert, Ditchingham		
Wales Geo., No. 8, Great St. Helen's, London		

	S.	C.

Earsham.

	S.	C.
Alborough Henry, Earsham		
Banham Robert, Earsham	—	
Burgess Richard, Earsham		
Calver William, Earsham	—	
Crowe Henry, Earsham	—	
Capon Edward, Earsham	—	
Clarke Harvy Robert, Earsham	—	
Clutton George, Earsham	—	
Cuddon Thomas, Ditchingham	—	
Drake Rivers Mayor, Earsham	—	
Drake Frederic, Earsham	—	
Dybell Robert, Bungay	—	
Fisk George, Earsham	—	
Goode William Peckham, Earsham	—	
Hammond Lomb William, Earsham	—	
Harris George, Earsham	—	
Hogg William, Earsham	—	
Haward Charles, Earsham	—	
Minns Charles, Earsham		
Neech Cornelius, Broome	—	
Parrington Fermore Thomas, Earsham		
Rackham John, Earsham	—	
Reeve Rising John, Bungay St. Mary	—	
Rope Charles, Earsham	—	
Roper John, Bungay		
Smith Samuel, Bungay St. Mary	—	
Smith Henry, Bungay St. Mary	—	
Thompson Thomas Hamond, Earsham	—	
	3	25
Cook Charles, No. 1, Rhodes-terrace, Queen's-row, Dalston, London		
Dalling Sir William Windham, Bart., Earsham		
Parrington William, Earsham		
Smith Robert, Earsham	..	

Ellingham.

	S.	C.
Butcher Robert, Ellingham	—	
Bonfellow Edmund, Yarmouth	—	
Cobb Rev. Robert, Ellingham	—	
Clarke Philip, Ellingham	—	
Ingate William, Ellingham	—	
Lodge Samuel, Ellingham	—	
Read Benjamin, Ellingham	—	
Smith Robert Rogers, Baylim-mill		
Spanton John, Ellingham	—	
Spurgeon William, St. Andrew's	—	
Ward James, Ellingham	—	
Walker John, Kirstead	—	
	6	6
Cannell John, jun., Ellingham		
Hayward Frederic, Ellingham		
Smith Henry, Ellingham		

Geldeston.

	S.	C.
Atkins Benjamin, Geldeston	—	
Bradnum William, Geldeston	—	
Dowson Edward Utting, Geldeston	—	
Dowson Septimus, Southtown	—	
Gower John Spurling, Geldeston	—	
Kerrich John, Geldeston	—	
Read John, Geldeston	—	
Turrell George, Geldeston	—	
	8	5
Cradock Edward Hartopp, Brazen Nose College, Oxford		
Dowson Henry Gibson, Geldeston		
Garden John Lewis, Redisham-hall		

	S.	C.
Hall Charles, Geldeston		
Mainwaring Rev. John, Swainswick, Somersetah.		
Neech Alfred, Bungay		
Rose William, Geldeston		

Gillingham All Saints.

	S.	C.
Balls Charles, Gillingham All Saints		
Balls James, Gillingham All Saints		
Banham George, Gillingham All Saints	—	
Farr John, Gillingham All Saints		
Nixon Charles, Gillingham All Saints		
Playford John, Gillingham All Saints		
Thacker William, Gillingham All Saints		
	5	2
Banham John, Gillingham All Saints		
Creak Henry Brown, Lightcliffe, near Halifax, Yorkshire		
Sturman Richard, Gillingham All Saints		
Woodthorpe William, Gillingham All Saints		

Gillingham St. Mary.

	S.	C.
Brundell Benjamin, Gillingham St. Mary		
Bexfield Benjamin, Gillingham St. Mary	—	
Beckett William, Gillingham St. Mary		
	1	2
Crowfoot William Edward, Beccles		
Crisp John, jun., Beccles		
Haward Samuel, Beccles		
Larke Robert, Geldestone		
Thompson John, Beccles		

Haddiscoe.

	S.	C.
Beckett John, Haddiscoe	—	
Brabben Henry, Thorpe next Haddiscoe	—	
Dawson Jonathan, Toft Monks	—	
Dawson Thomas, Haddiscoe		
Dye Thomas, Raveningham	—	
Flaxman James, Metfield, Suffolk	—	
Flaxman Robt., Ilketshall St. Lawrence, Suffolk		
Flaxman John, Haddiscoe	—	
Flaxman Benjamin, Haddiscoe	—	
Forder James, Toft Monks	—	
Garrood Charles Ling, Haddiscoe	—	
Grimmer Henry Septimus, Haddiscoe	—	
Hubbard William, Haddiscoe	—	
Jex William, Hopton, Suffolk	—	
Kett George, Haddiscoe	—	
Maddison William Haward, Herringfleet, Suffolk		
Nicholas Rev. George Frederic, Haddiscoe	—	
Palmer Ambrose Reeve, Haddiscoe-hall		
Rivett William, Gorleston, Suffolk	—	
Rushmer William, Haddiscoe	—	
	18	2
Bexfield Joseph, Thorpe next Haddiscoe		
Elliott Jacob, Haddiscoe		
Flaxman Robert, Haddiscoe		
Godfrey William, Haddiscoe		
Grimmer George, Haddiscoe		
Hoggett John, Yarmouth		
Shardalow William, Hales		
Woodthorpe Thomas, Gisleham, Suffolk		

Hales.

	S.	C.
Beckett John, Hales	—	
Brister Isaac, Hales	—	
Easter Charles, Hales	—	
Fuller Robert Freston, Hales	—	

	S.	C.
Hammond Thomas, Hales		
Spurgeon William, Raveningham	—	
Spurgeon Amos, Hales	—	
Whig Thomas, Hales	—	
	4	4
Easter Edward, Hales	—	
Freston Anthony, Hales	—	
Long John, Kirby Cane	—	
Long William, Hales	—	
Preston George, Hales	—	
Rodwell Geo., Loddon	—	
Youell Joseph, Kirby Cane	—	

Hardley.

	S.	C.
Belward John, Geldeston	—	
Brundall James, Hardley	—	
Carver William, Hardley	—	
Cross William Edward, Hardley	—	
Goddard Edward, Hardley	—	
Goddard William, Hardley	—	
Plow John, Hardley	—	
Shreeve Henry Isaac, Ashby	—	
	0	8
Manthorpe James, Hardley		

Heckingham.

	S.	C.
Blunderfield Henry, Heckingham	—	
Cooke John, Heckingham	·	
Forder James, Heckingham	—	
Gilbert Richard Henry, Chedgrave	—	
Hobson Rev. William Willis, Loddon	—	
Hunting Daniel, Loddon	—	
Lewin Charles Abbotts, Heckingham	—	
Riches Daniel, Loddon	—	
Shardlow Thomas, Norton	—	
	4	5

Hedenham.

	S.	C.
Appleton John, Hedenham	—	
Boon Charles, Hedenham	—	
Buck Richard, Hedenham	—	
Cattermole George, Hedenham	—	
Chambers Rev. John Peter, Hedenham	—	
Murrall Thomas Robert, Hedenham	—	
Stamford William, Hedenham	—	
Skinner Charles, Hedenham	—	
	2	6
Durrent Edward, Hedenham		
Hopper John, Hedenham		

Hellington.

	S.	C.
Martin William, Hellington	—	
	1	0

Howe.

	S.	C.
Allington Carman, Howe	—	
Briggs William, Howe-green	—	
Cole Robert, Howe Village	—	
	3	0
Cooper John Norton Valentine, Crescent, St. Stephen's, Norwich		
Tattersall William, Howe		

Kirby Cane.

	S.	C.
Boggis James, senr., Kirby Cane	—	
Boggis James, Ellingham	—	
Crickmore William, Kirby Cane	—	

	S.	C.
Doe John, Kirby Cane	—	
Doe John, jun., Kirby Cane	—	
Doe James, Kirby Cane	—	
Howes Edward, Kirby Cane	—	
Long Thomas, Kirby Cane	—	
Long John, Kirby Cane	—	
Mills Edward, Yarmouth, Norfolk	—	
Olley David, Kirby Cane	—	
Roberts John, Ditchingham	—	
Spall Henry, Bungay, Suffolk	—	
Sparkes Benjamin, Kirby Cane	—	
Upcher Abbott, Kirby Cane	—	
	11	4
Berners Right Hon. Lord, Keythorpe-hall, Leicestershire		
Florence William, Gorleston		
Pleasance Robert, Kirby Cane		

Kirstead.

	S.	C.
Butcher George, Kirstead	—	
Kent James, Brooke	—	
Kerrison Charles, Kirstead	—	
Martins William, Kirstead	—	
Paget Alfred Tolver, Kirstead	—	
Thrower James, Kirby Cane	—	
Tibbenham Charles James, Kirstead	—	
	4	3
Bence Henry, Thorington, Suffolk		
Bence Thomas Starkie, Thorington, Suffolk		
Smith Robert, Shottesham		
Whall Dring William, Kirstead		

Langley.

	S.	C.
Burton Thomas, Langley	—	
Cossey John, Langley	—	
Proctor Thomas Beauchamp, Langley-park	—	
Read John, Langley	—	
Rudd John, Langley	—	
Spence Robert, Langley	—	
Spence James, Langley	—	
	0	7
Cleveland James, Lowestoft		
Hargrave Thomas, Langley		
Long Robert, Blofield		
Proctor Sir William Beauchamp, Bart., Langley Park		

Loddon.

	S.	C.
Batchelder Samuel, Loddon	—	
Braddock Thomas, Loddon	—	
Blunderfield Francis, Loddon	—	
Baker William, Loddon	—	
Branch Daniel, Loddon	—	
Baker John, Loddon	—	
Crake John, Loddon	—	
Cannell John, Loddon	—	
Chapman John, Loddon	—	
Cumby William, Chedgrave, Norfolk	—	
Clarke Job Nickless, Loddon	—	
Cleveland Alfred, Loddon	—	
Copeman James, Loddon	—	
Cullum Thomas, Loddon	—	
Campbell Robert, King-street, Great Yarmouth	—	
Fayerman Henry, Great Yarmouth	—	
Feltham Jonathan, Loddon	—	
Gilbert Charles, Moulton, Norfolk	—	
Goff John Massingham, Loddon	—	
Greengrass John, Loddon	—	

	S.	C.
Groom Christmas, Loddon	—	
Gunton John, Loddon	—	
Hart David, Loddon	—	
Huson James, Chedgrave	—	
Harrod John Kitton, Loddon	—	
Jolley Guyton William, Loddon	—	
Kett Samuel, Loddon	—	
Lane Edward, Loddon	—	
Leman John (grocer), Loddon	—	
Leman William, Loddon	—	
Morriss Robert, Loddon	—	
Norriss Samuel, St. Peter's Hungate	—	
Osborne William, Loddon	—	
Pedgrift Robert, Loddon	—	
Plow John, senior	—	
Riches Henry, Loddon	—	
Riches William, Loddon	—	
Riches John, Loddon	—	
Spence Matthew, Loddon	—	
Snowling Daniel, Raveningham-hall, Norfolk	—	
Stronger John, Loddon	—	
Sparke John Henry, Gunthorpe, Norfolk	—	
Sparke Edward Bowyer, Feltwell, Norfolk	—	
Smith John James, clerk, Loddon	—	
Varvell William Edmonds, Loddon	—	
Ward Henry, Loddon	—	
Wilde William, London-road, Norwich	—	
Wilde Stephen, Unthank's-road, Norwich	—	
	15	33
Alecock Robert, Loddon	—	
Barwell John, sen., Surrey-street, Norwich	—	
Cadge Christopher Goulder, Loddon	—	
Goddard Edward, Hardley-hall	—	
Gilbert Rev. John Denny, Cantley	—	
Gilbert Edward, Chedgrave	—	
Holmes Edward, Heigham, Norwich	—	
Plow John jun., Loddon	—	
Pitts Robert Christopher, Thorpe	—	
Rodwell George, Loddon	—	
Singleton John, St. Michael's at Thorn, Norwich	—	
Spurgeon John, Loddon	—	
Thurtell James Watson, Loddon	—	

Mundham.

	S.	C.
Broughton Edward, Mundham	—	
Farrow Jonathan, Mundham	—	
Fairhead Richard, Mundham	—	
Tillett Thomas, Mundham	—	
Tillett Joseph, Mundham	—	
	4	1
Branch John, Mundham	—	
Clark Henry, Parham	—	
Clarke Edward Stephen Osmond, Yarmouth	—	
Flaxman William, Mundham	—	
Forder John, Seething	—	

Norton Subcourse.

	S.	C.
Andrews John, Norton Subcourse	—	
Denny Rev. Richard Cooke, Bergh Apton	—	
Evans William, Norton Subcourse	—	
Forder William, Toft Monks	—	
Hall John, Stockton	—	
Hayward Nelson, Norton Subcourse	—	
Leach Francis, Raveningham	—	
Melton Samuel, Chedgrave	—	
Nursey Daniel, Norton Subcourse	—	
Nursey Robert, Norton Subcourse	—	
Playford Mark, Norton Subcourse	—	
Playford John, Reedham	—	

E

	S.	C.
Reynolds Thomas, Norton Subcourse	—	
Shardalow William, Norton Subcourse	—	
Shardalow Francis, Norton Subcourse	—	
Shardalow James, Norton Subcourse	—	
Smijth Sir William Bowyer, Bart., Hill-hall, Theydon, Essex	—	
Wigg James, Norton Subcourse	—	
Woods Robert, Norton Subcourse	—	
	15	4
Bexfield James, Norton Subcourse	—	
Hunter Edward, Thurlton	—	
Manthorpe William, Thurlton	—	
Playford John, Beccles, Suffolk	—	
Read Robert, Norton Subcourse	—	
Shepherd Stephen, Norton Subcourse	—	
West Thomas Robert, Raveningham	—	
Yallop John, Norton Subcourse	—	

Raveningham.

	S.	C.
Andrews Robert, Beccles, Suffolk	—	
Andrews William, Norton Subcourse	—	
Andrews Christopher, Beccles, Suffolk	—	
Bacon Sir Edmund, Bart., Raveningham	—	
Banns George, Raveningham	—	
Beane Francis, Raveningham	—	
Easter Thomas, Raveningham	—	
Fuller William, Raveningham	—	
Herrod John, Raveningham	—	
Piller Jacob, Raveningham	—	
West Thomas R., Raveningham	—	
	2	9
Blunderfield Francis, Raveningham	—	
Dawson Jonathan, Toft Monks	—	
Farrow Stephen, Raveningham	—	
Kerrich John, Geldeston-hall	—	
Kerrich E., Arnold's chapel, Dorking, Surrey	—	
Shardalow George, Raveningham	—	
Ward Robert, Raveningham	—	

Seething.

	S.	C.
Burt John Toll, Seething	—	
Crabbe George, Seething	—	
Crickmore Robert, Seething	—	
Crickmore William, Seething	—	
Crickmore John, Seething	—	
Grimer Robert, Seething	—	
Harvey Thomas, Seething	—	
Lovick Robert, Seething	—	
Lovick William, Seething	—	
Lovick Charles, Seething	—	
Mann Edmund Scott, Seething	—	
Sparkes Benjamin, Seething	—	
Tate Robert, Seething	—	
	1	12
Austin Matthew, Seething	—	
Branch Daniel, Loddon	—	
Gooderham, William, Seething	—	
Johnson Samuel, Alburgh	—	
Nobbs Samuel, Rockland	—	

Sisland.

	S.	C.
Branch William, Sisland	—	
Hobson Rev. William, Sisland	—	
Tibbenham Edward, Sisland	—	
	8	0
Clarke Osmund, Stuston	—	
Lovick William, Seething	—	

Stockton.	S.	C.
Adams Thomas, Stockton	—	
Barber John, Stockton	—	
Barwick James, Stockton	—	
Morris Robert, Stockton	—	
Pearce Richard, Stockton	—	
	5	0
Brown George, Wordle, Uppingham, Rutlandsh.		

Thorpe next Haddiscoe.		
Bexfield Joseph, Thorpe	—	
Beckham James, Thorpe	—	
Blunderfield Francis, Thorpe	—	
Blunderfield Thomas, Thorpe	—	
Barrow Rev. George, Thorpe	—	
Last Samuel, Beccles, Suffolk	—	
Rivett James, Gorleston, Suffolk	—	
Shardalow William, Heckingham	—	
Shardalow Edward, Thorpe	—	
	3	6
Brabben Henry, Thorpe	—	
Gaymore Robert, Thorpe	—	

Thurlton.		
Boud Joseph, Thurlton	—	
Brabben Robert, Thurlton	—	
Chapman John, Thurlton	—	
Fox Thomas, Thurlton	—	
Goodwin Rev. Frederic George, Thurlton	—	
Hunt John, Thurlton	—	
Hunter Edward, Thurlton	—	
Jennis John, Thurlton	—	
Lamb George, Loddon	—	
Minister Robert, Thurlton	—	
Napp Thornton, Thurlton	—	
Pope William, younger, Thurlton	—	
Piper James, Beccles, Suffolk	—	
Rushmer James, Thurlton	—	
Sayer William, Thurlton	—	
Sayer John Eliott, Thurlton	—	
Sayer Burcham, Great Yarmouth	—	
Spore William, Thurlton	—	
Savory Edward, Thurlton	—	
Scarl Charles, Thurlton	—	
Shardalow John, Thurlton	—	
Wilkins John, Thurlton	—	
Wigg Freeman, Thurlton	—	
	6	17
Goodrich William Stannard, Corton, Suffolk		
Nursey Richard, Runham		
Playford John, Gillingham		
Pope William, Thurlton		
Pope Richard, Thurlton		
Rushmer Charles, Thurlton		
Scarlett James, Thurlton		
Taylor Robert, Thurlton		

Thurton.		
Burton Thomas, Thurton	—	
Cossey Stephen, Thurton	—	
Minns James, Thurton	—	
Oxborough Barington, Thurton	—	
	1	3
Gilbert Edward, Chedgrave		
Harber John, Thurton		
Webster Rev. Josias Gardner, Brunswick-house, Southampton		
Wright Robert, Bank-plain, Norwich		

Thwaite.	S.	C.
Hindle Thomas, Thwaite	—	
Herrod James, Thwaite	—	
Mackrell John, Thwaite	—	
Playford Robert, Thwaite	—	
	1	3
Cobb Robert, clerk, Ellingham		

Toft Monks.		
Bohun Richard, Esq., Beccles	—	
Bexfield James, Norton Subcourse	—	
Farrow Stephen, Toft Monks	—	
Fuller John, Toft Monks	—	
Mabson William, Great Yarmouth	—	
Morse Joseph Rama, Lound	—	
Maddle William, Toft Monks	—	
Sayer William, Toft Monks	—	
Tripp John, Gillingham,	—	
Winter Alfred, Toft Monks	—	
Wooltorton Robert, Toft Monks	—	
Wood Thomas, Toft Monks	—	
	8	4
Blacker Murray Mac Gregor, Claremont, Claremorris, Ely, Mayo, Ireland		
Colman Edward Hovell, Toft Monks		
Forder James, jun., Toft Monks		
Fuller James, Toft Monks		
Wooltorton John, Toft Monks		

Wheatacre All Saints.		
Briggs John, Burgh St. Peter	—	
Cooper James, Wheatacre All Saints	—	
Gardiner Samuel, Wheatacre All Saints	—	
Grimmer George, Wheatacre All Saints	—	
Greengrass William, Thurton	—	
Kittle Robert, Somerleyton, Suffolk	—	
Turner Robert, Wheatacre All Saints	—	
	2	5
Okes Rev. William, Wheatacre All Saints		

Woodton.		
Baley Thomas, Woodton	—	
Beckett Robert, Woodton	—	
Everett John Arthur, Woodton	—	
Feltham John, Saxlingham	—	
Foulger Joseph, Bungay	—	
Hawes William, Woodton	—	
Leeder Palmer, Brooke, Norfolk	—	
Newman Robert, Ber-street, Norwich	—	
Packer Richard Walgrave, Woodton	—	
Palmer Phillip, St. John's Sepulchre, Norwich	—	
Sayer Daniel, Woodton	—	
Shorten Richard, Woodton	—	
Tibb George Harvey, Woodton	—	
Varnell John, Woodton	—	
	11	3
Crabb George, Bredfield, Suffolk		
Dring William, Woodton		
Dring Last, Wymondham		
Everett Jeremy Everard, Cookley, Suffolk		
Howman George E., Barnsley, Gloucestershire		
Loynes John, Woodton		
Mimmacks George, Brooke		
Meek John, Morningthorpe		

Yelverton.		
Burrell John, Yelverton	—	
Postle Rev. Edward, Yelverton	—	
Thrower Alfred, Yelverton	—	
	1	2

NORTH WALSHAM DISTRICT,

COMPRISING THE PARISHES OF

Alby.	S.	C.
Clarke John Secker, Aylsham	—	
Gay George, Alby	—	
Govett Thomas Romaine, Alby	—	
Pedgrift Thomas, Alby	—	
Preston Thomas, Alby	—	
Richardson Richard, Alby	—	
Suffing Robert Russell, Alby	—	
Scottow John, Alby	—	
Temple John, Erpingham	—	
Watts John, Erpingham	—	
Watts William, Erpingham	—	
	5	6
Amos John, Alby		
Hanbury Osgood, Oldfield Grange, Great Coggeshall, Essex		

Alborough.

	S.	C.
Bone John, Alborough	—	
Chapman Stephen, Alborough	—	
Chapman William, Alborough	—	
Clarke Richard, No. 5, Crescent, Norwich	—	
Critoph Edmund, Westwich	—	
Durrant William, Alborough	—	
Durrant William, Alborough	—	
Gay James, jun., Alborough	—	
Gray Thomas, Alborough	—	
Miller Robert, Alborough	—	
Pank Charles, Runton	—	
Woods Robert, Bradfield	—	
	8	9
Fish Charles, Kingstone, Surrey		
Horner Francis, Alborough		
Hudson Randel James, Alborough		
Parke William Burcham, Reepham.		
Shuckburgh Rev. Robert, Alborough		

Antingham.

	S.	C.
Cranefield William, Antingham		
Dolphin John, clerk, Antingham		
Helsdon Benjamin, jun., Antingham		
Le Neve William, Antingham		
Watts Ireland, Antingham		
Wright Henry, Antingham		
	1	5
Helsdon Benjamin, Antingham		
Wright Henry, Antingham		

Ashmanaugh.

	S.	C.
Childs Edward, Southwold		
Popey James, Ashmanaugh		

Aylmerton.

	S.	C.
Cable Robert, Aylmerton		
Cooper John, Aylmerton		
Matthews Jasper, Aylmerton		
Simons Richard, Aylmerton		
	0	4

Baconsthorpe.

	S.	C.
Everett James, Bodham	—	
Everett Stephen, Baconsthorpe	—	
Fisher Philip, Baconsthorpe	—	
Harrison Robert, Baconsthorpe	—	
Harrison James, Baconsthorpe	—	
King Richard, Baconsthorpe	—	
Nichols Thomas, Baconsthorpe	—	
Philipo Robert, Baconsthorpe	—	
Rallison Nicholas, Baconsthorpe	—	
Seaman George Richard, Baconsthorpe	—	
Waller William, Blakeney	—	
Warnes Edmund, Baconsthorpe	—	
	8	9
Bumphrey James, Baconsthorpe		
Girling John, Baconsthorpe		
Partridge John Anthony, Baconsthorpe		

Bacton.

	S.	C.
Browne Wm., St. Michael's Coslany, Norwich	—	
Clarke John William, Bacton	—	
Cubitt William Partridge, Bacton	—	
Elliot William, Bacton	—	
Haggeth William, Bacton	—	
Jackson Thomas, Bacton	—	
Jeary John, Bacton	—	
Lound William, Bacton	—	
Marshall William, Bacton	—	
Marshall Francis, Bacton		
Maris Henry Ellis, Bacton	—	
Mason Samuel, Bacton	—	
Monsey George Bush, Bacton	—	
Neve William, Bacton	—	
Newman Robert, Bacton	—	
Nichols William, Bacton	—	
Sexton Robert, Bacton	—	
Sturgess William, Bacton	—	
Watts John, Witton	—	
Watts George, Catfield	—	
Wiseman Murray, Bacton	—	
Wodehouse Thomas, Bacton	—	
Wodehouse Campbell, Bacton	—	
	5	18
Alexander Joseph, Bacton		
Bond John Mayes, Bacton		
Claxton Rice, Bacton		
Lacy William, North Walsham		

Banningham.

	S.	C.
Bowles Barnard William, Banningham	—	
Coleby Charles, North Walsham	—	
Cranefield Corby, Antingham	—	
Elden William, Banningham	—	
Elden William, jun., Banningham	—	
Frost William, Banningham	—	
Frostick John, Banningham	—	
Fearman Thomas Hall, Westwick	—	
Griffen William Edward, Banningham	—	

	S.	C.
Glister John, Blickling	—	
Glister Joseph, Burgh	—	
Glister William, Aylsham	—	
Neech George Samuel, Banningham	—	
Rump William Elden, Banningham	—	
Sexton John Joseph, Banningham	—	
Sharpin Thomas, Banningham	—	
Woodcock John Gresham, Briston	—	
	11	6
Covell Joseph, Runton		
Fearman Thomas, Westwick		
Shephard John, Erpingham		
Tattam George, Aylsham		
Turner Robert, Banningham		

Barningham Norwood.

	S.	C.
Miller George, Barningham Norwood	—	
Willis William, Barningham Norwood	—	
	0	2
Cremer Rev. Marlow, North Walsham		

Barningham Winter.

	S.	C.
Anderson Jas. R., clerk, Barningham Winter	—	
Chapman James, Barningham Winter	—	
Mott John Thomas, Barningham Winter	—	
	1	2

Barton Turf.

	S.	C.
Abigall John Shaw, Smallburgh	—	
Amies Joseph, Barton Turf	—	
Amies John, Ingham	—	
Baldwin George, Barton Turf	—	
Baldwin John, Barton Turf	—	
Baldwin Matthew, Barton Turf	—	
Francis John, Barton Turf	—	
Gales John, Barton Turf	—	
Haylett John, Barton Turf	—	
Hewitt William, Hoveton St. Peter	—	
Hewitt James, Barton Turf	—	
Neave Jacob, Barton Turf	—	
Nockolds Henry, Barton Turf	—	
Postle John, Barton Turf	—	
Preston Thomas Edward, Barton Turf	—	
Watts James, Barton Turf	—	
Yaxley James, Smallburgh	—	
Yaxley John, Barton Turf	—	
	13	5
Butterfunt James, Lynn		
Cox James, Barton Turf		
Mack John, Tunstead		
Watts John, Dilham		
Watts Robert, Barton Turf		

Beckham East.

	S.	C.
Bird George, sen., Beckham East	—	
Bird George, jun., Beckham East	—	
Emery Robert, Beckham East	—	
Emery Benjamin, Beckham East	—	
Rounce Hilary, Beckham East	—	
Skipper John, Beckham East	—	
	0	6

Beckham West.

	S.	C.
Fuller Cook, Beckham West	—	
Ransom Henry, Beckham West	—	
Robins Richard, Aylmerton	—	
Seeley William Gladden, Bodham	—	
	1	3

	S.	C.
Ebbetts Daniel, Beckham West	—	
Emery William, Beckham West	—	
Emery James, Beckham West	—	
Gunton Rev. John, Marsham	—	
Howell John, Beckham West	—	
Martin Sir William, St. James' Palace	—	
Sayers Samuel, Beckham West	—	
	11	6

Beeston St. Lawrence.

	S.	C.
Long Weeds John, Beeston St. Lawrence	—	
Preston Sir Jacob Henry, Beeston-hall	—	
	0	2

Beeston Regis.

	S.	C.
Cremer Cremer, clerk, Beeston Regis	—	
Fuller Samuel, Beeston Regis	—	
Ward John, Beeston Regis	—	
West Christopher, Beeston Regis	—	
	1	3
Peckham Robert Collier, clerk, Rectory, Langdon-hills, near Horndon, Essex		

Belaugh.

	S.	C.
Allen William, Sustead	—	
Riches Anthony Blackburn, Belaugh	—	
Scales Robert, Belaugh	—	
	3	0
Allen Thomas, Norwich		
Cadge Christopher, Loddon		

Bessingham.

	S.	C.
Arden Rev. Henry Cotton, Sustead	—	
Puxley Timothy, Bessingham	—	
Puxley Thomas, Bessingham	—	
Spurrell Daniel, Bessingham	—	
Thursby Samuel, Bessingham	—	
	3	2
Brooke James, Bessingham		
Frankland George, Bessingham		

Bradfield.

	S.	C.
Booth Thomas William, Northrepps	—	
Larner James, Bradfield	—	
Smith Henry, Bradfield	—	
Sewell James, Bradfield	—	
	0	4
Harris Robert, North Walsham		

Brampton.

	S.	C.
Burcham George, jun., Brampton	—	
Sutton Richard, Twyford	—	
Threadwell John Kilbey, Marsham	—	
	0	3
Marsham Henry Philip, Marsham		
Seaman Greenacre John, Scottow		
Smith James, Stratton Strawless		

Brunstead.

	S.	C.
Comyn Horatio Nelson William, clerk, Brunstead	—	
Durrant Cubitt, Brunstead	—	
Durrant George, Surrey-street, Norwich	—	
Hewitt Charles, Ingham	—	
Newman Cubitt, Brunstead	—	
Wittleton George, Brunstead	—	
	6	0

	S.	C.

Burgh next Aylsham.

Browne William, Burgh	—	
Burr Edmund, Burgh	—	
Postle Robert, Burgh next Aylsham	—	
Wright Charles, Burgh	—	
	1	3
Holley James Hunt, Burgh		
Holley Edward, clerk, Hackford		
Holley Windham Hunt, Burgh-hall		

Buxton.

Allen Thomas, Buxton	—	
Beck William, Buxton	—	
Butterworth John, Buxton	—	
Bell John, Buxton	—	
Fulcher Thomas, Elmham	—	
Gambling John, Buxton	—	
Gambling John, jun., Buxton	—	
Hardiment Robert, Buxton	—	
Norman Richard Briton, St. Clement's, Norwich	—	
Nash Thomas Rump, Buxton	—	
Passon Benjamin, jun., Buxton	—	
Printer George, Felmingham	—	
Rayson George, Buxton	—	
Smith Edward, Brampton	—	
Stibbons James, Buxton	—	
Sutton James, Buxton	—	
Stracey William James, Buxton	—	
Taylor Edward, Tharston	—	
Wright John, Buxton	—	
	13	6
Dunning Daniel, Buxton		
Mack Robert, Hainford		
Watts Thomas, Buxton		

Calthorpe.

Newstead John Elden, Calthorpe		
	0	1
Gillam Stephen, Calthorpe		
Hook Richard, Calthorpe		
Ives Robert, Calthorpe		
Shepheard Samuel Marsh, Calthorpe		
Westney Stephen, Calthorpe		

Catfield.

Beck William, Catfield	—	
Barber George, Catfield	—	
Cubitt Henry Archibald, Catfield	—	
Cubitt Charles George, Catfield	—	
Dawson George, Catfield	—	
Dawson Robert, Hickling	—	
George Robert, Catfield	—	
Gibbs William, Catfield	—	
Myhill Edward, Catfield	—	
Moore John, Catfield	—	
Neve William, Catfield	—	
Norgate Thomas, Catfield	—	
Pig Philip, Catfield	—	
Rice Robert, Catfield	—	
Slipper William, Catfield	—	
	10	5
Beck James, Catfield		
Balls John, Catfield		
Crowe William, Catfield		
Cubitt Benjamin Lucas, Catfield		
Dye Richard, Catfield		

	S.	C.
Myhill John, Catfield		
Matthews George, Sutton		
Neve Edward, Catfield	—	
Sayer George, 19, Stonefield-street, Islington, London	—	
Southgate John, Catfield	—	

Colby.

Beck Daniel, Colby	—	
Barney Robert, Colby	—	
Coleby Rev. George, Colby	—	
Clover Joseph, Colby	—	
Fuller John, Colby	—	
Gaze George, Colby	—	
Lacey William, Colby	—	
Parlby Thomas, Keswick	—	
Roper Snelling Drosier, Colby	—	
Roper Leonard, Colby	—	
Shaw Henry, Heigham, Norwich	—	
Scottow Peter, Banningham	—	
Storey William, Bull-close, Norwich	—	
	5	8
Clover Thomas, Colby		
Chapman William, Ingworth		
Hayhoe Thomas, Colby		
Roper Snelling Drosier, Colby		
Windham Rev. Robt., Lowestoft		
Windham Charles Ash, Myton, Warwickshire		
Ward William, Saxlingham		

Coltishall.

Allen Robert, jun., Coltishall	—	
Allen Robert, sen., Coltishall		
Buck Samuel, Coltishall		
Barber Charles, Coltishall	—	
Burroughes William, Coltishall	—	
Coman Thomas John, Coltishall	—	
Fuller John, Coltishall	—	
Fitt Thomas, Coltishall	—	
Horner Wyatt, Coltishall	—	
Hornor Edward, Coltishall	—	
Hornor Robt. T., Post-office-street, Norwich	—	
Ives George, Coltishall	—	
Knights William Crowe, Scottow	—	
Massingham Joseph, Catton	—	
Mayes Henry, jun., Coltishall	—	
Payne James, Coltishall	—	
Rouse John, Coltishall	—	
Wright Thos., Nelson-st., Heigham, Norwich	—	
Willey John, Coltishall	—	
Wright Isaac, Coltishall	—	
Watts Robert, Coltishall	—	
	13	8
Blake Thomas Jex, 13, Sussex-square, Kemptown, Brighton		
Coman James, Coltishall		
Murphy Patrick, Coltishall		
Smith John, Coltishall		
St. John Charles Orlando, Coltishall		
Watson James, Chedgrave		
Wright Thomas, Coltishall		

Cromer.

Allen John, Cromer		
Allen James, Cromer		
Brooks Matthew, Cromer		
Burton Isaac Howes, Cromer		
Burton Lewis Gilbert, Cromer		

	S.	C.
Boulter Thomas, Cromer		
Cabbell Benjamin Bond, Cromer hall	—	
Covell Joseph, Runton	—	
Curtis Joseph, Cromer	—	
Earle Charles, Cromer	—	
Earle John Henry, Cromer	—	
Fitt Stephen, Cromer	—	
Fox John, Cromer	—	
Hardingham John, Cromer		
Harris George, Cromer	—	
Heath Edward, Cromer	—	
Herring Robert, Cromer	—	
Jacob Joshua, Cromer	—	
Johnson Herbert Jarrett, Runton, Norfolk	—	
Leake James Clear, Runton		
Neave Dan, Cromer	—	
Newstead Ellis, Cromer	—	
Nockels Henry, Cromer	—	
Nockels Hillery, Cromer	—	
Preston John, Cromer	—	
Pye John Stimpson, Cromer		
Riches George, Cromer	—	
Riches James, Cromer	—	
Rust Benjamin, Cromer	—	
Rust John William, Cromer	—	
Sandford Henry, Cromer	—	
Thurston Samuel William, Norwich		
	10	22
Bilham James, Cromer		
Breese George, Cromer		
Breese Charles, Cromer		
Breese Robert, Cromer		
Brown Edmund, Sydenham, Lewisham, Kent		
Buxton Sir Edward North, Bart., Cromer		
Cox Robert, junr., Sherringham		
Fitch Frederic, Cromer		
Forster Dowsing, Cromer		
Howard George, Cromer		
Paine William, Cromer		
Pank John Juler, Cromer		
Pank Thomas, Cromer		
Sharpe William, Cromer		
Simons Simeon, Cromer		
Smith Thomas, Cromer		
Vial David, Cromer		
Witting James, Cromer		

Crostwight.

Vale John Bartholomew, clerk, Crostwight

Dilham.

	S.	C.
Culley Henry Read, Dilham	—	
Deacle Hicks, Coltishall		
Frarey John, Dilham		
Johnson Samuel Lovick, Dilham	—	
Mattison William, Dilham	—	
Palmer James, jun., Walcott	—	
Taylor Henry, Dilham	—	
Walpole Richard, Dilham		
Watts John, Dilham	—	
	4	5
Austin Edward Griffith, Dilham		
Borrett Charles William, Queen Ann-street, Cavendish-square, London		
Borrett Francis Turner, Queen Ann-street, Cavendish-square, London		
Borrett Thomas, Gloucester-place, London		
Borrett, James, Yarmouth		
Gardiner William Drake, Dilham		
Palmer James, sen., Honing		

Edingthorpe.

	S.	C.
Bush Thomas, Edingthorpe	—	
Fuller Adam, Edingthorpe	—	
Landymore John, Edingthorpe	—	
Turner John, Paston	—	
Turner Charles, jun., Edingthorpe		
	1	4
Jay George, St. Peter of Mancroft, Norwich		
Sisson Rev. Joseph Lawson, Edingthorpe		
Turner William, Edingthorpe		
Turner Charles, sen., Aylsham		

Erpingham.

	S.	C.
Balls Edmund, Erpingham	—	
Cutting Thomas, Erpingham	—	
Crisp John, Erpingham	—	
Critoph Christopher, Erpingham	—	
Hardingham William Henry, Erpingham	—	
Johnson John, Erpingham	—	
Newstead Benjamin, Erpingham	—	
Smith Thomas, jun., Blickling	—	
Turner Samuel, Northrepps	—	
Tyrrell Henry, Wells	—	
Wilde John, Erpingham	—	
Watts, Joseph, Erpingham	—	
Woolsey Cardinal, Erpingham		
	8	5
Burrell Elden John, Calthorpe		
Coleman Henry John, Worstead		
Cooper Jonathan, Erpingham		
Durrant John, Erpingham		
Smith Thomas, Blickling		
Smith John, Erpingham		
Spurrell Richard, Long Stratton		
Watts George, Ingworth		
Woolsey John, St. Bennet's, Norwich		

Felbrigg.

	S.	C.
Clark John, Felbrigg		
Cawston Nicholas, Felbrigg		
	0	2

Felmingham.

	S.	C.
Atkins James, Felmingham	—	
Clarke James, Felmingham	—	
Field John, Felmingham	—	
Hayn William, Felmingham	—	
Hall John, North Walsham	—	
Hylton Richard, Felmingham	—	
Neech James, Felmingham	—	
Neech James Thomas, Felmingham	—	
Peters Edwin, Felmingham	—	
Postle William, Felmingham	—	
Postle John, Burgh, near Aylsham	—	
	1	10
Banyer John, Felmingham		
Hylton John, Felmingham		
Hylton Frederic, Felmingham		
Printer George, Felmingham		
Wortley John, Felmingham		

Gimingham.

	S.	C.
Allard Francis, Gimingham	—	
Allard William, Gimingham	—	
Blakelock Ralph, clerk, Gimingham	—	
Clarke John, Gimingham	—	
French William, Gimingham	—	
Gillam Robert, Gimingham	—	

	S.	C.
Lacey Robert, Gimingham	—	
Plumbly Thomas, Gimingham	—	
Porritt John Black, Gimingham	—	
Primrose Henry, Gimingham	—	
Pycroft Henry, Gimingham	—	
Rising Robert, Gimingham	—	
Waterson John, Gimingham	—	
	5	8
Milem John, Gimingham	—	

Gresham.

	S.	C.
Bird William, Hempstead	—	
Cooper James, Sustead	—	
Curtis Robert, Gresham	—	
Durrant John, Gresham	—	
Field Ellis, Cromer	—	
Gotts John, Gresham	—	
Leman Abraham, Edgefield	—	
Leman Barnabas, Gresham	—	
Sharpen Robert, Gresham	—	
Spurgin Arthur Dewing, Gresham	—	
Windham John Henry, Cromer	—	
	3	8
Brown John, Gresham	—	
Jordan Lewis, Gresham	—	

Hanworth.

	S.	C.
Chapman James, Hanworth	—	
Chapman Samuel, Hanworth	—	
Ebbetts James, Hanworth	—	
Emery George, Hanworth	—	
Heath Rev. Charles, Hanworth	—	
Helsdon Robert, Hanworth	—	
Hicks John, Hanworth	—	
Page Robert, Hanworth	—	
	0	8

Happisburgh.

	S.	C.
Clarke Thomas, Happisburgh	—	
Cooke Robert, Happisburgh	—	
Faulke James, Happisburgh	—	
Frarey Thomas Harvey, jun., Happisburgh	—	
Frarey Jonathan Harvey, Happisburgh	—	
Hall Browne, Ber-street, Norwich	—	
Holmes Rev. Richard, Ridlington	—	
Jimpson Robert, Happisbugh	—	
Lacey John, Happisburgh	—	
Long William, Happisburgh	—	
Nickels John Cubitt, Lessingham	—	
Palmer John, Happisburgh	—	
Pye Joseph, Happisburgh	—	
Siely James, jun., Happisburgh	—	
Siely John, Happisburgh	—	
Siely Andrew, Happisburgh	—	
Siely William, Stalham	—	
Storey Charles, Happisburgh	—	
Thirst Thomas, Happisburgh	—	
Thompson John, Happisburgh	—	
White Rev. John, Chevington, near Bury St. Edmund's	—	
Woodrow Joseph, Norwich	—	
Wright John, Happisburgh	.	
	18	5
Bartram Robert, Happisburgh		
Betts John, Happisburgh		
Frarey Thomas, sen., Lessingham		
Jimpson Robert, Barton Turf		
Newman John, Brunstead		
Siely James, sen., Happisburgh		
Storey John A., Happisburgh and Southrepps		

Hautbois Great.

	S.	C.
Crome Richard, Hautbois Magna	—	
Farman John, Hautbois Magna	—	
Fox John, Hautbois Magna	—	
Herne Robert, Hautbois Magna	—	
Hinde Ephraim Wilkin, Hautbois Magna	—	
Lambert Robert, Coltishall	—	
Moore Henry, Hautbois Magna	—	
Moore William, Hautbois Magna	—	
Southgate William, Hautbois Magna	—	
	2	7
Herne James, Hautbois Magna	—	

Hempstead with Eccles.

	S.	C.
Ives George, Calthorpe	—	
Littlewood William, Hempstead	—	
Pilgrim Postle, Hempstead	—	
Wilkins Rev. Edward, Hempstead	—	
Wilkins William, Hempstead	—	
	4	1
Croxton Cornelius, Eccles		
Dyball John, Hempstead		
Heseltine Edward, Blackheath-park, Kent		
Thompson William, Eccles		

Hickling.

	S.	C.
Aylmer John, Norwich	—	
Bishop James, Hickling	—	
Borrett John, Hickling	—	
Barber Jonathan, Hickling	—	
Cubitt Thomas, Hickling	—	
Clipperton John, Hickling	—	
Curtis Benjamin, Hickling	—	
Durrant Charles, Hickling	—	
Fenn Thomas Miles, Stalham	—	
Forster William, Aylsham	—	
Forster John, North Walsham	—	
Garrett Israel Royal, Hickling	—	
Gibbs George, senr., Hickling	—	
Goulder William, Hickling	—	
Harbord Robert, Hickling	—	
Lambert Joshua, Hickling	—	
Layton Thomas, Hickling	—	
Mack Edward, Hickling	—	
Micklethwaite Sotherton Nathaniel, Hickling	—	
Myhill John, Hickling	—	
Neal Samuel, Hickling	—	
Newman Samuel, Hickling	—	
Newman Samuel, jun., Hickling	—	
Nudd John, Hickling	—	
Slipper Benjamin, Hickling	—	
Skipper John, Hickling	—	
Trorey William, Yarmouth	—	
Trorey William, Hickling	—	
Turner Richard, Hickling	—	
	26	8
Brackenbury William, Hickling		
Bates George John, Stalham		
Deary Thomas, Hickling		
Hill Rev. Henry, Heacham		
Plummer Charles, Hickling		
Riches Richard, Catfield		
Slipper Rev. Robert Brown, Hingham		
Wright Joseph, Hickling		

Honing.

	S.	C.
Beck Warren, Honing		
Browne William, Honing		

	S.	C.
Bush Thomas, Honing		
Cole John, Honing		
Cubitt Edward George, Honing		
Ducker Charles, Honing		
Farman Thomas, Honing		
Gaze Charles, Honing		
Gedge James, Honing		
Howlett Henry, Honing		
Larter John, Honing		
Steward Robert, Honing		
Steward John, Honing		
Watkinson George, Honing		
Watson Thomas, Honing		
Watson Richard, Stratton Strawless		
Youngman Richard, Honing		
Youngman Thomas, Honing		
	16	2
Buffham Robert, Honing		
Gedge Richard, Honing		
Rump Hewitt, East Ruston		

Horning.

	S.	C.
Colman Thomas, Horning		
Cook Charles, Horning		
Crowe Robert, Horning		
Freeman John, Heigham, Norwich		
Grimes John, Horning		
Grimes Benjamin, Horning		
Jay William, Horning		
Jay George, Horning		
Lemon John, Horning		
Lemon Robert, Horning		
Platten Robert, Horning		
Pyne Rev. Augustus, Horning		
Thurtle Thomas, Horning		
Wright Fenn, Horning		
	18	1
Crowe Walter Thomas, Horning		
Grapes William, Horning		
Heath William, Ludham		
Wright John Horning		

Horsey.

	S.	C.
Gedge John, Horsey		
Grapes John, Horsey		
Green William, Horsey		
Neale Edward Pote, Horsey		
Rising Robert, Horsey		
	4	1
Gilbert Robert, jun., Ashby		
Johnson Thomas, Horsey		

Hoveton St. John.

	S.	C.
Blofield Thomas John, Hoveton St. John		
Boorne George, Hoveton St. John		
Besfor Leonard, Hoveton St. John		
Chamberlin John, Hoveton St. John		
Curtis Thomas, Hoveton St. John		
Hall Henry, Hoveton St. John		
Hall Martin, Hoveton St. John		
Miles James, Hoveton St. John		
Pell Edmund, Hoveton St. John		
Platten Jonathan, Hoveton St. John		
Spanton Benjamin, Hoveton St. John		
Wilkins, John, Hoveton St. John		
	11	1
Cadge Michael, Peterborough		
Cook Charles, Horning		

	S.	C.
Herne James, Hoveton St. Peter		
Littlewood John, Hoveton St. John		

Hoveton St. Peter.

	S.	C.
Allan Joseph, Neatishead		
Herne James, Hoveton St. Peter		
Mayes Charles, Hoveton St. Peter		
Riches Richard Cook, Hoveton St. Peter		
	3	1

Ingham.

	S.	C.
Beck William, Ingham		
Barcham Thomas, Ingham		
Bird Dunham, Ingham		
Croxton Cornelius, Hempstead		
Dye Charles, Ingham		
Florey Philip, Ingham		
Fiddes Joseph, Great Yarmouth		
Harris William, Ingham		
Harvey John, senr., Ingham		
Long Samuel, Ingham		
Lusher John, Ingham		
Lack William Wagg, Ingham		
Venimore James, Ingham		
Whaites Robert Francis, Ingham		
Whaites John Johnson, Ingham		
	9	6
Harvey John, jun., North Walsham		
Matthews George, Ingham		
Wilkins Robert, Lessingham		

Ingworth.

	S.	C.
Balls Robert Marshall, Ingworth		
Burrell Joseph, Erpingham		
Hart Henry Gardiner, Ingworth		
Watson James, Ingworth		
Watson James, jun., Aylsham		
Watts George, Ingworth		
	2	4
Fish Rev. George, Erpingham		
Goulder Robert, Ingworth		
Goulder Charles, Bradford, Yorkshire		
Kerr the Hon. and Rev. Lord Henry Francis Charles, Dittisham, Devonshire		
Smith Thomas, jun., Blickling		

Irstead.

	S.	C.
Gunn Rev. John, Irstead		
Scarland John, Irstead		
	1	1
Edrich Robert, Irstead		
Smith John, Irstead		
Shepherd S. Bowar, Irstead		

Knapton.

	S.	C.
Allison Thomas, Knapton		
Burton William, Knapton		
Cooke Stephen, clerk, Knapton		
Collings John Peed, Knapton		
Cremer Robert Marler, clerk, North Walsham		
Cobb John, Bungay		
Cooper James, Knapton		
Kemp Thomas Cooke, Eastmeon, Hants		
Long David, Knapton		
Robinson Sir Henry, Knapton		
Watts Robert, Knapton		
Watts Thomas, Knapton		
	8	4

	S.	C.

Atkinson Henry, Mundesley
Barnes Rev. William Lawson, Swafield
Coleman Abraham, Knapton
Mullen William Thomas, Knapton
Pratt James Wortley, Mundesley
Silvey Jonas, Knapton
Watts Ireland, Antingham

Lamas with Hautbois Parva.

Bransby Ransome, Lamas
Davy John, Ingoldisthorpe
Ladbrooke James, Hautbois Parva
Marsh Rev. William Heath, Lamas
Smith Alfred, Buxton
Stockings William, Lamas
Sutton George Ayers, Lamas

	4	3

Blake William Jex, Lamas
Lubbock John William, 25, St. James'-place, Westminster
Mack Robert, Hainford

Lessingham.

Bartram John, Lessingham
Frarey Robert, Lessingham
Fielding James, Stalham
Waterson George, Lessingham
Worts Thomas, Lessingham

Cubitt Benjamin, Lessingham
Wilkins Robert, Lessingham

	1	4

Ludham.

Annison Edward, Ludham
Berry Thomas, Ludham
Clarke John, Ludham
England William, Ludham
Fairhead George, Ludham
Fendick William, Ludham
Ford Thomas, Ludham
Garrett James, Ludham
Green William, Ludham
Grapes Simon, Ludham
Green Edward, Ludham
Harrison Robert, Ludham
Lacey James, Ludham
Nash Samuel, Ludham
Page Sherwood William, Ludham
Palgrave James, Ludham
Page George, Ludham
Slipper William Armine, Ludham
Wright Thomas, Ludham

	15	4

Annison Edward, jun., Hull
Bayles John, Ludham
Garrett Royal, Ludham
Greenacre James, sen., Neatishead
Heath William, Ludham
Mitchell Thomas, Ludham
Page William Sherwood, Oby
Rice Robert, Ludham
Slipper Robert Browne, Hardingham
Southgate George, Ludham
Sutton Sandle, Palling
Walker Henry, Ludham

F

Matlaske.

Langton Rev. Arthur, Plumstead
Spurgeon William, Matlaske

	0	2

Metton.

Amos William, Roughton
Bartram James, Metton
King Robert, Metton
Windham Rev. Robert, Metton

	0	4

Mundesley.

Barcham William, Mundesley
Barcham Thomas, Mundesley
Bear Edmund, Paston
Ducker Francis William, Lowestoft, Suffolk
Juniper Skoyles, Mundesley
Kirk John, Mundesley
Larter William, Mundesley
Miles Wakelin John, Shottisham
Pain John, Mundesley

	4	5

Mower John Thomas, North Walsham
Pycraft George Howlett, Mundesley
Steele Robert, clerk, Paston
Winch Job Turner, Mundesley
Wilder John Mac Mahon, clerk, Brandiston

Neatishead.

Allcock Richard, Neatishead
Allen Richard, Brooke
Banham John, Neatishead
Baldry Francis, Neatishead
Bayes Richard Henry, Neatishead
Cubitt Charles, Neatishead
Cubitt William Quincey, Neatishead
Greenacre James, Neatishead
Lonnen Charles, Neatishead
Meek William, Neatishead
Parr Thomas, Neatishead
Spanton Benjamin, Swaffham
Watts Robert, Sutton

	8	5

Allcock Richard, Neatishead
Clear Bulley James, Thorpe St. Andrew
Hall John, Neatishead

Northrepps.

Becket Joseph, Northrepps
Curties John, Northrepps
Curties Benjamin, Northrepps
Emery James, Northrepps
Emery George, Northrepps
Golden John, Northrepps
Law Patrick Comerford, Northrepps
Ling Edmund, Northrepps
Storey William, Northrepps
Summers Edmund, Northrepps

	2	8

Cushion Joseph, Northrepps
Lee Henry, Sidestrand
Ray William C. R., Eastford, Rochford

North Walsham.

	S.	C.
Alexander Joseph, North Walsham	—	
Baker Robert Summers, North Walsham	—	
Bradfield John, North Walsham	—	
Burton John, Bacton	—	
Butcher Henry, North Walsham	—	
Chamberlin John, North Walsham	—	
Chapman James, North Walsham	—	
Chipperfield John, Skeyton	—	
Cooper William, North Walsham	—	
Coleby John, North Walsham	—	
Crosswell Thomas, North Walsham	—	
Cubitt George, North Walsham		
Dyball Robert, North Walsham		
Dye James, North Walsham	—	
Dyke James, North Walsham	—	
Earl James, North Walsham	—	
England John, North Walsham	—	
Everard George, North Walsham	—	
Foreman John, North Walsham	—	
Fox Mark, North Walsham	—	
Fox William, North Walsham	—	
Fox Robert Salisbury, North Walsham	—	
Fox John, North Walsham		
Gales Robert, North Walsham		
Gedge Richard, North Walsham		
Gedge James, North Walsham		
Hall Thomas, North Walsham		
Harvey John, North Walsham		
Horsefield James, North Walsham		
Hunt John, North Walsham		
Johnson William Simms, North Walsham	—	
Juler George, North Walsham	—	
Lacey Richard Culley, North Walsham		
Learner Helsdon, North Walsham		
Lacock George, North Walsham	—	
Le Neve William, North Walsham	—	
Loads Joseph, North Walsham	—	
Loads William, North Walsham	—	
Love Martin, High-street, Stoke Newington	—	
Martin Robert, North Walsham	—	
Mace Joseph, North Walsham	—	
Morter William, North Walsham	—	
Mower John Thomas, North Walsham		
Murray James, North Walsham		
Neave Matthew, North Walsham		
Pank William Farrow, North Walsham	—	
Plowman William, North Walsham	—	
Plumbly John, North Walsham	—	
Riches John, Farmer, North Walsham	—	
Randall John, North Walsham	—	
Roofe Robert, North Walsham		
Rounce Everett, Rollesby		
Saunders Charles, North Walsham		
Scott George, North Walsham		
Sharpe William, North Walsham		
Shepheard Martin James, North Walsham		
Sewell Samuel, North Walsham		
Sewell Samuel, North Walsham		
Simpson Joseph, North Walsham		
Smith John, North Walsham		
Storey John Henry, North Walsham		
Thornton Charles, Antingham		
Trollop George Thomas, North Walsham	—	
Vincent Robert, North Walsham		
Walpole Richard, North Walsham		
Waterson Henry, North Walsham		
Ward George, North Walsham		
Webster William, North Walsham		
White Edward, North Walsham		

	S.	C.
White Timothy, North Walsham	—	
Wilkinson George, North Walsham	—	
Wilkinson John, North Walsham	—	
Williamson Joseph, North Walsham	—	
Wortley John, North Walsham	—	
Wright Cook Henry Lane, East Dereham	—	
Youngman Isaac, North Walsham	—	
Youngman Richard Gedge, North Walsham	—	
Youngman John, North Walsham	—	
	81	47
Andrews William, Magdalen-street, Norwich	—	
Baker Robert, North Walsham	—	
Barcham Jedediah, North Walsham	—	
Burton Thomas, North Walsham	—	
Clipperton William, North Walsham	—	
Deyns John Fuller, North Walsham	—	
Dyball John, Felmingham	—	
Johnson William, North Walsham	—	
Lane Thomas Angell, Hickling	—	
Lindo John, North Walsham	—	
Newton William, North Walsham	—	
Plumbly George, North Walsham	—	
Rippingall Rev. Stephen Frost, Langham	—	
Randall James, North Walsham	—	
Sadler Richard, North Walsham	—	
Sadler Samuel, North Walsham	—	
Steward Charles, North Walsham	—	
Tills Thomas, North Walsham	—	
Warner Thomas, North Walsham	—	
Woolsey Benjamin Postle, Swafield	—	
Wright William, Aylsham	—	

Overstrand.

	S.	C.
Cross Jeremiah, Overstrand	—	
Hutson William, Northrepps	—	
Howes John, Overstrand	—	
Pilgrim John, Overstrand	—	
Rogers Joseph, Overstrand	—	
Rogers Robert, Overstrand	—	
Rogers William, Overstrand	—	
Spinks John, Overstrand	—	
	0	8
Johnson Rev. Paul, Overstrand		
Peters Edwin, Gunton		

Oxnead.

	S.	C.
Spinks William Atkins, Oxnead		
	1	0
Ellis Thomas Richard, Oxnead Hall		
Smith John, Oxnead		

Palling.

	S.	C.
Barber George, Palling	—	
Chapman William Stamp, Potter Heigham	—	
Crowe Alfred, Palling	—	
Empson Thomas, Palling	—	
Hallock William, Palling	—	
Sutton Sandall, Palling	—	
Warnes Henry, Palling	—	
Wright James, Palling	—	
	4	4
Amis Robert, Palling		
Bond George, Palling		
Manship James, Palling		
Palmer Robert, Palling		
Pestell Samuel, Palling		
Thain Samuel, Palling		

Paston.

	S.	C.
Gaze Thomas, Paston	—	
Gaze James, Paston	—	
Hastings Joshua, Paston	—	
Hennesy Michael, Paston	—	
Lee William, North Walsham	—	
Mack John, Paston	—	
Purdy Thomas, Paston	—	
	4	8
Beare Edmund, Paston		
Larter Edward, Paston		
Rising Robert, Gimmingham		
Suffolk William, Paston		
Turner Charles, Paston		

Plumstead.

	S.	C.
Buck Thomas, Barningham Parva	—	
Overton John Buck, Plumstead	—	
Pull William, Plumstead	—	
Rowland James, Plumstead	—	
	0	4
Brett William, Plumstead		
Harrison James, Plumstead		

Potter Heigham.

	S.	C.
Applegate William, Potter Heigham	—	
Bower Edmund, Potter Heigham	—	
Boyce Symonds, Potter Heigham	—	
Blaxell John, Potter Heigham	—	
Blackburn William, Potter Heigham		
Grapes John, Potter Heigham		
Grapes Benjamin, Potter Heigham		
George Henry, Potter Heigham		
Howlett Robert Clark, West Bradenham	—	
Kidd Rev. Richard Bentley P., Potter Heigham		
Mace James, Yarmouth		
Neve James, Potter Heigham	—	
Pye William, Potter Heigham	—	
Rudd George, Potter Heigham	—	
Thaxter Samuel, Potter Heigham	—	
	8	7
Daniels George, Potter Heigham		
Grapes Thomas, Southtown		
Gurney Thomas C., Newmarket-road, Norwich		
Neve Jacob, Barton Turf		
Slipper John, Lound, Suffolk		

Ridlington.

	S.	C.
Flavell Rev. John Webb, Ridlington	—	
Green Thomas, Ridlington	—	
Grimes William, Magdalen-street, Norwich	—	
Marler Robert, Ridlington	—	
	4	0
Alexander Joseph, Bacton		
Banyer Robinson, Ridlington		
Bush John, Ridlington		
Fish Richard, North Walsham		

Roughton.

	S.	C.
Denny Joshua, Roughton	—	
Fox Amies Lee, Roughton	—	
Gwyn Rev. Richard Hamond, Roughton	—	
Huitt Robert, Roughton	—	
Hust Samuel, Roughton	—	
Hust Samuel, jun., Roughton	—	
Hewitt Robert, Roughton	—	

	S.	C.
Jonas James, Roughton	—	
Kittle James (alias Riches), Roughton	—	
Knights Sims Edward, Roughton	—	
Lemon John, Roughton	—	
Perkins George, Roughton	—	
Sutton Stephen, Roughton	—	
	4	9
Clarke James, Felbrigg		
Joy Robert, Roughton		
Melton James, Sustead		
Wortley Leonard, Roughton		

Runton.

	S.	C.
Abbs John, Runton	—	
Abbs Thomas, Runton	—	
Abbs James, Runton	—	
Abbs Matthew, Runton	—	
Abbs Thomas, Runton	—	
Cox John Sims, North Walsham	—	
Dennis John, Runton	—	
Knowles Matthew, Runton	—	
Pank Thomas, Runton	—	
Pegg Isaac, Sheringham	—	
Shore Stephen, Runton	—	
	1	10
Buxton Sir Edward North, Cromer		
Bolding William Johnson J., Weybourne		
Hill John David Hay, Gressinghall-hall		
Riches William, Cromer		

Ruston East.

	S.	C.
Atthill Anthony John, East Ruston	—	
Balls Thomas, Worstead	—	
Barber Benjamin, East Ruston	—	
Bates Samuel, Trimingham	—	
Bacon John, East Ruston	—	
Cubitt William Francis, clerk, Fritton, Suffolk	—	
Durrell William, East Ruston	—	
Durrell Samuel, East Ruston	—	
Gaze Robert, East Ruston	—	
Gaze Robert, East Ruston	—	
Hammond Joseph, East Ruston	—	
Hewitt Stephen, East Ruston	—	
Le Neve Charles, East Ruston	—	
Love John, Crostwight		
Lubbock John, East Ruston	—	
Newman William, Ridlington		
Page John, Antingham	—	
Plummer William, East Ruston	—	
Plummer Charles, East Ruston	—	
Plummer William, Walcott	—	
Rump Hewitt, East Ruston		
Riches Thomas, Brumstead		
Riches William, East Ruston	—	
Turner John Rudd, East Ruston	—	
Wiseman John, East Ruston	—	
Wittleton Walter George, East Ruston	—	
	19	7
Durrell John, East Ruston	—	
Durrell Charles, East Ruston	—	
Rudd Ash, East Ruston		
Symondson W., Bury St. Edmonton, Middlesex		
Wenn William, Walcott		
Wittleton Robert, East Ruston		
Youngman John, East Ruston		

Sco Ruston.

	S.	C.
Betts Benjamin, Sco Ruston	—	
Wells Thomas, Horstead	—	
	0	2
Wells Thomas Hayn, Sco Ruston		

Scottow.

	S.	C.
Allen Thomas, Scottow	—	
Betts John Girling, Scottow	—	
Bird Robert, Scottow	—	
Colk John, Scottow	—	
Durrant Sir Thomas Henry Estridge, Bart., Scottow	—	
Knights Thomas, Scottow	—	
Waterson George, Scottow	—	
	0	7
Harbord Robert, Scottow	—	

Sherringham.

	S.	C.
Barcham Barcham Benjamin, Sherringham	—	
Barcham Barcham, Lower Sherringham	—	
Breese Elmer, Lower Sherringham	—	
Breeze Robert Cooper, Bodham	—	
Bird Richard, Old Buckenham	—	
Coke Edward Keppel Wentworth, Longford-hall, Derbyshire	—	
Chestney Thomas, Waybourne	—	
Cox Richard, Sherringham	—	
Cox Robert, Lower Sherringham	—	
Critoph Samuel, Sherringham	—	
Chamberlin Corba, Sherringham	—	
Emery Lewis, Sherringham	—	
Gidney Samuel, Sherringham	—	
Grice John, Lower Sherringham	—	
Grimes William, Lower Sherringham	—	
Hammond Robert, Sherringham	—	
Hendry William, Sherringham	—	
Jordon Matthew, Lower Sherringham	—	
Leeder Thomas, Sherringham	—	
Long John, Lower Sherringham	—	
Long Robert, sen., Holt	—	
Little Robert, Lower Sherringham	—	
Lown Leonard, jun., Lower Sherringham	—	
Middleton James, Lower Sherringham	—	
Middleton William, Sherringham	—	
Pegg Henry, Lower Sherringham	—	
Pigott Robert, Sherringham	—	
Pike William, Gresham	—	
Pulleyne Rev. Benjamin, Holt	—	
Skipper Martin, Sherringham	—	
Upcher Henry Ramey, Sherringham	—	
Ward John, Lower Sherringham	—	
Wodehouse Robert, Lower Sherringham	—	
West Henry, Lower Sherringham	—	
West Edmund, Lower Sherringham	—	
Wilson Henry, Sherringham	—	
Wilson John, Sherringham	—	
	1	36
Brooks Robert, Sherringham		
Cooper John, Lower Sherringham		
Craske George, Sherringham		
Hart Walter William, Sherringham		
Kerrison George, Sherringham		
Pearce John, Hempstead		
West Edmund, Lower Sherringham		
West Christopher, junr., Sherringham		

Sidestrand.

	S.	C.
Breese Robert, Sidestrand	—	
Hedge George, Sidestrand	—	
Lee Henry, Sidestrand	—	
Moore Robert Norman, Sidestrand	—	
Ray William Carpenter Riston, Eastwood, near Rochford	—	
Starling John, Sidestrand	—	
	2	4
Curtis John, Northrepps		
Johnson Paul, Overstrand		
Ray Walter John, 13, Albert Terrace, Paddington, Middlesex		
Spurrell Flaxman, Bexley, Kent		

Skeyton.

	S.	C.
Bidewell Henry, Aylsham	—	
Bugden Henry, Skeyton	—	
Buck Richard, Skeyton	—	
Bugden Edward, Norwich	—	
Dyke James, Skeyton	—	
Galley John, Skeyton	—	
Leggett Laverocke Barnard, Skeyton	—	
Mace Joseph, Heigham	—	
Moore John William, Skeyton	—	
Otway Robert, Skeyton	—	
Pooley William, Skeyton	—	
Postle John, Skeyton	—	
Roofe William, Skeyton	—	
	6	7
Blake William Jex, Swanton Abbott		
Buck Miles, Skeyton		
Jones Samuel, Norwich		
Rice George, Skeyton		

Sloley.

	S.	C.
August Simon, Sloley	—	
Colman Samuel, Sloley	—	
Cole John, Sloley	—	
Colman Charles Shepherd, Sloley	—	
Kerrison John, Sloley	—	
Middleton Joseph, Sloley	—	
Scott Henry William, Aylsham	—	
Steward William, Sloley	—	
Thirtle John, Sloley	—	
Taylor Phillip, Sloley	—	
White James, Sloley	—	
	9	2
Postle William, Smallburgh		

Smallburgh.

	S.	C.
Baldwin John, Neatishead	—	
Chapman James, Smallburgh	—	
Cole Joseph, Smallburgh	—	
Dix John, Smallburgh	—	
Denham James Samuel, Smallburgh	—	
Deyns William, Smallburgh	—	
Deyns John, North Walsham	—	
Howes John, Smallburgh	—	
Harmer James, Smallburgh	—	
Knights Elijah, Smallburgh	—	
Lacey William, Smallburgh	—	
Long George, Smallburgh	—	
Neave Edward, Smallburgh	—	
Ormsby William Arthur, Smallburgh	—	
Pratt Robert, Smallburgh	—	
Postle William, Smallburgh	—	

	S.	C.
Spanton William, Tunstead		
Trorey Richard, Smallburgh	—	
	16	2
Knights Henry, Smallburgh		
Mattison William, Dilham		

Southrepps.

	S.	C.
Cooke John, Southrepps	—	
Ducker John, Southrepps	—	
Glover George Genville, Southrepps	—	
Golden John, Thorpe Market	—	
Golden Benjamin, Southrepps	—	
Green Priest, Southrepps	—	
Hewitt Robert, Southrepps	—	
Hutson William, jun., Northrepps	—	
Haddon Leonard, Southrepps	—	
Hern John, Southrepps	—	
Legood Samuel, Southrepps	—	
Lubbock John, Southrepps	—	
Martin William, Southrepps	—	
Painter Edmund, Southrepps	—	
Sharpen James, Southrepps	—	
Starling Samuel, Southrepps	—	
Theobald George, Southrepps	—	
Temple William, Southrepps	—	
Temple John, Southrepps	—	
Vince Samuel, Southrepps	—	
Woods Christopher, Southrepps	—	
	0	21
Barber Robert, Southrepps		
Bull Rev. Edward, Pentlow Rectory, Essex		
Breeze James, Southrepps		
Copeman Robert, Southrepps		
Carter James, Antingham		
Carter John, Southrepps		
Crowe Thomas, Soutreps		
Flower Cooke Sibbs, Aylsham		
Glover Rev. George, Southrepps		
Nichols John, Southrepps		
Plumbly James Spurrell, Southrepps		
Ray William C. R., Eastwood, Rochford, Essex		
Taylor William, Costessey		
Thornton Thomas, Antingham		

Stalham.

	S.	C.
Allcock Robert, Stalham	—	
Bates George John, Stalham	—	
Clarke Joseph, Stalham	—	
Clowes William, Stalham	—	
Cooke Robert, Stalham	—	
Cooke William Miller, Stalham	—	
Gaze Robert, Stalham	—	
Gibbons John, Weston	—	
Harvey Robert, Stalham	—	
Jay William Howard, Stalham	—	
Johnson George Randall, Bury St. Edmund's	—	
Keeler Samuel, Stalham	—	
Le Frank James, Stalham	—	
Richardson Robert, Stalham	—	
Salmon William, Stalham	—	
Salmon John, Stalham	—	
Sharp Joseph, Broadway, Deptford, Kent	—	
Silcock Richard Boardman, Stalham	—	
Salmon Henry, Stalham	—	
Salmon William, jun., Stalham	—	
Trorey James, Dilham	—	
West John Merriman, Stalham	—	
White Rev. Joseph Neville, Stalham	—	
	12	11

	S.	C.
Amiss John, Ingham		
Barber James, Stalham		
Burton Jonathan, Stalham		
Clarke John Elph, Winterton		
Clarke Henry, Stalham		
Jay William, Stalham		
Pestell Peter, Stalham		
Pestell John Ralls, Stalham		
Webb John Craske, Stalham		

Suffield.

	S.	C.
Cook Thomas, Suffield	—	
Kendle John, Suffield	—	
Lacy Richard, Suffield	—	
Wortley Robert, Suffield	—	
	0	4

Sustead.

	S.	C.
Le Neve Charles, Sustead	—	
Landymore Jonathan, Sustead	—	
Melton James, Sustead	—	
	0	3

Sutton.

	S.	C.
Barber George Simpson, Sutton	—	
Beane John, Sutton	—	
Flowarday Edward, Sutton	—	
Minner Edward, Hickling	—	
Moore Rev. Barnard, Sutton	—	
Richardson Joseph, Sutton	—	
Rudd John, Sutton	—	
	8	4
Annison Robert, Kessingland		
Breeze John, Sutton		
Bygrave John, sen., Sutton		
Beane John, Ashmanhaugh		
Bygrave John, jun., Sutton		
Crowe Robert, Sutton		
Cubitt Charles George, Catfield		
Durrant John, Sutton		
Smith Samuel, Sutton		

Swafield.

	S.	C.
Bastard John, Swafield		
Christopher Robert, Swafield	—	
Cork James, Swafield	—	
Codling Thomas, Westwick	—	
Dolphin Thomas, Swafield	—	
Layard John Thomas, Swafield	—	
Lark Burrell William, Swafield	—	
Steward John, Swafield	—	
Woollsey Benjamin Postle, Swafield	—	
Wrench Henry, Swafield	—	
	9	1
Wilden John, Thornham	—	

Swanton Abbott.

	S.	C.
Arnold Robert A., Lower Westwick, Norwich	—	
Balls Thomas Cadge, Scottow	—	
Ducker Richard, Swanton Abbott	—	
Jex Blake William Lubbock, Swanton Abbott	—	
Knights John, Swanton Abbott	—	
	2	3
Bidewell Henry James, Swanton Abbott		
Brett William, Plumstead		
Evans Henry, clerk, Lyng		
Jex Blake William Jex, clerk, Lamas		

38   THE POLL AND REGISTER—NORTH WALSHAM DISTRICT.

	S.	C.
Richardson Isaac, Swanton Abbott		
Spink Robert, Swanton Abbott		
Sturmy Herbert, 8, Wellington-st., St. Saviour's, Southwark		

Thorpe Market.

	S.	C.
Clark George, Thorpe Market	—	
Cushion Philip, Thorpe Market	—	
Martin Richard, Thorpe Market	—	
	0	3

Thurgarton.

	S.	C.
Balls Thomas, Thurgarton	—	
Chapman Dennis, Thurgarton	—	
Roper Snelling, Thurgarton	—	
Spurrell William Dewing, Thurgarton	—	
Woods Robert, Thurgarton	—	
Woods James, Thurgarton	—	
Wrench Benjamin Emery, Aylsham	—	
	1	6
Robins William Burton, Thurgarton		

Thwaite.

	S.	C.
Dix Thomas, clerk, Thwaite	—	
	1	0
Bradford John, Thwaite		
Cook John, Thwaite		
Elden John, Thwaite		

Trimingham.

	S.	C.
Buxton Chas., Grosvenor-crescent, St. George's, Hanover-square, Middlesex		
Buxton Thomas Fowell, Leytonstone-house, Leytonstone, Essex		
Bullamore John, Trimingham		
Ducker John Benjamin, Southrepps		
Gillam Stephen, Trimingham		
Hall Thomas, Trimingham		
	0	6
Hacon William, Ludham		
Steele Robert, Paston		

Trunch.

	S.	C.
Bidwell Thomas Blaxland, Trunch	—	
Buck William, North Walsham	—	
Bugden Cornelius, Trunch	—	
Clarke Matthew, Trunch	—	
Chapman Robert, Trunch	—	
Greenacre Charles, Trunch	—	
Hust Richard, Trunch	—	
Jarrett Rev. Thomas, Trunch	—	
Juniper Robert, Mundesley	—	
Miller John, Trunch	—	
Primrose William, jun., Trunch	—	
Thompson James, Trunch	—	
Townrow James, Trunch	—	
	6	7
Bullen Samuel, Trunch		
Hastings Daniel, Misterton, near Bawtry		
Johnson William, North Walsham		
Juniper Skyles William, Shoreham, Sussex		
Primrose William, Trunch		
Wright Henry, Antingham		

Tunstead.

	S.	C.
Appleton James, Tunstead	—	
Bailey Henry Negus, Tunstead	—	
Breeze George, Tunstead	—	
Case Henry, Tunstead	—	
Mack John, Tunstead	—	
Mack John, jun., Tunstead	—	
Purdy George, Tunstead	—	
Pointer Thomas, Tunstead	—	
	7	1
Garrod William, Tunstead		
Johnson Randall, Tunstead		
Mack Thomas, clerk, Tunstead		
Scottow John, Tunstead		
Sharpe Thomas, Tunstead		

Tuttington.

	S.	C.
Bowles Benjamin Brettingham, Tuttington	—	
Beck Philip, Tuttington	—	
Gowing Zachariah, Tuttington	—	
Hobson Rev. Samuel, Marsham	—	
Hall John, Tuttington	—	
Hardy Cozens Hardy William Clement, Letheringsett, Norfolk	—	
Vincent John, Tuttington	—	
	1	6

Walcott.

	S.	C.
Baldwin Thomas Cubitt, Shereford	—	
Lyall Robert, Walcott	—	
Palmer James, Walcott	—	
Riches Thomas, Walcott	—	
Sandell William, Walcott	—	
Wenn William, Walcott	—	
	5	1
Bush John, Walcott		
Palmer John, Happisburgh		
Siely Andrew, Walcott		
Warner Siely John, Yarmouth		

Waxham.

	S.	C.
Harvey Henry, Waxham	—	
Ready Rev. Henry, Hickling	—	
Whitaker Henry, Waxham	—	
	1	2
Cubitt Samuel, Waxham		
Gibbs Alfred, Waxham		
Tuck John, Waxham		

Westwick.

	S.	C.
Fearman Thomas, Westwick	—	
Goose Thomas, Westwick	—	
Lacey John Flaxman, Westwick	—	
Wymer Rev. Edward, Smallburgh	—	
	4	0
Petre John Berney, Westwick		

Witton.

	S.	C.
Monsey Thomas, Witton	—	
Marshall Francis, Witton	—	
Proctor Rev. Francis, Witton	—	
Smith William, Witton	—	
Youngman George, Witton	—	
	2	3
Bates William, East Ruston		
Cubitt Thomas, Witton		
Marshall Francis, Bacton		

Worstead.

	S.	C.
Cooke Henry, Worstead		
Cross Thomas, Worstead	—	
Cole John, Worstead	—	
Cooper Robert, Worstead	—	
Cross John, Worstead	—	
Denham James, Worstead	—	
Durrell Joseph, Worstead	—	
Greenacre Everard, Honing	—	
Greenacre Thomas, Westwick	—	
Greenacre Robert, Worstead	—	
Goose John, Worstead	—	
King Rev. George, Worstead	—	
Kirk Thomas, Worstead	—	
Lacey John, Worstead	—	
Loveday Henry, Worstead	—	
Mace John, Coltishall	—	
Nash William, Worstead	—	
Neave Jeremiah, Worstead	—	
Ostler Robert, Worstead	—	
Rous Hon. William Rufus, Worstead	—	
Salmon Richard, Stalham	—	
Tooley James, Worstead	—	

	S.	C.
Tooley Henry, Sloley	—	
Watson Richard, Worstead		—
Wiseman Thomas, Worstead	—	
Watts Henry, Worstead	—	
Watts Christmas, Swanton Abbott		—
Woodrow William, Worstead	—	
Watts Christopher, North Walsham	—	
	16	18
Beloe Henry, Gorleston		
Barnard Henry Riches, Worstead		
Boult Thomas, Worstead		
Clarke Matthew, Trunch		
Greenacre James, Hempstead		
Morse Charles, Horstead		
Petre John Berney, Westwick	—	
Sedgwick the Rev. Richard, the Close, Norwich		
Wenn Richard, Worstead		

Outvoters.

	S.	C.
Girling Colk John, Cromer	—	
Woolbright William Henry, King-st., Norwich		—
	0	2
Rudd John, Sutton	—	

REEPHAM DISTRICT,

COMPRISING THE PARISHES OF

Aylsham.

	S.	C.
Bane William, Aylsham		
Bellward William, Aylsham	—	
Buston John, Aylsham	—	
Bartram William, Aylsham	—	
Bartram Robert, Aylsham	—	
Bulwer James, clerk, Hunworth		
Case James Lee, Aylsham		
Colk John, Aylsham	—	
Cory Thomas, Aylsham	—	
Clover John Wright, 44, Mortimer-street, Cavendish-square, London	—	
Clover John, Aylsham	—	
Copeman George, Aylsham		
Davison James, Aylsham	—	
Duffield James, Aylsham		
Edwards John, Aylsham	—	
Freeman John, Aylsham		
Harrod Henry, Priory-lane, King-st., Norwich	—	
Huddleston George James, Upwell, Isle of Ely	—	
Horstead John, Aylsham		
Hall William, Aylsham	—	
Laxen Henry, Aylsham		
Lemon Benjamin, Aylsham	—	
Lockton John, Blickling		
Mayston John, Aylsham	—	
Neech John, Aylsham	—	
Pert David, Aylsham		
Pratt Robert, Aylsham		
Proudfoot John, Aylsham	—	
Poll Henry, Aylsham		
Postle Robert, Aylsham	—	
Roe Daniel Frederick, Aylsham		
Robson William, Aylsham	—	
Scott George, Aylsham	—	
Shreeve George, Aylsham		
Soame Henry Edward, Aylsham	—	
Soame George, Aylsham	—	
Sutton John, Aylsham	—	
Symonds John, Aylsham	—	
Tipple George, Aylsham	—	
Tipple Thomas, Oulton	—	
Ulph Richard, Erpingham	—	
Waller John Clear, Aylsham	—	
Wilson William, Aylsham	—	
White George, Aylsham	—	
Yates Rev. Edmund Telfer, Aylsham		
	24	21
Bane John Pedder, Downham, Norfolk		
Copeman Thomas, Aylsham		
Chapman John, Aylsham		
Clark Richard, Aylsham		
Clarke George, Aylsham		
Digings James, Belvidere-road, London		
Dickino Tomyns S., Kirby Melzeard, Yorkshire		
Elvin Robert, Aylsham		
Frostick Daniel, Aylsham		
Fitt John, Aylsham		
Glister Thomas, Aylsham		
Harrod James, Aylsham		

	S.	C.
Mann Samuel, Ingworth		
Parmeter Robert William, Aylsham		
Repton William, Aylsham		
Saunders James Warnes, Sampford, Peverell, Devonshire		
Sexton Joseph, Aylsham		
Wright William, Aylsham		
Wickes William Watts, Thetford		

Barningham Parva.

	S.	C.
Hardy Thomas, Barningham Parva		—
Leake Rev. Custance, Holt		
Page Christopher Thomas, Stiffkey		
Page George Thomas, Stiffkey		—
	1	3
Case Edward, Barningham Parva		
Cubitt Samuel, Barningham Parva		
Page Robert Brereton, Stiffkey		

Bawdeswell.

	S.	C.
Allen John, Bawdeswell		—
Bacon Thomas, Bawdeswell		
Bush Arthur, Bawdeswell		
Bidewell William, junr., Bawdeswell		
Breese Thomas, Bawdewell		
Breese William, Bawdeswell		
Brown John, Bawdeswell		
Catton Alfred, Bawdeswell		
Floyd Henry, Castleacre		
Frost John James, Bawdeswell		
Haylett Stephen, Bawdeswell		
Leeds Robert, Bawdeswell		
Pearce Robert, Bawdeswell		
Pulley Henry, Carrow-hill, Norwich		
Purdy John, Bawdeswell		
Purdy Thomas, Eaton, near Norwich		
Scott Robert, Shouldham		
Tann Benjamin, Bawdeswell		
Twaites Barnabas, Strumpshaw		
	4	15
Hall Charles, Bawdeswell		
Hyh John, Wickhampton		
Parke William, Bawdeswell		
Pynsent Ferdinand Alfred, Bawdeswell		

Billingford.

	S.	C.
Blomfield John, Warham		—
Dashwood Charles John, Billingford		
Gill William Brook, Billingford		
Good Philip, Weston		
Leeder Thomas, Union-place, Lynn		
Millatt James, Billingford		
Spooner George, Briston		
Thomas William Savory, Billingford		
Whiteman George Freeman, Billingford		
	2	7
Freeman Whiteman G., Billingford		
Millett William, Billingford		
Watson William, Billingford		

Bintry.

	S.	C.
Burrell William, Bintry	—	
Francis Benjamin, Twyford	—	
Gedge George, Alderford	—	
Goggs Nathaniel Duffield, Fakenham	—	
Kitton George Rodwell, East Basham	—	
Kitton Thomas Samuel, East Basham	—	
Milles Watson George, Elmham-hall, Norfolk	—	
Rackham Willoughby Breare Still, Lincoln's Inn Fields, London	—	
Rodwell Lionel, Burnham Norton	—	
Sillett Robert, Fakenham	—	
Upton William, North Elmham	—	
Wrightup Thomas, Ashill	—	
	6	6
Dashwood Rev. Augustus, Thornage	—	
Durrant William, Hoe	—	
Harrison Robert, Bintry	—	
Parmeter Francis, Booton	—	

Blickling.

	S.	C.
Barker Robert Charles, Blickling	—	
Custance Rev. John, Blickling	—	
Palmer Robert, Blickling	—	
Raymes John, Blickling	—	
Smith Thomas, Blickling	—	
Wells Robert Utting, Blickling	—	
	6	0
Kent Rev. Frederic, Ryde, Isle of Wight	—	
Sharpin Samuel, Blickling	—	

Booton.

	S.	C.
Bircham Samuel, Booton	—	
Elwin Whitwell, Booton	—	
Parsons Benjamin, Booton	—	
Parsons Robert, Booton	—	
Rodham Richard Sewell	—	
	3	2

Brandiston.

	S.	C.
Atthill Rev. William, Horsford Vicarage	—	
Page Isaac, Brandiston	—	
Wilder John Mc Mahon, Brandiston	—	
	3	0

Bylaugh.

	S.	C.
Taylor Joseph, Bylaugh	—	
Warnes Stephen, Bylaugh	—	
Lombe Charles, Upper Harley-street, London	—	
	0	2

Cawston.

	S.	C.
Austin Matthew, Cawston	—	
Austin Watts, Cawston	—	
Bird Edward, Cawston	—	
Bambridge Waller, Cawston	—	
Buck Samuel, Hackford	—	
Blythe Jacob, Cawston	—	
Brett James, Guestwick	—	
Bird Bailey, Norwich	—	
Cotterill William, Heydon	—	
Cook William, Cawston	—	
Craske Samuel, Holt	—	
Dix Robins, Cawston	—	
Dix Thomas, Cawston	—	

	S.	C.
Dewing William, Cawston	—	
Dewing Robert, sen., Cawston	—	
Douglas James, Cawston	—	
Easton Isaac, Cawston	—	
Easton James, Cawston	—	
Easton William, Cawston	—	
Easton Edward, Cawston	—	
Easton Joseph, Cawston	—	
Hickling John Shepheard, Cawston	—	
Hodgson David, Norwich	—	
Howes John, Cawston	—	
Howes John, Cawston	—	
Lewis Leo, sen., Cawston	—	
Marsh Theodore Henry, Cawston Rectory	—	
Oliver John, Norwich	—	
Pye Samuel, Cawston	—	
Richmond William, Cawston	—	
Saul Thomas, Buxton	—	
Saul William, jun., Cawston	—	
Saul William, Cawston	—	
Slipper George, Cawston	—	
Tuddenham James, Cawston	—	
Tuddenham John, Cawston	—	
Tuddenham William, Cawston	—	
Wakeford William, Cawston	—	
Williams Brettingham, Cawston	—	
Watts William, Cawston	—	
Wiggett William, Cawston	—	
Watts William, jun., Cawston	—	
	5	37
Brett John Augustine, Wisbech, Cambridgeshire	—	
Dix James, Cawston	—	
Easton Thomas, East Sheen, Mortlake, Surrey	—	
Easton John Groom, Cawston	—	
Page Samuel, Cawston	—	
Robins Joseph, Dartford, Kent	—	
Scottow Robert, Saxthorpe	—	
Taylor Thomas, Cawston	—	

Corpusty.

	S.	C.
Barber James, Wood Dalling	—	
Blogg Stephen Money, Norwich	—	
Bulwer William Earle G. Lytton, Heydon	—	
Goldsmith Samuel, Corpusty	—	
Godfrey Robert, Blickling	—	
Hastead Benjamin, Bridgham	—	
Kiddell George, Corpusty	—	
Platten Robert, Corpusty	—	
	3	5
Austin Matthew, Seething	—	
Barber George, Guestwick	—	
Bulwer Edward Gascoyne, Heydon	—	
Flogdell John, Corpusty	—	
Gooch James, Corpusty	—	
Ireland Henry John, Guestwick	—	
Ives Jeremiah Robert, Bentworth-hall, Alton, Hampshire	—	
Wright John, Saxthorpe	—	

Elsing.

	S.	C.
Brown Richard Charles, Elsing	—	
Freeman William Robert, Swanton Morley	—	
Isbell John, Elsing	—	
Kent John Pryme, Elsing	—	
Large Benjamin, Elsing	—	
Lewell Edward, Elsing	—	
Lewell John, Elsing	—	
Miles John, Elsing	—	
Rix George, Elsing	—	

G

	S.	C.
Sharman Peter, Elsing		—
Shickle James, Elsing		—
Valpy Rev. Julias John Culpepper, Elsing		—
Waters Richard Curl, Elsing		—
Wier James, Elsing		—
Wier Charles Elsing		—
	4	11
Evans Thomas Browne, Dean-house, Oxfordshire		
Goward William, Elsing		
Hart Edward Fair, Distillery-street, Heigham, Norwich		
Ling William, Swanton Morley		

Foulsham.

	S.	C.
Allen George, Foulsham		—
Austin Thomas, Foulsham		—
Body Henry, Foulsham		—
Body Henry, Foulsham		—
Blanchflower John, Fakenham		—
Blogg James, Foulsham		—
Body Edmund, Foulsham		—
Chapman Thomas, Bintry		—
Cubitt Benjamin, Foulsham		—
Chamberlain Edward, East Dereham		—
Cooke George, Avely, Essex		—
Clarke Robert, Foulsham		—
Craske Thomas, Foulsham		—
Craske William Ireland, Barningham Winter		—
Dawson Michael, Foulsham		—
Gant Robert, Foulsham		—
Gibbs Frederick, Foulsham		—
Girling Christopher Andrews, Foulsham		—
Leaman Richard, Foulsham		—
Leaman Charles, Foulsham		—
Moore Jonathan, Foulsham		—
Neal Valentine, Foulsham		—
Pratt Richard, Foulsham		—
Pratt Charles, Hindolveston		—
Peterson William, Foulsham		—
Rieve West, Hackford		—
Saunders Charles, Foulsham		—
Saunders James, Foulsham		—
Sawyer John, Foulsham		—
Shepherd Allen, Aylmerton		—
Spooner Robert, Worthing		—
Spooner James, Foulsham		—
Stroulger Isaac, Foulsham		—
Seaman Henry, Guestwick		—
Sherringham Edward William, Gt. Massingham		—
Thurling Peter, Foulsham		—
	13	23
Aufrere George Anthony, Bowness, Westmoreland		
Amis Richard, Hackford next Reepham		
Austin Watts, Foulsham		
Bird James Waller, Foulsham		
Curson Robert John, Wood Dalling		
Hastings Jacob Lord, Melton Constable		
Ireland Anthony Woodhouse, Guestwick		
Leaman Edmund, Foulsham		
Lunness Joseph, Foulsham		
Woods Robert, Thurgarton		

Foxley.

	S.	C.
Barker James, Foxley		
Elvin James David, Bawdeswell		
Fox George Thomas, Foxley		
Lewell Isaac, Foxley		
Meal John, Foxley		

	S.	C.
Norgate the Rev. Louis Augustus, Foxley		—
Parker Thomas Christmas, Little Snoring		—
Pegg John, Foxley		—
Ramsdale Robert, Dereham		—
Spinks John Lane, Valentine-street, Heigham, Norwich		—
White William John, Foxley		—
	8	8
Grounds William, Hoe		
West Thomas, North Elmham		

Guestwick.

	S.	C.
Barstard William, Guestwick		—
Butler Robert, Houghton		—
Chad Joseph Stonehewer Scott, Pinkney-hall, Tattersett, Fakenham		—
Colman William, Swanton Novers		—
Cooper Thomas, Mileham		—
Drane Robert, Guestwick		—
Gayford George, Guestwick		—
Goldsmith Thomas, Guestwick		—
Ireland Anthony Woodhouse, Guestwick		—
Neale George, Foulsham		—
Seaman John, Guestwick		—
Smith Samuel, Plumstead		—
	2	10
Barber George, Guestwick		
Drane Robert, Guestwick		
Heath William Macclesfield, Langdown Lawn, Hythe, Southampton		
Page Thomas Christopher, Stiffkey		
Sherringham Valentine Dennis, Thornage		
Shand Rev. George, Guestwick		

Guist.

	S.	C.
Abbey John, Guist		—
Bircham William, Guist		—
Cooper Henry, Guist		—
Dack Matthew, Guist		—
Griggs Money, South Creake		—
Harrison Robert, Guist		—
Kendall William, Guist		—
Mallan William, Guist		—
Money John, Guist		—
	5	4
Drosier Robert Margetson, Buckenham Palace		

Hackford.

	S.	C.
Bircham Francis Samuel, Hackford		—
Bircham William, Hackford		—
Bircham William, junr., Hackford		—
Bircham William, Hackford		—
Briggs James, Hackford		—
Burton John, Hackford		—
Burton Thomas, Hackford		—
Davidson James, Hackford		—
Gladden Robert Peters, Hackford		—
Hart Robert, Worthing		—
Hart Thomas Grounds, Hackford		—
Holley Edward, clerk, Hackford		—
Howard George, Hackford		—
Howes Samuel, Hackford		—
Isaacks Nathaniel, Cromer		—
Keeler John, Hackford and Mattishall		—
Keeler Robert, Hackford		—
King John, Hackford		—
Leeds Stephen, Kerdiston		—
Lincoln Thomas, Hackford		—

	S.	C.
Parmeter Francis, Booton	—	
Perry Charles Henry, Hackford	—	
Roberson Henry, Heald's-hall, Leeds	—	
Sands Alexander, Hackford	—	
Sewell William Pescod, Hackford	—	
Springall Thomas West, Hackford	—	
	5	21
Bambridge Martin, junr., Fakenham	—	
Bush John, Hackford	—	
Collyer John, Impington-hall, near Cambridge	—	
Dunham John, Hackford	—	
George William, Hackford	—	
Rodham William, Hackford	—	
St. John George, Hackford	—	
Scurll Brettingham, Hackford	—	
Staples Thomas, Hackford	—	

Haveringland.

	S.	C.
Fellowes Edward, Haveringland	—	
Muskett William, Haveringland	—	
	2	0
Leamon Philip, Haveringland	—	

Hevingham.

	S.	C.
Basey Francis, Hevingham	—	
Beck William, Hevingham	—	
Beevor Edward Rigby, clerk, Hevingham	—	
Blyth George, Hevingham	—	
Brooks Benjamin, Hevingham	—	
Bowman Benjamin, Hevingham	—	
Burton John, Hevingham	—	
Basey Robert, Hevingham	—	
Bowman James, Hevingham	—	
Burton James, Hevingham	—	
Breeze James, Aylsham	—	
Case Thomas Henry, Hevingham	—	
Case Robert, Lammas	—	
Dack Charles, Hevingham	—	
Dack Francis, Hevingham	—	
Fuller John, Hevingham	—	
Gilham James, Hevingham	—	
Gibson William, Hevingham	—	
Gooch George, Hevingham	—	
Lawse John, Swaffham	—	
Marsham George Augustus, Aylsham	—	
Medler William, Hevingham	—	
Medler Charles, Hevingham	—	
Matthewson James, Hevingham	—	
Matthewson Joseph, Hevingham	—	
Medler Henry, Hevingham	—	
Mitchell Erasmus, Hevingham	—	
Mitchell John, Hevingham	—	
Nobbs Charles, Hevingham	—	
Pamment Thomas, Hevingham	—	
Pratt William, Hevingham	—	
Preston Thomas, Stratton Strawless	—	
Pye Jeremiah, Hevingham	—	
Smith John, St. Augustine's, Norwich	—	
Stearman James, Hevingham	—	
Wade Mark, Hevingham	—	
Willimott William, Hevingham	—	
	4	33
Austin Matthew, Cawston	—	
Bowman Robert, Stratton Strawless	—	
Browne William, Burgh	—	
Fellowes Edward, Haveringland	—	
Gladdon John, Stratton Strawless	—	
Mack Robert, Hainford	—	
Marsham Rev. Henry Philip, Marsham	—	

	S.	C.
Marsham Rev. Thomas John Gordon, Wramplingham	—	
Medler Charles, Hevingham	—	
Newton Edward, Hevingham	—	

Heydon.

	S.	C.
Bulwer William Earle Lytton, Heydon-hall	—	
Golding William Lawrence, Heydon	—	
Ireland Benjamin, Heydon	—	
Kiddell John, Heydon	—	
Leeds Stephen, Heydon	—	
	0	5
Nepean Rev. Evan, Bolton-street, London	—	

Hindolveston.

	S.	C.
Adkins John, Hindolveston	—	
Astley Francis Le Strange, Burgh-hall	—	
Butters John, Hindolveston	—	
Burrell Daniel, Fakenham	—	
Boulter Edward, Stibbard	—	
Dent William, Hindolveston	—	
Dobson Henry, Hindolveston	—	
Dobson John, Hindolveston	—	
Forrow Robert, Hindolveston	—	
Fulcher Thomas, Hindolveston	—	
Gidney John, Melton Constable	—	
Johnson Thomas, Hindolveston	—	
Moore John Bell, Hindolveston	—	
Martins James, Hindolveston	—	
Newman Thomas, Hindolveston	—	
Pegg Matthew, Hindolveston	—	
Pegg John (baker), Hindolveston	—	
Pegg John, jun., Hindolveston	—	
Reynolds Robert, Hindolveston	—	
Slyman Thomas, 4, Montague-street, Portman-square, London	—	
Thaxter Samuel, Hindolveston	—	
Taylor John, Hindolveston	—	
Thurlow Thomas, South Creake	—	
	0	23
Brereton John, Brinton	—	
Cook William, Glandford	—	
Love Osborne John, Holt, Norfolk	—	
Margerson William, Stody	—	
Nurse James, Hindolveston	—	

Irmingland.

	S.	C.
Clark Richard, Irmingland	—	
Tipple Thomas, Irmingland	—	

Itteringham.

	S.	C.
Bayes Thomas Henry, Itteringham	—	
Browne James, Itteringham	—	
Copeman Frederick, Blickling	—	
Randle William, North Walsham	—	
Shepherd Brooks Crowe, Itteringham	—	
	4	1
Elwin Peter James, Itteringham	—	
Lee Robert, Itteringham	—	
Starling Thomas, Burnham Thorpe	—	
Tipple James, Itteringham	—	
Walpole Henry, 7, Connaught-square, London	—	

Lyng.

	S.	C.
Bidwell George, Stanton rectory, near Ixworth, Suffolk	—	

	S.	C.
Bunn William, Lyng		—
Brand William, Lyng		—
Brett Benjamin, Lingwood		—
Bullock Stephen, Lyng		—
Comer Isaac, Lyng		—
English James, Lyng		—
Frost William, Lyng		—
Isbell Charles, Lyng		—
Lincoln James, 64, Cambridge-terrace, Hyde-park, London		—
Marcon Edward George, Lyng		—
Money William, Lyng		—
Nicholson John, Lyng		—
Partrick Dennis, Lyng		—
Robberds Charles Augustus, Norwich		—
Speakman Austin, Lyng		—
Spendlove William, Lyng		—
Spragg Samuel, Lyng		—
	5	18
Blythe James, Lyng		
Colson Charles, clerk, Great Hormead Vicarage, Herts.		
Evans Rev. Henry, Lyng		
Eglington Mark, Whitwell		
Mills Thomas, Tolmers, Herts		

Mannington.

	S.	C.
Cook John, Thwaite		
Gay William Paul, Mannington		

Marsham.

	S.	C.
Blyth Thomas, Marsham		—
Bowles Robert Jeckell, Marsham		—
Cook Thomas, Marsham		—
Edridge Thomas, Marsham		—
Elvin William, Marsham		—
Greenwood Charles, Aylsham		—
Howlett John, Marsham		—
Jones Charles, Marsham,		—
Lake William, Aylsham		—
Lambert John, Marsham		—
Mack Robert, Marsham		—
Moore Edward, Marsham		—
Moore Edward, Marsham		—
Nave John, Marsham		—
Neal Christmas, Marsham		—
Neal James, Marsham		—
Rounce Benjamin, Marsham		—
Shreeve Edward, Marsham		—
Story William, Grove-place, Norwich		—
Spink Peter, Marsham		—
Watts James, Marsham		—
Watts Needham, Marsham		—
Watts William, Marsham		—
	14	9
Bowles Benjamin Brettingham, Tuttington		
Edwards Luke, Marsham		
Ellis William, Wymondham		
Gambling John, Buxton		
Gunton Rev. John, Marsham		
Hastings Henry, Marsham		
Moore William, Morton		
Nave James, Marsham		
Reynolds Joseph, Hindolveston		
Soame Peter, Marsham		

Morton.

	S.	C.
Berney Thomas French, Morton		—
Berney George Ducket, Morton		—
Large John, Morton		—
Palmer John, Morton		—
Bunn James, Morton		
	3	1

Oulton.

	S.	C.
Crisp Rayner Stillingfleet, Oulton		—
Gay William, Oulton		—
Golding John, Corpusty		—
Hunt Thomas Maxwell, Oulton		—
Jeffery Edward, Oulton		—
Keeler Thomas, Oulton		—
Lake James, Oulton		—
Middleton Charles, Holkham		—
Moore John Dyball, Oulton		—
Seaman Robert, Oulton		—
Seaman Thomas, Oulton		—
	7	4
Golding William Lawrence, Corpusty		
Martins William, Oulton		
Pitman Samuel, Rumwell-lodge, Taunton, Somersetshire		
Pegg Robert, Oulton		
Rice James, Oulton		
Tipple James, Oulton		

Reepham with Kerdistone.

	S.	C.
Alderton Thomas, Reepham		—
Blake Francis John, King-street, Norwich		—
Dye Henry, Kerdistone		—
Eglington Samuel Sewell, Hackford		—
Eglington Freeman, Kerdistone		—
Eacher John, Corpusty		—
Filby John William, Kerdistone		—
George Henry, Kerdistone		—
Hardingham James, Reepham		—
Leeds John Parmeter, Billingford		—
Leeds William, Hackford		—
Partridge Thomas John, Reepham		—
Pumfrey James, Kerdistone		—
Seely Barnabas, Kerdistone		—
Seely Barnabas Lemon, Kerdistone		—
Tann Thomas, Kerdistone		—
Watson Job Henry, Reepham Moor		—
	7	10
Besford John, Kerdistone		
Edwards James, Heydon		
Field Rev. Frederic, Reepham		
George Robert, Kerdistone		
Parke William Bircham, Reepham Moor		
Sewell Samuel, Reepham		

Ringland.

	S.	C.
Abel Jeremiah, Ringland		—
Caston John, St. Benedict's, Norwich		—
Dunham James, Bawburgh		—
Garrould William, Ringland		—
Millatt Jonathan, Ringland		—
	3	2
Brickdale Richard, Felthorpe		
Howes James, Ringland		

	S.	C.
Sall.		
Austin Frederick, Sall	—	
Ireland Thomas, Sall	—	
Leeds Joseph, Sall	—	
Marsh Rev. Charles Earle, Sall Rectory	—	
Perowne Rev. John, Chapel-field, Norwich	—	
Seely James, Sall	—	
Seely Barnabas Lemon, Sall		
	2	5
Joddrell Sir Richard Paul, Sall House	—	
Saxthorpe.		
Ashby Rev. Samuel, Saxthorpe	—	
Goldsmith J. Barker, Saxthorpe	—	
Goldsmith Samuel, jun., Corpusty	—	
Gooch Robert Parker, Hackford next Reepham	—	
Hase Thomas, Saxthorpe	—	
Woods Edmund, Briston		
	1	5
Bacon John, Saxthorpe	—	
Breese Stephen, Aylsham	—	
Crowe John, Saxthorpe	—	
Cubitt John, Stratton Strawless	—	
Dixon Abel, Saxthorpe	—	
Farrow James, Saxthorpe	—	
Goldsmith Samuel, Corpusty	—	
Howes William, Saxthorpe	—	
Lake Charles, Saxthorpe	—	
Witherell Thomas, Fincham	—	
Sparham.		
Clarke John, Sparham	—	
Forby Robert Wright, Sparham	—	
Foster Lambert Blackwell, Fritton, Suffolk	—	
Middleton Edmund Plane, Hindringham	—	
Norgate Rev. Thomas Starling, Sparham	—	
Nelson James, Mattishall, Norfolk	—	
Savory John, jun., Sparham	—	
Verdon John, Great Witchingham		
	0	8
Bloomfield Miles, South Wootton	—	
Canham Henry, Sparham	—	
Hazel Robert, Sparham	—	
Nelson Thomas, Sparham	—	
Stoughton Clarke, Sparham	—	
Taylor James, Sparham	—	
Stratton Strawless.		
Bowman Robert, Stratton Strawless	—	
Laws Thomas, Stratton Strawless	—	
Powell Peter, Stratton Strawless		
	3	0
Cubitt John, Stratton Strawless	—	
Gladden John, Stratton Strawless	—	
Marsham Rev. Edward, Sculthorpe	—	
Marsham Rev. Henry Philip, Marsham	—	
Preston Thomas, Stratton Strawless	—	
Smith James, Stratton Strawless	—	
Swanington.		
Artis Matthew, Swanington	—	
Hildyard Rev. Frederick, Swanington	—	
Lowe Robt, Cold Fair-green, Knodishall, Suffolk	—	
Pye William, Swanington	—	
Sparks Daniel Sidney, Swanington	—	

	S.	C.
Spinks William, Swanington	—	
Ulph John Hook, Aylsham		
	7	0
Grimer John Leist, Swanington	—	
Waters Richard, Elsing	—	
Themelthorpe.		
Amias William, Themelthorpe	—	
Fish James Henry, Stamford	—	
Gay John, Thurning, Norfolk, and Magdalen College, Cambridge	—	
Jarvis John, Themelthorpe	—	
Pumfrey John, Themelthorpe	—	
Wegg Robert, Themelthorpe	—	
Yarham Edmund, Themelthorpe		
	2	5
Thurning.		
Barber James, Thurning	—	
Bidewell John, Thurning	—	
Buck Richard, Thurning	—	
Gay James, Thurning-hall	—	
Leakey William, Thurning	—	
Margarson William, Thurning	—	
Scarf Samuel, Thurning		
	0	7
Blake Rev. Henry William, Thurning	—	
Ireland Anthony Woodhouse, Guestwick	—	
Twyford.		
Curties Sir Thomas Isaac, Twyford	—	
Massingham Henry, Twyford	—	
Packe Lieut.-Colonel Henry, Twyford	—	
Spurgeon Rev. John, Twyford		
	2	2
Weston.		
Bussey John, Weston	—	
Baker Charles, Weston	—	
Barrett John, Weston	—	
Besford John, Weston	—	
Conyngham Rev. J., Weston	—	
Coker Richard, Weston	—	
Comer William, Themelthorpe	—	
Fuller Robert, Weston	—	
Gray William, Weston	—	
Hubbard John, Weston	—	
Hubbard William, Weston	—	
Juby Edmund, Weston	—	
Knights George, Weston	—	
Milk David, Weston	—	
Salisbury Bowles, Weston	—	
Salisbury Thomas, Weston		
	8	8
Carman John, Weston	—	
Custance Hambleton Francis, Weston	—	
Collison John, East Bilney	—	
Collison Rev. Henry, East Bilney	—	
Whitwell.		
Bacon John, Whitwell	—	
Eglington Mark, Whitwell	—	
Leamon Robert, Whitwell	—	
Leeds Stephen, jun., Whitwell	—	
Leeds Robert, West Lexham		
	0	5

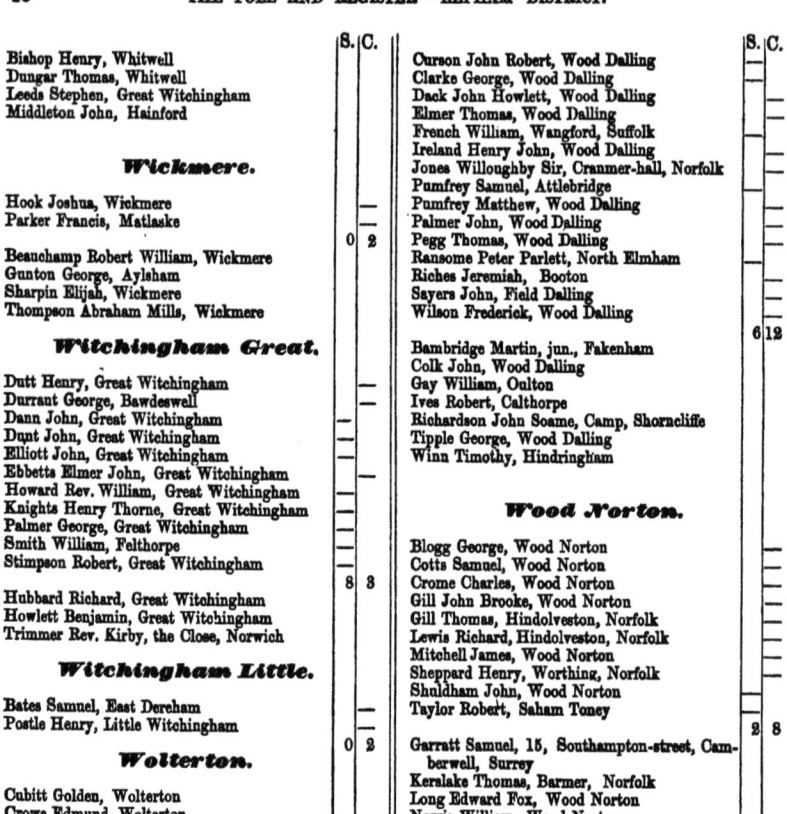

	S.	C.
Bishop Henry, Whitwell		
Dungar Thomas, Whitwell		
Leeds Stephen, Great Witchingham		
Middleton John, Hainford		

Wickmere.

	S.	C.
Hook Joshua, Wickmere	—	
Parker Francis, Matlaske	—	
	0	2
Beauchamp Robert William, Wickmere		
Gunton George, Aylsham		
Sharpin Elijah, Wickmere		
Thompson Abraham Mills, Wickmere		

Witchingham Great.

	S.	C.
Dutt Henry, Great Witchingham	—	
Durrant George, Bawdeswell	—	
Dann John, Great Witchingham		
Dunt John, Great Witchingham	—	
Elliott John, Great Witchingham	—	
Ebbetts Elmer John, Great Witchingham	—	
Howard Rev. William, Great Witchingham	—	
Knights Henry Thorne, Great Witchingham	—	
Palmer George, Great Witchingham		
Smith William, Felthorpe	—	
Stimpson Robert, Great Witchingham	—	
	8	3
Hubbard Richard, Great Witchingham		
Howlett Benjamin, Great Witchingham		
Trimmer Rev. Kirby, the Close, Norwich		

Witchingham Little.

	S.	C.
Bates Samuel, East Dereham	—	
Postle Henry, Little Witchingham	—	
	0	2

Wolterton.

	S.	C.
Cubitt Golden, Wolterton		
Crowe Edmund, Wolterton		
Orford Right Hon. Earl of, Wolterton		

Wood Dalling.

	S.	C.
Bussens James, Wood Dalling	—	
Brownsell William, Wood Dalling	—	
Clark Alfred, Wood Dalling	—	

	S.	C.
Curson John Robert, Wood Dalling	—	
Clarke George, Wood Dalling	—	
Dack John Howlett, Wood Dalling	—	
Elmer Thomas, Wood Dalling	—	
French William, Wangford, Suffolk		—
Ireland Henry John, Wood Dalling		—
Jones Willoughby Sir, Cranmer-hall, Norfolk		—
Pumfrey Samuel, Attlebridge		—
Pumfrey Matthew, Wood Dalling	—	
Palmer John, Wood Dalling	—	
Pegg Thomas, Wood Dalling	—	
Ransome Peter Parlett, North Elmham		—
Riches Jeremiah, Booton		—
Sayers John, Field Dalling	—	
Wilson Frederick, Wood Dalling	—	
	6	12
Bambridge Martin, jun., Fakenham		—
Colk John, Wood Dalling		—
Gay William, Oulton	—	
Ives Robert, Calthorpe		—
Richardson John Soame, Camp, Shorncliffe	—	
Tipple George, Wood Dalling	—	
Winn Timothy, Hindringham	—	

Wood Norton.

	S.	C.
Blogg George, Wood Norton		
Cotts Samuel, Wood Norton		
Crome Charles, Wood Norton		
Gill John Brooke, Wood Norton		
Gill Thomas, Hindolveston, Norfolk		
Lewis Richard, Hindolveston, Norfolk		
Mitchell James, Wood Norton		
Sheppard Henry, Worthing, Norfolk		
Shuldham John, Wood Norton		
Taylor Robert, Saham Toney		
	2	8
Garratt Samuel, 15, Southampton-street, Camberwell, Surrey		
Kerslake Thomas, Barmer, Norfolk		
Long Edward Fox, Wood Norton		
Norris William, Wood Norton		
Phillippo William Skinner, Barney		
Sawyer Edmund, Wood Norton		
Winn Timothy, Field Dalling, Norfolk		

Outvoter.

	S.	C.
Sewell Philip, Wareham, Suffolk	—	

LONG STRATTON DISTRICT,

COMPRISING THE PARISHES OF

Alburgh.	S.	C.
Basden Frederick Sherrerd, Denton	—	
Blofield William Watling, Denton	—	
Bond Barnabas, Alburgh	—	
Bond John, Alburgh	—	
Bootman John, Alburgh	—	
Buck William, Hempnall	—	
Coombe John Adams, Alburgh	—	
Doughton Michael, Alburgh	—	
Dunn Samuel, Alburgh	—	
Edge George, Alburgh	—	
Johnson Samuel, Alburgh	—	
Kerrich Edward Richard, Cambridge	—	
Legood Jeremiah, Alburgh	—	
Legood Samuel, Bedingham	—	
Miles Isaac Cannell, Alburgh	—	
Smith Benjamin, Alburgh	—	
Spelman Isaac, Alburgh	—	
	10	7
Fosberry Vincent Thomas, Gunton, Suffolk		
Fowler Cooke Robert, Gunton-hall, Suffolk		
Hurst Samuel Sheppard, Parker's Piece, Cambridge		
Moore William, Alburgh		
Powles Isaac, Aldeby		
Spelman Isaac Gower, Shimpling		
Youngs Samuel, jun., Alburgh		
Youngs Samuel, sen., Alburgh		

Ashwelthorpe.	S.	C.
Browne Thomas, Ashwelthorpe	—	
Browne Charles, Wymondham	—	
Balls Able, Ashwelthorpe	—	
Bunn William, Ashwelthorpe	—	
Browne Edward, Ashwelthorpe	—	
Green Charles, Ashwelthorpe	—	
Harvey Thomas, Ashwelthorpe	—	
Sizeland Adam, Bethel street, Norwich	—	
	7	1
Browne Edward, Ashwelthorpe		
Whitehand James, London		

Aslacton.	S.	C.
Arnold John, Aslacton	—	
Boulton Edward, Aslacton	—	
Brown William, Aslacton	—	
Filbee Edmund, Aslacton	—	
Grimes John, Aslacton	—	
Hammond John, Stratton St. Michael	—	
Holl Lewis, New Buckenham, Norfolk	—	
Lester William, Aslacton	—	
Moss John, Bunwell	—	
Utting John, Stratton St. Mary	—	
	8	3
Fisher Joseph, Aslacton		
Goose Agas, Theatre-street, Norwich		

Bedingham.	S.	C.
Burgess Joseph, Bedingham	—	
Bailey James, Bedingham	—	
Banham James, Bedingham	—	
Barber Thomas, Bedingham	—	
Borrett Samuel, Bedingham	—	
Everett George, Bedingham	—	
Flood George, Buckenham	—	
Lohr Charles the Rev. William, Bedingham	—	
Lodge Frederick, Bedingham	—	
Patrick William, Bedingham	—	
Pole Robert, Bedingham	—	
Rackham George, Bedingham	—	
Walker Tiffard, Bedingham	—	
	4	9
Cooper Benjamin, Bedingham		
Fisher Samuel, Bungay		
Legood William, Bedingham		
Overton William, 25, Old Jewry, London		

Billingford.	S.	C.
Beales Thomas W. L., Billingford	—	
Blomfield John, Billingford	—	
Cooper Rev. Augustus, Syleham, Suffolk	—	
King George, Billingford	—	
	8	1
Bartram Samuel, Billingford		
Bartram Robert, Billingford		
Drake Francis, Billingford		
Drake James, Billingford		
Holland Rev. Edmund, Benhall-lodge, Suffolk		

Bressingham.	S.	C.
Betts Christopher, North Lopham	—	
Bun Robert, Bressingham	—	
Bidwell George Henry, clerk, Bressingham	—	
Chenery Edgar, Castle, Eye	—	
Clamp Henry, Bressingham	—	
Coe Charles, Bressingham	—	
Dix James, Bressingham	—	
Eston George, Little Thornham, Suffolk	—	
Eaton Peter, Bressingham	—	
Eaton John, Bressingham	—	
Fisher Nathaniel, Bressingham	—	
Fowell Frederick, Blo Norton, Norfolk	—	
Haws George, Bressingham	—	
Henniker Major John Lord Henniker, Thornham Magna, Suffolk	—	
Hoskins James, Bressingham	—	
Knights Robert, Bressingham	—	
Kent John, Diss	—	
Landamore John, Bressingham	—	
Moore Frederick Edwin, 9, Great George-street, London	—	
Murtin William, Bressingham	—	
Muskett Charles, Bressingham-house	—	
Moore Foster Grand, Mount Pleasant, Norwich	—	
Mason William, Necton	—	

	S.	C.
Palmer Leonard, Snetterton	—	
Strachen James, Guildhall Tavern, Norwich	—	
Tacon James, Bressingham	—	
Thwaites James, Bressingham	—	
Woodcock Robert, Bressingham	—	
	11	17
Betts Thomas D'Eye, Martlesham, Suffolk		
Baldry John, Bressingham		
Copping Zachariah, Mellis, Suffolk		
Davy John, Bressingham		
Eaton Isaac, Bressingham		
Howard Edward Granville Fitzalan, commonly called Lord Edward Howard, 19, Rutland-gate, Knightsbridge, London		
Huson Henry, Bressingham		
Potter Robert Roper, Bressingham		
Rolph John, North Lopham		
Rolfe William Walter, North Lopham		
Whitmore Richard, Bressingham		
Wright John, Bressingham		

Brockdish.

	S.	C.
Crickmore William, Scole	—	
Garrod John King, Beccles		
Garrod William Henry, Beccles		
Hart George, Palgrave		
Mason Cornelius, Harleston		
Prime Henry, Harleston	—	
Read Alfred, Syleham		
Smith George, Thorpe Abbotts		
Warne Charles, Syleham	—	
Walne Daniel Henry, Guildford-street, Russell-square, London		
Walne Daniel, Brockdish		
	5	6
Aldous Jabez, Brockdish		
Brigham Thomas, Brockdish		
Coleman Charles, Brockdish		
Dobson William, Blofield		
France George, clerk, Brockdish		
Holmes Edward Adolphus, St. Margaret's Rectory		
Mullenger John, Brockdish		
Minister James, Plumstead		
Peak John, Billingford		
Whitear Rev. William, Croydon		

Bunwell.

	S.	C.
Austin William, Bunwell		
Ayton Isaac, Bunwell	—	
Bryant Richard, Kenninghall	—	
Burton William, Bunwell		
Bale William, Bunwell		
Benson William, Bunwell		
Barker Thomas, Bunwell		
Betts William, Bunwell		
Branch Robert, Bunwell		
Brown William, Bunwell		
Coleman James, Bunwell		
Downes Robert, Bunwell		
Everett Richard, Bunwell		
Fordham Charles, Tibenham		
Feltham Henry, Bunwell		
Grant Stephen, Bunwell		
Gunns George, Banham	—	
Hinchley Charles, Bunwell		
Holman Edward, Bunwell		
Kemp Samuel, Bunwell	—	
Lister John, Bunwell		

	S.	C.
Lingwood William, Bunwell		
Laws John Porter, No. 5, St. George's Terrace, Great Yarmouth	—	
Long John, Bunwell		
Morley David, Carleton Rode		
Page George, St. Clement's, Norwich		
Struman James, Bunwell		
Smith Robert, Bunwell		
Smith James, Bunwell		
Stubbings Thomas, Bunwell		
Smith James, Bunwell	—	
Thurston Thomas, Bunwell		
Thouless James, Pottergate-street, St. Giles', Norwich		
West William James, Bunwell		
Winter Robert, Lower Westwick-street, St. Benedict's, Norwich	—	
Youels James, Bunwell		
	28	8
Abon Jeremiah, Bunwell		
Beeston John, Wymondham		
Barker George, Morley St. Botolph		
Blomfield Miles, Keswick Mills		
Coleman Dennis, Wattlefield, Wymondham		
Coleman William, Carleton Rode		
Dawson Henry, clerk, Hopton, Suffolk		
Everett Robert, Bunwell		
Howes James, Bunwell		
Lanham Nelson, Bunwell		
Long William, Bunwell		
Mitchell John, Esq., Wymondham		
Palmer Ellis, Caines, Worcester		
Phillipo Elisha, Tacolnestone		
Stevenson James, Weybread		
Wild Francis, St. Faith's-lane, Norwich		

Burston.

	S.	C.
Bell James, Burston		
Bartram Charles, Burston		
Carter Robert, Burston		
Cooper William, Burston		
Dixon William, senr., Burston		
Dixon William, junr., Burston		
Esling John, Burston		
Fisher Joseph, Burston		
Frere Henry Temple, Rectory, Burston		
Kerry Joseph, Burston		
Ling Joseph, Burston		
Ling Jabez, Burston		
Martin Richard, Burston		
Ruddock Thomas, Burston		
Sandy John, Burston		
Scales Robert, Burston		
Self Thomas, Burston		
Tacon Joseph, Winkfield, Suffolk		
	12	6
Green John, Burston		
Gooderham William, Rickenhall Superior		
Saunders Richard, Ipswich, Suffolk, Parish of St. Margaret		
Wood Edward Negus, Melton-hall, Suffolk		
Wood John, Melton-hall, Suffolk		

Carleton Rode.

	S.	C.
Austin Edward, New Buckenham		
Austin James, New Buckenham		
Bevan Rev. Stephen Frederic, Carleton Rode		
Brock Robert, Carleton Rode		

	S.	C.
Brown William, Carleton Rode	—	
Bond Edward Fisher, New Buckenham	—	
Burcham Robert, Carleton Rode	—	
Bateman Elijah, Carleton Rode	—	
Bateman Elisha, Carleton Rode	—	
Brown Blackbourn John, Carleton Rode	—	
Brown Zacariah, Carleton Rode	—	
Banham James, Carleton Rode	—	
Blake Nazareth, Carleton Rode	—	
Cann Samuel Thomas, Carleton Rode	—	
Chatton Robert, Carleton Rode	—	
Coulson John, Kenninghall	—	
Coulson Samuel, Kenninghall	—	
Davey John, Carleton Rode	—	
Dawdrey George, Carleton Rode	—	
Day Robert, Carleton Rode	—	
Everett George, Carleton Rode	—	
Freeman William Henry, Carleton Rode	—	
French George, New Buckenham	—	
Foster James, Carleton Rode	—	
Gall John, New Buckenham	—	
Gibbs Charles, Carleton Rode	—	
Glover George, Carleton Rode	—	
Hardy Robert, Carleton Rode	—	
Hewett James Simonds, New Buckenham	—	
Howard Horace, New Buckenham	—	
Page William, Carleton Road	—	
Phillipo James, Carleton Rode	—	
Pottle James, Carleton Rode	—	
Reeve Richard, Old Buckenham	—	
Self John, Forncett	—	
Smith Robert, Carleton Rode	—	
Stevenson John, Carleton Rode	—	
Scott John, Carleton Rode	—	
Scott Uriah, Carleton Rode	—	
Stebbings James, Carleton Rode	—	
Thompson Thomas William, New Buckenham	—	
Thurston John, Carleton Rode	—	
	19	23
Barnard Robert, Carleton Rode	—	
Brown James, Carleton Rode	—	
Beevor Rigby Edward, Hevingham	—	
Coleman John, Carleton Rode	—	
Edwards Robert, Carleton Rode	—	
Ellis Richard, Shelfanger	—	
Merrison Timothy, Carleton Rode	—	
Newell Robert, Banham	—	
Parr William Burrell, St. Giles', Norwich	—	
Self James, Carleton Rode	—	
Taylor George, Norwich	—	

Denton.

	S.	C.
Bowler Benjamin, Denton	—	
Button William Rodwell, Denton	—	
Burgess Edward, Denton	—	
Burgess Benjamin, Denton	—	
Bidwell Mark, Bungay	—	
Butcher William, Bungay	—	
Buggs Daniel, Denton	—	
Chambers Francis, Denton	—	
Devereux Benjamin, Denton	—	
Elliot John, Denton	—	
Farrall Joseph, Denton	—	
Holland William, Denton	—	
Johnson Charles, Denton	—	
Mutt John, Mutford, Suffolk	—	—
Mutt George, Denton	—	
Massey Alfred, Mount Pleasant, Norwich	—	
Nurse James, St. Andrew's, Ilketshall, Suffolk	—	—
Payne John, Denton	—	

	S.	C.
Sandby Rev. George, Flixton	—	
Turner William, Great Ryburgh	—	
Umphelby Charles, Denton	—	
Walne Thomas, Tasburgh	—	
Whitton Henry, Denton	—	
	14	9
Bouverie William Arundell, Denton	—	
Howlett Jonathan, Wissett	—	
Middleton William, Denton	—	
Thorpe William Smyth, Shropham	—	
Todd Noah, Denton	—	
Wegg Robert, Dickleburgh	—	

Dickleburgh.

	S.	C.
Abbott Joseph, Diss	—	
Bartram Samuel, Langmere	—	
Booty James, Dickleburgh	—	
Bartram James, Langmere	—	
Bunyan John William, Diss	—	
Burgess James, Langmere	—	
Campling James, Golden Ball-street, Norwich	—	
Crisp William, Dickleburgh	—	
Cobbold Robert Knipe, Bredfield	—	
Cooper Charles, Dickleburgh	—	
Cobbold John, Ipswich	—	
Coleby John, Langmere	—	
Cole James, 4, High-street, Ipswich	—	
Dye John, Dickleburgh	—	
Edwards James, Dickleburgh	—	
Garland Robert, Dickleburgh	—	
Harvey Robert, Dickleburgh	—	
Knights Simon, Dickleburgh	—	
Le Grys James, Langmere	—	
Mickleburgh John, Dickleburgh	—	
MoorThomas S., Warham All Saints, near Wells	—	
Nurse Edward, Langmere	—	
Perfit Robert Stephen, Stratton St. Mary	—	
Pymar John, Ipswich-road, Norwich	—	
Smith William, senior, Dickleburgh	—	
Smith William, junior, Dickleburgh	—	
Smith Robert, Dickleburgh	—	
Sheldrake James, Dickleburgh	—	
Stevenson Rev. George, Dickleburgh	—	
Seaman William, Dickleburgh	—	
Tinker Horace, Thorpe, near Norwich	—	
Vyse Nicholas, Dickleburgh	—	
Wilton Edmund, Dickleburgh	—	
Woods James, Shimpling	—	
	17	17
Bartram Samuel, Dickleburgh	—	
Barrett Colin, Metfield	—	
Cole James, Langmere	—	
Dent Robert, Dickleburgh	—	
Dix Francis, Dickleburgh	—	
Edwards Benjamin, Friston	—	
Howlett Henry, Langmere	—	
Hubbard Thomas, Dickleburgh	—	
Holmes Robert, Tacolneston	—	
Macro Abraham, Diss	—	
Saunders David, Pulham St. Mary the Virgin	—	
Thrower Noah, Dickleburgh	—	
Wells Benjamin, Dickleburgh	—	
Woolsey William, Langmere	—	

Diss.

	S.	C.
Abbott Edward Edmund, Diss	—	
Angold Samuel, Diss	—	
Angold John, Mount-street, Diss	—	—

H

	S.	C.
Angold Henry, Diss	—	
Anness John, Diss	—	
Atkins George, Diss	—	
Atkins George, junior, Diss	—	
Barkham Thomas, Diss	—	
Bloomfield John, Diss	—	
Bobby James Horatio, Diss	—	
Bobby Henry, Diss	—	
Brook Samuel, Diss	—	
Berrett Benjamin, Diss	—	
Burrows Robert, Diss	—	
Burrows Gibson Lucas, Diss	—	
Brown Henry, clerk, Neatishead, Norfolk	—	
Calver Philip, Diss	—	
Carter Samuel, Diss	—	
Chaplyn William, Diss	—	
Cobb Samuel, Diss	—	
Cuthbert Henry, Diss	—	
Cooke James, Diss	—	
Cornell Samuel, Diss	—	
Chapman John, Southolt, Suffolk	—	
Cracknell John, Diss	—	
Drake Samuel, Diss	—	
Ellis William, Diss	—	
Ellis Stimpson, Diss	—	
Elsey Robert, Diss	—	
Elsey Philip, Diss	—	
Ealing John, Diss	—	
Eglington Solomon, Diss	—	
Farrow Samuel, Diss	—	
Farrow Charles, Diss	—	
Fincham Robert, Diss	—	
Foulser Robert, Diss	—	
Foulser Isaac, Walcot green, Diss	—	
Garrett Sylvester Bond, Diss	—	
Goldsmith Mark, Diss	—	
Gostling Thomas Preston, Diss	—	
Harvey Martin, Diss	—	
Houchen George, Diss	—	
Harrison William, Diss	—	
Harrison Phillip, Diss	—	
Jarrett John, Diss	—	
Keeble William, Diss	—	
Leech John, Diss	—	
Leech John, Diss	—	
Lewis Jonathan Preston, Cock-street, Diss	—	
Lock Edward, Debenham, Suffolk	—	
Lyus George, Diss	—	
Leeder Simon, Diss	—	
Manning Charles Robinson, Diss	—	
Middleton Richard, Diss	—	
Moore William, Diss	—	
Murton Robert, Diss	—	
Muskett Benjamin, Diss	—	
Muskett John, Diss	—	
Nicholson Terah, Diss	—	
Parr Robert, Diss	—	
Parker John, Diss	—	
Pearce Robert, Diss	—	
Plummer John, Diss	—	
Rout John, Diss	—	
Sayer John Watling, Diss	—	
Self John, Diss	—	
Simpson Zachariah, Diss	—	
Smith Edward, Diss	—	
Slack Richard, Diss	—	
Spurling John, Diss	—	
Towell William, Diss	—	
Ward Henry, Diss	—	
Ward William, Huntingdon	—	
Wallace Thomas Edward, Diss	—	

	S.	C.
Witting Charles, Diss	—	
Woodrow William, Diss	25	51
Balding Henry, Wortham, Suffolk	—	
Browne George Frederick, Diss	—	
Church William, Diss	—	
Coe John, Diss	—	
Cupiss Francis, Diss	—	
Cupiss Philip, Edlaston, Ashbourne, Derbyshire	—	
Cooper David, Diss	—	
Elsey Robert, Blackthorn Farm, Walcot Green	—	
Easto Richard, Diss	—	
Grear William, Islington, London	—	
Heffill Henry, Diss	—	
Herne John, Diss	—	
Juby Thomas, Diss	—	
Leech Thomas, Diss	—	
Luccock James, Diss	—	
Mann Thomas, Stoke Newington	—	
Manning William Woodward, Coldbrook-park Abergavenny	—	
Mason George, jun., Ipswich	—	
Murch Jerome, Evanwells, Bath	—	
Prime Thomas, Diss	—	
Quadling Benjamin, Diss	—	
Roper Samuel, 6, Clapham-square, Middlesex	—	
Ready Richard, Diss	—	
Smith Edmund, Diss	—	
Stollery Jonathan, Diss	—	
Taylor George, Leeds, Yorkshire	—	
Taylor Dennis, Mere-street, Diss	—	
Wharton George, M.D., Norwich	—	
Whaite Thomas, Diss	—	

Fersfield.

	S.	C.
Algar John, Fersfield	—	—
Bloomfield George, Necton	—	—
Darby George William, Fersfield	—	—
Garrood Robert, Fersfield	—	—
Greenwood James, Fersfield	—	—
Muskett Charles, Fersfield	—	—
Mison Samuel, Fersfield	—	—
Page Henry, Bressingham	—	—
Page William, Fersfield	—	—
Wharton John, Aslacton	—	—
Waites Robert, Fersfield	—	—
Woods George, Fersfield	8	9
Bryant Henry, Fersfield	—	—
Green Charles, North Lopham	—	—
Howard Henry Granville Fitzalan, Earl of Arundel and Surrey, Carlton-terrace, St. James' Parish, Westminster	—	—
Palmer Leonard, Snetterton	—	—
Palmer Richard, Fersfield	—	—

Forncett St. Mary.

	S.	C.
Baker Benjamin, Forncett St. Mary	—	—
Barnes George, sen., Forncett St. Mary	—	—
Baxter Samuel, Tasburgh	—	—
Caley Samuel, Forncett St. Mary	—	—
Cooper Rev. John Edward, Forncett St. Mary	—	—
Harvey Elijah, Forncett St. Mary	—	—
Harvey Canham, Forncett St. Mary	—	—
Knights Rayner, Forncett St. Mary	—	—
Ludkin John, Forncett St. Mary	—	—
Moore George, Forncett St. Mary	—	—
Potter George, Forncett St. Mary	2	9

	S.	C.
Alborough William, Forncett St. Mary		
Freestone Edwd., St. Peter's Mancroft, Norwich		
Jeffries Robert, Forncett St. Mary		
Mickleburgh Jonas, Forncett St. Mary		
Self John, Forncett St. Mary		
Spicer John, Finningham, Suffolk		
Spicer John, Finningham, Suffolk		

Forncett St. Peter.

	S.	C.
Alexander William, Forncett St. Peter	—	
Aldborough Jeremiah, Yarmouth	—	
Bassingthwaighte James, Forncett St. Peter	—	
Bloom Thomas, Forncett St. Peter	—	
Colman Henry, Forncett St. Peter	—	
Cannell John, Forncett St. Peter	—	
Feltham William, Forncett St. Peter	—	
Greenacre Robert, Forncett St. Peter	—	
Harvey James, Forncett St. Peter	—	
Humphreys James, Forncett St. Peter	—	
Lansdell William, Forncett St. Peter	—	
Lain John, Forncett St. Peter	—	
Maddeys George, Forncett St. Peter	—	
Marshall Solomon, Forncett St. Peter	—	
Moore James, Forncett St. Peter		
Nash Spooner, Forncett St. Peter	—	
Ringer John, West Harling		
Smith William, Forncett St. Peter	—	
Todd John, Forncett St. Peter	—	
West John Gill, Forncett St. Peter	—	
Wilson William Greene, Forncett St. Peter	9	12

	S.	C.
Aldborough George, Forncett St. Peter		
Bloom Thomas, Melton		
Colman Thomas, 18, Pritchard-street, Bristol		
Johnson Edward Amon, Swaffham		
Moore William, Forncett St. Peter		
Oakley John, Forncett St. Peter		
Palmer Thomas, Forncett St. Peter		
Reynolds Francis, Beeston, Norfolk		
Ringer George, Walcott-green, Diss		
Ward Richard, Forncett St. Peter		

Fritton.

	S.	C.
Nash William, Fritton	—	
White William, Fritton	—	
Wilson Rev. Herbert, Fritton	—	
Drake Daniel, Fritton	3	0
Howes Edward, Morningthorpe		

Fundenhall.

	S.	C.
Bacon Francis, Fundenhall	—	
Clarke Robert, Fundenhall	—	
Howes James, Wymondham	—	
Harvey Robert, Ashwellthorpe	—	
Harvey Charles Watts, Ashwellthorpe	—	
Holloway Charles, the Close, Norwich	—	
Newman William, Fundenhall	—	
Peel Henry, Fundenhall	—	
Ringwood Benjamin, Fundenhall	.	
Tye Francis, Fundenhall	9	1
Feltham Jonathan, Fundenhall		
Howes William, Wymondham		
Harvey Thomas, Fundenhall		
Hubbard Daniel Wm., Hackford next Reepham		
Rattee Daniel, Fundenhall		
Woolbright William Henry, King-st. Norwich		

Gissing.

	S.	C.
Ayton William, Gissing	—	
Brooks William, Gissing	—	
Brooke John, Gissing	—	
Carter William, Gissing	—	
Haddock Joseph, Gissing rectory		
Haunton Robert, Gissing		
Hewitt James, Gissing		
Kemp Sir William Robert, Gissing		
Norman John, Gissing		
Norman Richard, Gissing		
Shelverton Isaac, Gissing		
Start John, Gissing		
Smith William, Gissing		
Simonds John, Gissing	9	5
Barrett George, Norwich,		
Flogdell Richard, Gissing		
Fryer Thomas, Gissing		
Saunders Charles, Gissing		
Shaw John, Gissing		

Hapton.

	S.	C.
Edwards Thomas, Keswick	—	
Hubbard Daniel William, Hackford	—	
Knapton James, Hapton	—	
Lamb Henry James, Hapton	—	
Lansdell William Walker, Forncett St. Peter	—	
Smith John, Tacolneston	0	6
Barnes George, jun., Hapton		
Dix Francis, Norwich		
Hart William, Gisborough, Yorkshire		

Hardwick.

	S.	C.
Copping Samuel, jun., Stratton St. Mary		
Copping Benjamin, Hardwick	—	
Cox John, Hardwick	—	
Lighton Robert, Hardwick		
More Robert, Hardwick		
Parson Samuel, Hardwick		
Pimer William, Stratton St. Mary		
Smith James, Morningthorpe		
Vipond George, Hardwick		
Vipond James, Hardwick		
Willby Richard, Hardwick	7	4
Bacon Rev. William, Fring		
Constable James, Hardwick		
Cattley Rev. Stephen, Fulham		
Goldsmith John, Pulham St. Mary the Virgin		
Hill George Frederick, Acle		
Pooley George Frederick, Cransford, Suffolk		
Willby James, Thelton		

Hempnall.

	S.	C.
Arnold William, Hempnall	—	
Bunn John, Bunwell		
Capon Charles, Bungay St. Mary		
D'Oyley Henry French, Hempnall		
Greene Charles, Dedham		
Gower William, Hempnall		
Grice Le Jonas, Hempnall		
Hylton Richard, Hempnall		
Hylton Walter Henry, Hempnall		
Hipperson Samuel, Hempnall		
Kennedy John, Hempnall	—	

	S.	C.
Leskey Henry, Hempnall-street	—	
Lodge John, Mattishall	—	
Mayor William, Oakley	—	
Meek Edward, Hempnall	—	
Morriss John, King-street, Norwich	—	
Richards Robert, Horsham St. Faith's	—	
Riches John, Hempnall	—	
Roberts Henry, Hempnall	—	
Roberts James, Hempnall	—	
Roberts William, Hempnall	—	
Roberts John, Hempnall	—	
Read William, Hempnall	—	
Read William, Hempnall	—	
Read John, Hempnall	—	
Spinks Edward, Hempnall	—	
Sporle Robert, Hempnall	—	
Thorold Edmund, Hempnall	—	
Thrower Alexander, Hempnall	—	
Warmoll Edward, Woodton	—	
Webb Joseph Cater, Hempnall	—	
Wright John, Stoke Holy Cross	—	
	18	14
Arnold William, jun., Hempnall		
Bunn John, Topcroft		
Carsey John, Hempnall		
Ellis William, Saxlingham		
Edwards Thomas, Keswick		
Edwards Thomas, Wymondham		
Green Edward, Farnborough Hill, Hampshire		
Gowing William, Hempnall		
Gowing William, Hempnall		
Hall George Thomas, Hempnall		
Hickling James, Hempnall		
Meek John, Morningthorpe		
Mott John Thomas, Barningham		
Parr William Burrell, St. Giles', Norwich		
Read Jonathan, Saxlingham		
Riches William, Loddon		
Sheldrake Robert, Framingham Pigot		
Scarnell John Evered, senr., Earsham, Norfolk		
Sporle John, Hempnall		
Todd John, Hempnall		

Mendham.

	S.	C.
Baas Robert, Halesworth	—	
Beaumont John, Mendham	—	
Borrett Robert, Harleston	—	
Buck Charles, Redenhall	—	
Francis James, Mendham	—	
Friston George Gooderham, Redenhall	—	
Gedney Frank James, Mendham	—	
Jeffes Leonard Palmer, Weybread, Suffolk	—	
Mayhew Elias, Mendham	—	
Whitaker Thomas Wright, clerk, Stanton by Bridge, Derbyshire	—	
	4	6
Barnaby James, Mendham		
Bunn William, Mendham		
Caley James, Needham		
Clutter James, Denham		
Donnison James Watson Stote, clerk, Mendham		
Edwards Thomas, Mendham		
Parker John William, Postwick		
Scrivener John Fredk. Pike, Ramridge, Andover, Hants, and 20, Bryanstone-square, London		
Thurston James, Fressingfield, Suffolk		
Whitaker George Ayton, clerk, Knoddishall		

Moulton.

	S.	C.
Aldis George, Moulton	—	
Betts Thomas, Moulton	—	
Betts Edward, Moulton	—	
Death Ambrose, Forncett St. Peter	—	
Elvin Benjamin, Aslacton	—	
Fish John, Moulton	—	
Hall John, Wymondham	—	
Hurn William, Moulton	—	
King Robert, Moulton	—	
Master Alfred, St. Giles', Norwich	—	
Miller Joseph, Moulton	—	
Neave Riches, Moulton	—	
Peake Thomas, Thorpe Hamlet	—	
Potter Robert, Moulton	—	
Seaman Robert, Moulton	—	
Smith Christopher, Wacton	—	
Smith James, Moulton	—	
Snelling Edward, Moulton	—	
Watling William, Moulton	—	
Webster Isaac, Tasburgh	—	
Wells Thomas, Diss	—	
Zipfel Charles, Stratton St. Mary	—	
	17	5
Bignold Edward Samuel, Bracondale, Norwich		
Master George, 22, Duke-street, Grosvenor-square, Middlesex		
Tuttle Henry, Moulton		
Walton William, Moulton		
Weston Nathaniel, Hemblington		
Witherly William, Moulton		

Morningthorpe.

	S.	C.
Claxton Richard, Morningthorpe	—	
Goldworth Alfred, Morningthorpe	—	
Howes Edward, Morningthorpe	—	
Irby Frederick William, Boyland-hall	—	
Meek John, Morningthorpe	—	
Rolfe Edmund Nelson, clerk, Morningthorpe	—	
Waite John Newman, Morningthorpe	—	
Pallant Samuel, 17, Beaufort-court, Chelsea, London	4	8

Needham.

	S.	C.
Algar Henry, Needham	—	
Bayles John, Needham	—	
Blackmur John, senr., Needham	—	
Chase George, Weybread, Suffolk	—	
Caley James, Needham	—	
Edwards Alfred, Needham	—	
Knevet John, senr., clerk, Syleham	—	
Prime Mounser William, Needham	—	
Rivett William, the younger, Needham	—	
Seaman Robert, Harleston	—	
Smith William, Needham	—	
Taylor Samuel, Needham	—	
Watchman William, Needham	—	
	9	4
Algar George, Pulham St. Mary		
Blackmur John, jun., Shoreditch, London		
Bridge Thomas, Croydon, Surrey		
Chambers Peter John, clerk, Hedenham		
Chappell Samuel, Harleston		
Drane Henry, Weybread, Suffolk		
Feaviour Robert, Stradbroke, Suffolk		
Feltham Clement Mingay, Dunton		
Matthews Thomas, Needham		
Pratt Burford James, Needham		

	S.	C.

Pulham St. Mary Magdalen.

	S.	C.
Aldrich John, Pulham St. Mary Magdalen	—	
Baxter James, Pulham Magdalen	—	
Barnes Samuel, Pulham Magdalen	—	
Bell Robert, St. Cross, South Elmham, Suffolk	—	
Bullock Robert, Pulham Magdalen	—	
Burcham Samuel, Pulham Magdalen	—	
Carpenter Thos., Pulham St. Mary Magdalen	—	
Churchyard Sidney, Pulham Magdalen	—	
Crisp Robert, Pulham Magdalen		
Elmar James, Pulham Magdalen	—	
Edwards George, Pulham Magdalen	—	
Edwards James, Denton		
Edwards William, Pulham St. Mary Magdalen	—	
Folkard James, Pulham Magdalen		
Field William, Pulham Magdalen	—	
Goff William, Pulham Magdalen	—	
Goldsmith James, Pulham Magdalen	—	
Gooderham John, Pulham St. Mary Virgin	—	
Hart George, Pulham St. Mary Magdalen		
Harris Charles, Pulham Magdalen	—	
Howlett Edward, Pulham Magdalen	—	
Howlett Elisha, Pulham Magdalen	—	
King George, Pulham Magdalen	—	
Kerrison Samuel, Pulham Magdalen	—	
Kersey Edward A., Pulham Magdalen	—	
King William Horn, Pulham Magdalen	—	
King William, Lowestoft		
Leggett John, Pulham St. Mary Magdalen	—	
Leggett Laverocke, Pulham Magdalen	—	
Levell Richard, Pulham St. Mary Magdalen	—	
Manclarke William Palgrave, Pulham St. Mary Magdalen	—	
More James, Pulham Magdalen	—	
Myhill Benjamin, New Buckenham		
Nurse William, Pulham Magdalen	—	
Palmer John, Pulham Magdalen	—	
Read John, Pulham Magdalen	—	
Read Zachariah, Pullam Magdalen	—	
Rayson George, Pullam Magdalen	—	
Rayson Robert, Pullam Magdalen	—	
Rayson John, Trafalgar Buildings, Ipswich		
Reeve Thomas, Pulham Magdalen	—	
Reeder John, Hardwick		
Skinner Benjamin, Pulham Magdalen	—	
Salter William, Pulham Magdalen	—	
Walne Daniel, Long Stratton, Norfolk		
Warn John, Harleston		
Weston Robert, Pulham Magdalen	—	
	18	29
Frost William, clerk, Thorpe, Norwich		
Goldsmith Philip, Aslacton, Norfolk		
Harden Jacob, jun., Pulham Magdalen		
Humphrey James, Harleston		
Shepperson Matthew, 43, Sloane-street, Chelsea		
Tubby Robert, Pulham St. Mary the Virgin		

Pulham St. Mary the Virgin.

	S.	C.
Adair Sir Shafto, St. James'-square, London, and Flixton-hall, Suffolk		
Baker Robert, Starston		
Bond Thomas, Pulham St. Mary Virgin	—	
Bentfield John, Pulham St. Mary the Virgin	—	
Burgess James, Pulham St. Mary Virgin	—	
Brown Joshua, Pulham St. Mary Virgin	—	
Bullen Benjamin, Pulham St. Mary Virgin	—	

	S.	C.
Goldsmith Thomas, Pulham St. Mary Virgin	—	
Goldsmith John, Pulham St. Mary the Virgin	—	
Gook Jonathan, Pulham St. Mary the Virgin	—	
Goldsmith Philip, Pulham St. Mary Magdalen	—	
Gowing John, Pulham St. Mary Virgin	—	
Harrison Samuel, Pulham St. Mary Virgin	—	
High John, Pulham St. Mary the Virgin	—	
Kerrison Henry, Pulham St. Mary Magdalen	—	
Mason Edwin, Harleston	—	
Mayes William, Pulham St. Mary Virgin	—	
Mills Charles Andre, Pulham St. Mary Virgin	—	
Patten Schofield, 17, Upper Woburn-place, St. Pancras, Middlesex	—	
Patten Jas., 17, Upper Woburn place, Middlesex	—	
Pearce Seales, Pulham St. Mary the Virgin	—	
Pritty Samuel, Pulham St. Mary Virgin	—	
Pratt Simpson, Pulham St. Mary Virgin	—	
Poppy David, Pulham St. Mary Virgin	—	
Ray Thomas, Sedgeford-lane, King's Lynn		
Reeve John, Fressingfield, Suffolk		
Reeve James, Pulham St. Mary Virgin	—	
Roebotham Thomas, Pulham St. Mary Virgin	—	
Self Samuel, Pulham St. Mary Virgin	—	
Stanton William, Harleston		
Saunders William Clutton, Pulham St. Mary Virgin	—	
Thrower John, Pulham St. Mary Virgin	—	
Tills Joseph, Pulham St. Mary Virgin	—	
Vipond Jeremiah, Pulham Virgin	—	
Waller Josiah, Pulham St. Mary Magdalen	—	
Williams Thomas, Pulham St. Mary Virgin	—	
	18	18
Bentfield Edmund, Pulham St. Mary Virgin		
Bond Barnabas, Alburgh		
Comyn John, Nottingham		
Leigh Rev. Wm., Pulham St. Mary the Virgin		
Millican Charles, Weybread		
Mullenger Thomas, Starston		
Nurse John, Pulham St. Mary the Virgin		
Stanton James, Pulham St. Mary the Virgin		
Tubby Robert, Pulham St. Mary the Virgin		
Youell John, Pulham St. Mary the Virgin		

Redenhall with Harleston.

	S.	C.
Aldous James, Harleston, &c.	—	
Aldous William Poole, Harleston	—	
Aldis Josias Lines, Harleston	—	
Asten John, Redenhall	—	
Asten Robert, Redenhall	—	
Bellward Robert, Redenhall	—	
Brown William Henry, Harleston	—	
Barber William, jun., Ipswich		
Barber Thomas, Harleston	—	
Carthew George, Harleston	—	
Carthew George Alfred, East Dereham		
Corbould Pelham, Harleston	—	
Chappell George William, Harleston	—	
Carman Samuel, Harleston	—	
Chappell Samuel, Harleston	—	
Chappell James, Harleston	—	
Crisp Benjamin John, Harleston	—	
Crowe Thomas, Lowestoft		
Diggins Henry, Starston		
Dordery William, Mendham		
Fevearyear Absalom, jun., Wingfield, Suffolk		
Fevearyear Robert, Redenhall	—	
Freston Jonathan, Harleston	—	
Gedney George, Redenhall	—	
Huse William, jun., Denham	—	

	S.	C.
Hudson Henry Lombard, Harleston	—	—
Keable William, Redenhall	—	
Kersey Henry Augustus, Mendham		
Muskett James, Harleston	—	
Meen James, Redenhall with Harleston	—	
Moore James, Eye	—	
Parker Nathaniel, Redenhall		
Parker Alfred, Alburgh		
Parker Henry, Redenhall	—	
Pashley Alexander William, Harleston	—	
Prentice Samuel, Harleston		
Pratt Jonathan Burford, Newbury, Berkshire	.	
Robinson George, Redenhall	—	
Rolfe Richard, Harleston	—	
Rudlin James, Redenhall	—	
Shepherd Charles, Harleston	—	
Smith Joseph, Mendham		
Smith Verdon, Harleston	—	
Smith Samuel, jun., Harleston	—	
Squire George, Harleston		
Tacon William Henry, Westhall, Suffolk		
Vipond John, Weybread, Suffolk	—	
Wilson John, Harleston		
Wilson Edward, Harleston		
Welton Charles, Redenhall with Harleston	—	
	17	33
Aldous Arthur Henry, Ipswich		
Barnaby James, Mendham		
Baldwin Richard, Wortham, Suffolk		
Buck William, St. Paul's Churchyard, London		
Colls John, Redenhall with Harleston		
Delf Samuel Newton, Topcroft		
Etheridge Benjamin Cotton, Eye		
Feltham William, Harleston		
Foulger William, Harleston		
Gilbert Samuel G., Redenhall with Harleston		
Hazard William Martin, Harleston		
Juby Jeremiah, Harleston		
Lillistone William, Harleston		
Montgomerie Frederick Molineux, St. Leonard's Sussex		
Ormerod Thomas Johnson, Redenhall Rectory		
Robinson William, Redenhall		
Squire David, jun., Putney-place, Golden-square, London		

Roydon.

	S.	C.
Anness William, Roydon	—	
Aldrich Robert, Diss	—	
Brook Calver John, Diss	—	
Cason Hugh, No. 6, Windmill-street, Union-place, Lambeth, Surrey		
Cobb George, Roydon		
Frere Temple Robert, No. 9, Queen-street, Mayfair, Westminster		
Frere George Edward, Roydon-hall		
Good George, Roydon		
Kerry John Copeman, Wortham		
Linstead John, jun., Roydon		
Lister Phillip, Wortham, Suffolk	—	
Matholi Michael, jun., Roydon	—	
Miles Stephen, Roydon		
Musk Phillip, Stuston, Suffolk	—	
Poarcher John, Roydon	—	
Saunders John, Roydon		
Scace Robert Baldry, Roydon		
Soame Isaiah, Roydon	—	
Tuck John Johnson, Sydenham, Kent		
Waters Robert, Roydon		

	S.	C.
Websdale Robert, Roydon		
Woodrow Samuel, Roydon		
	15	7
Bryant John, Roydon		
Fowell Frederick, sen., Blo Norton, Norfolk		
Frere Rev. Temple, Roydon		
Muskett Charles, Bressingham		
Richerson John, Foulden, Norfolk		
Wood Searles Valentine, St. Stephen's-house, Twickenham, Middlesex		

Rushall.

	S.	C.
Cooper Robert, clerk, Dickleburgh, Norfolk		—
Daniels Thomas, Rushall		
Fairhead Samuel, Rushall		
Fish William, Rushall		—
Howes Joshua, Rushall		
Le Grys Charles, Rushall		
Mills Henry, Rushall		
Mills John, Rushall		
Mills James, Bury St. Edmund's, 6, Westgate-street		
Mullenger James, Rushall		—
Pearce Henry, Rushall		
Stanton John, Rushall		
Stanton Thomas Smith, Rushall		
Smith John, Bungay		
Smith Robert, Bungay		
Smith James, Bungay		
	9	7
Aldous Frederick, Rushall		
Pearce Seales, Pulham St. Mary Virgin		

Saxlingham Nethergate.

	S.	C.
Alcock Edward, Saxlingham Nethergate		
Brown Thomas, Saxlingham Nethergate		
Beckett Samuel, Saxlingham Nethergate		
Ellis Henry, St. Catherine's-plain, New Lakenham, Norwich		
Ellis Robert, Saxlingham Nethergate		
Ellis Thomas, Thorn-lane, Curtis' Buildings, Norwich		
Ellis William, Trowse, near Norwich		
Francis Edward, clerk, Shottisham, Suffolk		
Guyett Thomas, Saxlingham Nethergate		
Gordon John, Saxlingham Nethergate		
King Samuel Wm., clerk, Saxlingham Rectory		
Lansdell Abraham, Balaclava-terrace, Bishopgate-street, Norwich	—	
Lincoln William, Saxlingham Nethergate		
Mayhew Thomas, Westleton, Suffolk		
Owles William, Saxlingham Nethergate		
Redgrave John, Saxlingham Nethergate		
Redgrave Thomas, Saxlingham Nethergate		
Whittaker Samuel, Saxlingham Nethergate		
Watson Robert, near Boys' Home, Norwich		
Wilson Thomas, Saxlingham Nethergate		
	7	13
Branford Ezra, Swainsthorpe		
Bilham James, Saxlingham Nethergate		
Capon Charles, Bungay St. Mary, Suffolk		
Daniels Jeremiah, Saxlingham Nethergate	—	
Ellis William, Saxlingham Nethergate	—	
Heard George H., Shottisham All Saints		
Hobart Robert, Saxlingham Nethergate		
Rolfe Joseph Reason, Saxlingham Nethergate	—	
Swann John, East Carleton		
Snart Alfred, Waldringfield Rectory		
Wooltorton Robert, Saxlingham Nethergate		

	S.	C.

Saxlingham Thorpe.

	S.	C.
Bush Barnabas, Saxlingham Nethergate	—	
Candler Lawrence, Saxlingham Thorpe	—	
Reeder William, Saxlingham Thorpe	—	
Sallitt Matthew, Saxlingham Thorpe	—	
Sayer John, Saxlingham Thorpe	—	
Want John Henry, Saxlingham Thorpe	—	
	0	6
Feltham William, Saxlingham Thorpe	—	
Lincoln Jeremiah, Dunston	—	
Meek William, Saxlingham Thorpe	—	

Scole with Frenze and Thorpe Parva.

Alecock John, Scole	—	
Aldous Robert, Scole	—	
Bailey James, 118, Northgate-street, Bury	—	
Blomfield James, Frenze	—	
Bowen Wilby, Scole	—	
Clarke Osmond, Stuston	—	
Coates Henry, Scole	—	
Chambers William, Scole	—	
Harrold George, Scole	—	
Hill George, Scole	—	
Hunt Levi, Scole	—	
Mayhew George, Stradbroke, Suffolk	—	
Mole Robert, Scole	—	
Pettett Charles, Scole	—	
Read George, Scole	—	
Read Ezekiel, Scole	—	
Rodwell Robert, Scole	—	
Show William, Scole	—	
Smith Sheldrake, Frenze	—	
Tacon Charles, Eye	—	
Tacon Richard, Eye	—	
White Thomas, Scole	—	
	10	12
Costerton Charles Fisher, Eye, Suffolk	—	
Dyball Robert, Buugay	—	
Kerrison Edward Clarance, Broome Hall	—	
Lines John, Thorpe Parva	—	
Thrower Charles, Chelmsford, Essex	—	

Shelfanger.

Anness Lillystone, Shelfanger	—	
Anness William Rudland, Shelfanger	—	
Baker Edward, Shelfanger	—	
Ellis Charles, Shelfanger	—	
Ellis Richard, Shelfanger	—	
Ellis Robert, Shelfanger	—	
Ellis William, Shelfanger	—	
Goodchild Arthur, Shelfanger	—	
Hammond John, Winfarthing	—	
Holmes Rev. William, Scole House	—	
Marner John, Attleborough	—	
Morris Rev. Thomas Brooke, Shelfanger	—	
Macro Robert, Shelfanger	—	
Morley John, Shelfanger	—	
Matthew George Jeremiah, Knettishall	—	
Page William, Shelfanger	—	
Reeve William, Shelfanger	—	
Simonds Charles, Shelfanger	—	
Wright Samuel, Shelfanger	—	
	4	15
Freeman C. Bailey, Norwich		
Reeve Richard, Old Buckenham		
Vassar Philip, Shelfanger		

Shelton.

	S.	C.
Blanchflower William, Hardwick		
Curteis Rev. Jeremiah, Shelton	—	
Cann William, Shelton	—	
Howlett William, Shelton	—	
Moore Richard, Shelton	—	
Moore Robert, Shelton	—	
Nobbs John, Shelton	—	
Starke Ezekiel Shelton		
Shaw Charles, R.N., King-street, Norwich	—	
Trimmer Kirby, clerk, St. Simon's, Norwich	—	
Thrower Cornelius, Shelton	—	
Wilby James, Shelton	—	
Westgate Michael, Shelton	—	
	8	5
Calver Michael, Shelton	—	
Corneby Wales, Shelton	—	
Deacon Rev. James, Pottergate-street, Norwich	—	
Eaton Edward Jarrett, Shelton	—	
Elliott William Waller, Shelton	—	
Goodwin Rev. William, Norwich	—	
Havers Thomas, Shelton-hall	—	
Kemp Rev. Robert, Walpole, Suffolk	—	
Kemp Isaac, Heigham, Norwich	—	
More William George, Shelton	—	
Wells Henry, Shelton	—	
Ward James, Shelton	—	

Shimpling.

Bond John, Botesdale, Suffolk	—	
Etheridge John, Dickleborough	—	
Hammond Edmund, Shimpling	—	
Kerridge Richard, Shimpling	—	
Millard Jeffrey Watson, Shimpling, Norfolk	—	
Spelman Gower Isaac, Shimpling	—	
Wilton Thomas, Shimpling		
	4	3
Bate William, Shimpling		
Calver George, Palgrave, Suffolk		
Ford George, Shimpling		
Harrison Philip, Diss		
Hawes Samuel, Shimpling		
Turner Thomas Joseph, Colchester, Essex		

Shottesham All Saints.

Baxter Thomas, Shottesham All Saints	—	
Boyce Francis, Shottesham All Saints	—	
Burgess Thomas, Shottesham All Saints	—	
Edwards Robert, Shottesham All Saints	—	
Fellowes Rev. Charles, Shottisham All Saints	—	
Godfrey Thomas, Shottesham All Saints	—	
Huggins Thomas, Shottesham All Saints	—	
Kerridge Thomas, 9, Mason's-alley, Bassinghall-street, City, London	—	
Merry Francis William, Shottesham All Saints	—	
Pilgrim John, jun., Chapel-field, St. Giles', Norwich	—	
Sayer James, Shottesham All Saints	—	
White Thomas, Shottesham All Saints	—	
White Jeremiah, St. Michael at Thorn, Norwich	—	
Winter John, Shottesham All Saints	—	
	11	3
Burwood Edward, Stoke Holy Cross		
Barlow William, Newcastle-upon-Tyne		

	S.	C.

Shottesham St. Mary and St. Martin.

	S.	C.
Fellowes Robert, Bitteswell-hall, Leicestershire	—	
Grice Saul, Shottesham St. Mary	—	
Lee Walter Henry, Shottesham St. Mary		
Mitchell John, Shottesham St. Mary	—	
Nicholls James, Shottesham St. Mary	—	
Raven Beverley William, Shottesham St. Mary	—	
Traxton Thomas, Shottesham St. Mary	—	
Warmoll John, Shottesham St. Mary	—	
	7	1
Boyce Francis, Shottesham All Saints		
Fellowes Robert, Shottesham St. Mary		

Starston.

	S.	C.
Arthy John, clerk, Caister St. Edmund's	—	
Coleby David, Starston	—	
Drewell Samuel, Starston	—	
Etheridge Jonathon, Starston	—	
Feaveryer David, Starston	—	
Gipson William, Starston	—	
Hopper Augustus Macdonald, Starston	—	
Lanham James, Starston	—	
Mullenger Thomas, Starston	—	
Redgrave Thomas, Starston	—	
Self George, Starston	—	
Smith John, Tindall hall farm, Ditchingham	—	
Tennant James, Starston	—	
Taylor Thomas Lombe, Starston	—	
Thurling George, Starston	—	
Wase Jeremiah, Starston	—	
	8	13
Barker Matthew, Starston		
Burgess Edward, Denton		
Dodd Edward, clerk, St. Giles', Cambridge		
Etheridge Charles, Starston		
Henniker Lord John, Thornham Magna, Suffolk		
Howard James, Starston		
Pratt James Burford, Needham		
Parke George, Heigham, Norwich		
Saunders Francis, Starston		
Wase Jeremiah, sen., Starston		

Stratton St. Mary.

	S.	C.
Back Leonard, Stratton St. Mary	—	
Barber John, Stratton St. Mary		
Basey Robert, Haynford		
Burroughes Randall E., Thorpe-hamlet, Norwich	—	
Burroughes Robert Randall, Stratton St. Mary	—	
Bunn Abraham, Stratton St. Mary	—	
Bassingthwaite John, Stratton St. Mary	—	
Brown George, Stratton St. Mary		
Bishop William, Wacton		
Deacon James, Pottergate-st., Norwich		
Everitt Samuel, Stratton St. Mary		
Farrow John, Stratton St. Mary		
Fiske James, Stratton St. Mary		
Fryer Benjamin, Stratton St. Mary	—	
Grys Le Willism, Stratton St. Mary		
Hotson Wales, Stratton St. Mary		
Hotson John, Stratton St. Mary		
Jarrard Frederick W. H., Stratton St. Mary		
Kemp Thomas John, Gissing		
Rous Samuel, Wrentham		
	16	4

	S.	C.
Gwyn William, Tasburgh-lodge		
Nudds Samuel, Stratton St. Mary		
Ringer William, Tharston		
Smith Garle Frederick, Finchley, near Loddon		

Stratton St. Michael.

	S.	C.
Bayly Rev. Charles H., Stratton St. Michael	—	
Crane William, Stratton St. Michael	—	
Dix Robert, Stratton St. Michael	—	
Spurrell Richard James, Stratton St. Michael	—	
	2	2
Atmore Bowles Richard, East Harling		
Field Robert, Stratton St. Michael		
Gwyn Richard Hammond, Northrepps		
Hotson John, Stratton St. Mary		
Rayner Thomas, Stratton St. Michael		
Robertson William, Stratton St. Michael		

Tacolnestone.

	S.	C.
Bassingthwaighte John, Tacolnestone	—	
Barnes William, Redenhall with Harleston	—	
Corbould Warren William, Tacolnestone	—	
Coleman William, Tacolnestone		
Goodrum Ephraim, Tacolnestone		
Hambleton John, Tacolnestone		
Howes Thomas, Tacolnestone		
Holmes Robert, Tacolnestone	—	
Hales William, Tacolnestone		
Kirk Thomas, Tacolnestone		
Knights Robert, Tacolnestone		
Ludkin George, Tacolnestone		
Newman John, Tacolnestone		
Newman Robert, Forncett St. Mary		
Phillipo Elisha, Tacolnestone		
Reeve James, Snetterton		
Spratt James, Tacolnestone		
Stebbings Francis, Tacolnestone		
White William Frederick, Tacolnestone		
	8	16
Boileau Sir John Peter, Ketteringham-hall		
Bloomfield William, Ketteringham		
Caston James, Forncett St. Peter		
Kirk William, Tacolneston		
Steward Edward, Eaton, Norwich		

Tasburgh.

	S.	C.
Buck Henry, Hethersett	—	
Cooper John, Tasburgh	—	
Dye Samuel, Newton Flotman	—	
Foulsham Samuel, Gildencroft, Norwich	—	
Francis Ephraim, Stratton St. Michael	—	
Gwyn William, Tasburgh	—	
Muskett John, Bury St. Edmund's	—	
Preston Rev. Henry, Tasburgh	—	
Rix John, Tasburgh	—	
Wright William, Tasburgh	—	
	2	8
Alexander Stephen, Tasburgh		
Betts William, Tasburgh		
Balls John, Tasburgh		
George Zachary, Tasburgh		
Smith James, Newmarket-road, Norwich		
Webster Isaac, Tasburgh		
White Henry, Tasburgh		

Tharston.

	S.	C.
Abbs Robert, Tharston		
Banfather Henry, Sprowston		
Beckett James, Tharston		
Biggs Rev. William, Tharston	—	
Bright Ezra, Tharston		
Bush James, Tharston		
Claxton James, Tharston		
Huggins Thomas, Tharston		
Pearce Robert, Tharston	—	
Pearce James, Tharston	—	
Ringer Wm., St. Peter's Mancroft, Norwich	—	
Smith Charles, Tharston	—	
Seaman James, Tharston		
Sword John, Tharston		
Thurston John Manhood, Tharston	—	
Thurston Robert, Tharston		
Vansittart Augustus Arthur, 49, Brook-street, Grosvenor-square, London		
Wicks' John, Tharston		
	12	6
Fitch Robert, Market-place, Norwich		
Harvey Sir Robert John, Mousehold-house, Thorpe, Norwich		
Harvey Harvey Robt. J., Bracondale, Norwich		
Kitson John, Hamlet of Thorpe, Norwich		
Mear Shadrach, Tharston		
Page William, Fersfield		

Thelton.

	S.	C.
Carver Michael, Thelton	—	
Eaton Edward Jarrett, Thelton	—	
Elliott William Waller, Thelton	—	
Havers Thomas, Esq., Thelton-hall	—	
More William George, Thelton	—	
Wells Henry, Thelton	—	
	0	6

Thorpe Abbotts.

	S.	C.
Chenry John, Thorpe Abbotts	—	
King John Lanchester, Thorpe Abbotts		
Rayner Robert Raymond, Thorpe Abbotts		
Soanes Daniel, Thorpe Abbotts		
Smith James, Thorpe Abbotts		
Wallace Rev. William, Thorpe Abbotts		
	3	3
Belwade Henry B. M., Lamberhurst, Kent		
Debenham Robert, Scole		
Holland Rev. Edward, 42, Grosvenor-place, London		
Knights John, Thorpe Abbotts		

Tibenham.

	S.	C.
Buxton Sir Robert Jacob, Shadwell-court	—	
Blomfield Frederick, Tibenham		
Barker George, Shipdham		
Betts John, Tibenham		
Brewster Henry, Tibenham	—	
Chaseney William, Tibenham		
Cook James Young, Semer, Suffolk	—	
Catchpole Robert, Tibenham	—	
Dordery William, Tibenham	—	
Everett John, Tibenham	—	
Everett George, Tibenham	—	
Etheridge William, Tibenham	—	
Farrow Joseph, Bungay, Suffolk	—	
Feltham William, Harleston, Norfolk	—	
Hales Jas., St. John's Maddermarket, Norwich	—	
Holmes Robert, Tibenham	—	

	S.	C.
Hardy Robert, Tibenham		
Kett Jacob, Tibenham		
Lester William, Tibenham		
Lant Joseph, Tibenham		
Mayes John, Gissing		
Nudds Robert, Tibenham		
Pearson John, senr., Tibenham		
Pearson John, jun., Tibenham		
Read John, Tibenham		
Robertson Thomas, Tibenham		
Self Edward, jun., Tibenham		
Self Charles, Tibenham		
Turner Thomas, Ixworth, Suffolk		
Turner George, Tibenham		
Wells George, Banham		
	17	14
Bobby Thomas, Tibenham		
Coulson Walter, 3, New-square, Lincoln's Inn, London		
Dixon Rev. Thomas, Tibenham		
Garrood Thomas, Tibenham		
Hart Charles, Tibenham		
Leech Stephen, West Somerton		
Leech Shawl, Tibenham		
Lester George, Tibenham		

Tivetshall St. Margaret.

	S.	C.
Coleby Caleb, Pulham St. Mary Virgin	—	
George William, Tivetshall St. Margaret		
Gibson Frederick, Tivetshall St. Margaret		
Norris Geo. Dennis, clerk, Kessingland, Suffolk	—	
Rayson Samuel, Tivetshall St. Margaret		
Rayson Ziba, Pulham St. Mary Magdalen		
Watling George, Tivetshall St. Margaret		
	4	3
Carpenter John, Tivetshall St. Margaret		
Howard James, Tivetshall St. Margaret		
Shepherd John, Tivetshall St. Margaret		
Steward James, Tivetshall St. Margaret		
Spratt John, Tivetshall St. Margaret		
Tillett William, Tivetshall St. Margaret		

Tivetshall St. Mary.

	S.	C.
Andrews John, Tivetshall St. Mary	—	
Barrett George, Norwich		
Bignold Samuel F., clerk, Tivetshall St. Mary	—	
Bond Robert, Tivetshall St. Mary		
Bond Henry, Tivetshall St. Mary		
Gowing William, Tivetshall St. Mary		
Gowing Lionel, Tivetshall St. Mary		
Hill James, Tivetshall St. Mary		
Le Grys James, Tivetshall St. Mary		
Newman James, Tivetshall St. Mary		
Thrower James, Tivetshall St. Margaret		
Wilby John, Tivetshall St. Mary		
	11	1
Aldous John, Tivetshall St. Mary		
Bell John, Crook's-place, Norwich		
Barney William, Tivetshall St. Mary		
Holmes Robert, Tibenham		
Jeffries Robert, Tivetshall St. Mary		
Le Grys John, Wacton		
Taylor George, Beccles		
Vyse George, Dickleburgh		
White James, clerk, Sloley		

Topcroft.

	S.	C.
Borrett Samuel, Topcroft	—	
Bunn Richard, Topcroft	—	

I

	S.	C.
Butten John, jun., Topcroft	—	
Cheney Edmund, Topcroft	—	
Chaney Edmund the younger, Topcroft	—	
Cunningham John, Topcroft	—	
Cunningham Henry, Topcroft	—	
Delf Samuel, sen., Topcroft	—	
Delf Samuel Newton, Topcroft	—	
Delf Daniel, Topcroft	—	
Fuller Curtis, Topcroft	—	
Laidler Stephen, Redenhall	—	
Rounce John, Topcroft	—	
Townrow John, Topcroft	—	
	3	11
Fairhead John, Topcroft		
Forster Francis, Hethersett		
Gowing William, Topcroft		
Hickman Francis Fairfax, Chester		
Mills Charles, Plumstead, Kent		
Smith William John, clerk, Cringleford-hall		
Safford Rev. Charles Cutting, Meltingham-castle, Suffolk		
Wilson Rev. Edward, Topcroft		

Wacton.

	S.	C.
Alexander Richard, Wacton		
Batley Charles, Wacton		
Cook John, Wacton	—	
Grain Rev. Charles, Wacton		
Grain P., jun., Great Shelford, Cambridgeshire	—	
Holmes John Colby, Wacton		
Le Grys John, Wacton	—	
Lincoln Edmund, Thorpe, Norwich	—	
Peck James, Wacton	—	
Rivett Ellis, Wacton	—	
Sheldrake Daniel, Stratton St. Mary	—	
Stane John Bramston, Forest-hall, Ongor, Essex	—	
Weston John, Wacton	—	
Weston William, Wacton	—	
	11	3
Delf William, Wacton		
Holmes Henry Tuke, Sendall-grove, Yorkshire		
Smith Robert, Stratton St. Michael		
Walford Charles, Esq., Melton, Suffolk		

Winfarthing.

	S.	C.
Atmore Richard, East Harling	—	
Banham George, Winfarthing	—	
Burch James, Grundisburgh, Suffolk	—	
Barker Robert, Winfarthing	—	
Bobby John, Winfarthing	—	
Brazeworth Robert, Winfarthing	—	
Catchpole Nathaniel, Winfarthing	—	
Catchpole John, Winfarthing	—	
Capes John, Winfarthing	—	
Coleman Robert, Winfarthing	—	
Everett Thomas, Winfarthing	—	
Filby Henry, Winfarthing	—	
Fox John, Winfarthing	—	
Filbee William, Winfarthing	—	
George Samuel, Winfarthing	—	
Hart Samuel, Winfarthing	—	
Hewett James, Banham	—	
Humphrey George, Winfarthing	—	
Jarrett Jonathan William, Winfarthing	—	
Keppel Hon. Edward Southwell, Quidenham Parsonage	—	
Lansdell George, New Buckenham	—	
Palmer Richard, Winfarthing	—	
Potter Joel, Winfarthing	—	
Rudd William Bloss, Winfarthing	—	

	S.	C.
Sharman John, Winfarthing	—	
Simonds John, Winfarthing	—	
Scarfe Robert, Shelfanger	—	
Sparrow Jeremiah, Winfarthing	—	
Taylor John, Winfarthing	—	
Taylor Francis Oddin, Winfarthing	—	
Utting Daniel, Winfarthing	—	
Wragg Elliss, Winfarthing	—	
Wragg Eliss, Winfarthing	—	
Youngman John, Winfarthing	—	
	5	29
Filby Edmund, Winfarthing		
Glanfield Robert, Lowestoft		
Hart Charles, Tibenham		
Nicholson Noah, Winfarthing		
Rich Thomas, Banham		
Snelling Robert, Diss		
Taylor Francis Oddin, Winfarthing		

Wortwell.

	S.	C.
Arnold Richard Aldous, Ellough, Suffolk		
Aldrich John, West Pottergate-street, Norwich	—	—
Bear William, Redenhall		
Borrett Robert, Wortwell	—	
Borrett George, Wortwell	—	
Bridges James, 30, Great Bath-street, Clerkenwell, Middlesex	—	
Calver William, Wortwell	—	
Cooper Robert, Flixton	—	
Drake Charles, Bungay	—	
Fuller James, Haddiscoe	—	
Goodwin John, Wortwell	—	
Hall James, Magdalen-street, Norwich	—	
Johnson Christopher Betts, Wortwell	—	
Jeffries Josiah, Wortwell	—	
Johnson Robert, Wortwell	—	
Larter Thomas, Wortwell	—	
Ling Isaac, Bungay	—	
Long William, Harleston	—	
Meen John Flatman, Metfield, Suffolk	—	
Palmer William, Wortwell	—	
Simmons John, Wortwell	—	
Stockdale John, Bungay	—	
Staff John, Wortwell	—	
Websdale Henry, Homersfield	—	
Whiting William, Wortwell	—	
	12	18
Alger Henry, Needham		
Boatwright Ambrose, Bungay, Suffolk		
Buxton Richard, Wortwell		
Barber William, Wandsworth, Surrey		
Colls, Edward, Wortwell		
Denny John Harvey, Mendham, Suffolk		
Girling Thomas, Rendham, Suffolk		
Guiat James, Wortwell		
Johnson John, Wortwell		
Mowles Samuel, Aldershot, Hants.		
Powell Arthur, Debenham, Suffolk		
Rayner James, Wortwell		
Richardson John, Wortwell		
Smith Samuel, Blunston		
Youngs Henry, Wortwell		
Youngs Sharman, Wortwell		

Outvoters.

	S.	C.
Gwyn Hamond Weston, Tasburgh, Norfolk		
Howlett Joseph, Pulham St. Mary Magdalen		
	0	2
Gwyn Charles Frederick, Tasburgh, Norfolk		
Irby Frederick Wm., Boyland-hall, Stratton		
Middleton Sir William, Shrubland-park, Suffolk		

GREAT YARMOUTH DISTRICT,

COMPRISING THE PARISHES OF

	S.	C.		S.	C
Ashby with Oby.			***Caister.***		
Davey William, Oby			Andrews George, No. 23, South-street, East-		
Harrison Henry, Oby			road, Cambridge		
Page William, Oby			Branford Womack William, Godwick		
Taylor Henry, Oby			Bond William Mayers, Yarmouth		
Wiseman John, Oby			Bond J. Mayes, Caister		
	4	1	Brown Thomas, Caister		
			Blyth Thomas, Caister		
Billockby.			Blyth John, Caister		
			Burton John, Caister		
Gown Robert, Billockby			Burton Clement, Caister		
Haywood Robert, Clippesby			Burton George, Caister		
	2	0	Bullock Edward, Caister		
			Brown Frederick, Bracondale, Norwich		
Garrett James, Billockby			Clowes Richard Septimus, Caister		
			Chase Robert, Caister		
			Chase John, Caister		
Burgh St. Margaret.			Crane Thomas, Caister		
			Cole William, Caister		
Beverley William, Burgh St. Margaret			Cross Jeremiah, Caister		
Bond George, Burgh St. Margaret			Daniels William Thomas, Stokesby		
Brooks William, Burgh St. Margaret			Davy Samuel, Caister		
Coppin William, Burgh St. Margaret			Edmunds Martin, Caister		
Day Quinton Richard, Burgh St. Margaret			Fellowes Henry, Caister		
Durrant George, Burgh St. Margaret			George Sheals John, Caister		
Elliott Edward, Ranworth			George Robert, Caister		
Florence Thomas, Burgh St. Margaret			George James, Caister		
Gibson Benjamin, Burgh St. Margaret			George Thomas, Caister		
Green John, Burgh St. Margaret			George Thomas, jun., Caister		
Green William, Burgh St. Margaret			George Samuel, Caister		
Green William, Burgh St. Margaret			Gunton Simon, Great Yarmouth		
Greenacre Simon, Burgh St. Margaret			Haylett John, Caister		
Greenacre Charles, Burgh St. Margaret			Haylett James, Caister		
Hales William, Burgh St. Margaret			Haylett Isaiah, Caister		
Howes Richard, Burgh St. Margaret			Horth Thomas, Caister		
Lucas Rev. William, Burgh St. Margaret			Hodds Benjamin, Caister		
Lucas Rev. William N., Burgh St. Margaret			Humphrey Joseph, Caister		
Lucas Rev. Charles John, Burgh St. Margaret			Kerridge English William, Caister		
Littlewood Fabb Charles, Hoveton St. John			Key Henry, Caister		
Monsey Benjamin, Burgh St. Margaret			Knowles Samuel, Caister		
Moore Edward, Burgh St. Margaret			Knowles William, Caister		
Newman John, Burgh St. Margaret			Nuthall Charles Christopher, Great Yarmouth		
Nicholas Jeremiah, Burgh Margaret			Purdy Jonathan, Hythe in Hampshire		
Nicholds William, Burgh St. Margaret			Ruthan James, Caister		
Nockolds John, Burgh St. Margaret			Smith George, Caister		
Nolbrow John, Burgh St. Margaret			Simmons Samuel, jun., Caister		
Saunders Jonathan, Flegg Burgh			Sneller Olive William, Caister		
Steward John, Burgh St. Margaret			Sneller James, Caister		
Shreeve Charles, Burgh St. Margaret			Spendlove John, Caister		
Thurtle William, Burgh St. Margaret			Tubby William, Caister		
Turner Robert, Burgh St. Margaret			Watson James, Caister		
Turner James, Burgh St. Margaret			Webster James, Caister		
Waller Turpin John, Burgh St. Margaret			Wigg Mays, Caister		
Youngs John, Burgh St. Margaret			Wigg William Shank, Great Yarmouth		
	22	13	Wincott John, Caister		
			Wright James, Caister		
				16	38
Claxton William, Burgh St. Margaret					
Kettle Robert, Somerleyton, Suffolk			Bell John Penrice, Leamington		
Kittle Joseph, Burgh St. Margaret			Bratt John, Caister		
Rice Samuel, Stratford-upon-Avon			Debbage William, Caister		

	S.	C.
Dowson Edward William, Geldestone		
Durrant Henry, Caister		
George Philip John, Caister		
George Dennis, Caister		
King Aaron, Caister		
Munford William, Caister		
Pettingill William, Caister		
Plummer John, Caister		
Purday Jonathan, jun., Southampton		
Purday Thomas, jun., Caister		
Purday George Cassell, Hythe, Hampshire		
Steward Rev. George William, Caister		
Smith George, Caister		
Squires William, Caister		
Topps William, Great Yarmouth		
Youell William, Saltburn, Yorkshire		
Yeomans James, Caister		

Clippesby.

	S.	C.
Coleby Rev. William, Gorleston	—	
Garrett Edward, Clippesby	—	
Gown Thomas, Clippesby	—	
Muskett Rev. Joseph Henry, Clippesby	—	
Skinner Thomas, Yarmouth	—	
Wiseman John, Clippesby	—	
	5	1
Barwood George, Clippesby		
Barwood James, Clippesby		
Debbage Benjamin, Clippesby		

Filby.

	S.	C.
Allard Francis, Filby	—	
Allard John, Filby	—	
Chase George, Filby	—	
Chalker James, Filby	—	
Crisp William, Filby	—	
Everson James, Filby	—	
English William, Filby	—	
Green Robert, Filby		
Green John, Filby		
Gorble Michael, Filby		
Hewitt John, Filby		
Humphrey Benjamin, Filby		
Lingwood James, Filby		
Lucas Rev. Charles, Filby		
Lucas George, Esq., Filby		
Nockolds Robert, Filby		
Palmer Edmund, Filby		
Parker John, Filby		
Parker George, Filby		
Skoyles James, Filby		
Skoyles Henry, Filby		
Walpole Clement, Filby		
Walpole William, Filby		
	22	1
Harrison William, Filby		
Kennion Robert Winter, Old-square, Lincoln's Inn, London		
Squire Henry, Yarmouth		
Skoyles Thomas, Filby		

Hemsby.

	S.	C.
Barnes Stephen, Hemsby	—	
Chaney John, Hemsby	—	
Clowes Francis, Norwich	—	
Copeman Robert, Hemsby	—	
Copeman Robert, jun., Hemsby	—	
Chapman William, Filby	—	

	S.	C.
Cooper James, Cromer	—	
Durrant Edmond, Hemsby	—	
Edmonds Joseph, Hemsby	—	
Gallant James, Hemsby	—	
George Edward, Scratby	—	
Gilbert Clement, Hemsby	—	
Green Robert, the elder, Hemsby	—	
Hewett Stephen, Hemsby	—	
Long William, Hemsby	—	
Myhill Samuel, Hemsby	—	
Nichols William, Hemsby	—	
Pickstone Robert, Hemsby	—	
Silcock Cubitt, Hemsby	—	
Saunders John, Hemsby	—	
Temple William, Hemsby	—	
Took Edward, Hemsby	—	
	12	10
Browne John Tubby, Winterton		
Barnes Edward, Hemsby		
Cubitt James, Hemsby		
Dow Pettingill Edward Frederick, Hemsby		
Gillett Edward, Hunham-hall		
Harbord John, Hemsby		
Manship Benjamin, Ormesby St. Margaret		
Pettingill Richard Fabb, Somerleyton-street, Unthank's-road, Norwich		
Woolstone Mark, Hemsby		

Martham.

	S.	C.
Barber George, Martham	—	
Braddock William, Martham	—	
Bushell Thomas, Martham	—	
Bane James, Martham	—	
Belson Robert, Martham	—	
Browne James, Martham	—	
Corbould Rev. Thomas, Norwich	—	
Crisp Anthony, Martham	—	
Clowes Francis, 87, New Bridge-street, Black-friar's, London	—	
Dawson John, Martham	—	
Deary John, Martham	—	
Dunt Nathaniel Hindle, Hemsby	—	
Durrent Robert, Martham	—	
Dyball Humphrey, Martham	—	
Faulke James Cooper, Martham	—	
Garnham Robert, Martham	—	
Gaze William, Martham	—	
Gedge William, Stokesby	—	
Gedge John, Martham	—	
Gillett William, Martham	—	
Grimson William, sen., Martham	—	
Greenacre Richard, Martham	—	
Green Robert, Martham	—	
Harmer William, Martham	—	
Jeary John, Martham	—	
Johnsons James, Martham	—	
Knights Richard, Martham	—	
Lusher James, 19, Holborn-hill, London	—	
Linford William, Martham	—	
Manship Daniel, Martham	—	
Manship Thomas, Rollesby	—	
Payne William, Martham	—	
Pearse Rev. George, Martham	—	
Piggin Thomas, Martham	—	
Proctor Thomas, Martham	—	
Pollard John, Somerton	—	
Rising George, Martham	—	
Rogers William, Martham	—	
Rising Thomas Sutfield, Rollesby	—	
Rising William, Somerton-hall	—	

	S.	C.
Rumming William, Cowley Arms, North Brixton, London	—	
Rust Daniel, Martham	—	
Spargoe John, Martham	—	
Watson George, Martham	—	
Watson Long John, Martham	—	
Watson Short John, Martham	—	
Ware Joseph, Martham	—	
Wright James, Martham	—	
Woods Nichols, Martham	—	
	18	31
Braddock James, Martham		
Braddock George, Martham		
Bane Frederick, Horning		
Cooper Charles, Martham		
Conyard John, jun., Martham		
Clowes William, Stalham		
Garnham Captain John, R.N., Southtown		
Garnham Richard Enoch, Highgate,Middlesex		
Houchen Richard, Norwich		
Hunt John Lee, Martham		
Lambert Henry, Martham		
Littleboy Robert, Martham		
Moore Robert, Burgh		
Nichols John, Martham		
Purdy Charles, Martham		
Webb Robert, 15, Shaftesbury Crescent, London		

Mautby.

	S.	C.
Browne Henry, senr., Mautby	—	
Browne Henry, jun., Mautby	—	
Hewitt David, Mautby	—	
Waters Mark, Mautby	—	
	4	0
Gibbs Alfred George, Mautby		

Ormesby St. Margaret with Scratby.

	S.	C.
Agus William, Ormesby St. Margaret	—	
Augur William, Ormesby St. Margaret	—	
Catchpole William, Scratby	—	
Carr Thomas, Ormesby St. Margaret	—	
Catchpole Robert Trett, Scratby	—	
Clowes John, Yarmouth	—	
Chapman William, jun., Ormesby St. Margaret	—	
Chapman George, Ormesby St. Margaret	—	
Collyer George B., Ormesby St. Margaret	—	
Crisp Joseph, Ormesby St. Margaret	—	
Davis William, Ormesby St. Margaret	—	
Daniels Benjamin, Scratby	—	
Derry Stephen, Ormesby St. Margaret	—	
Dunt John, Ormesby St. Margaret	—	
Dyball Christmas, Ormesby St. Margaret	—	
English Matthew Neave, Scratby	—	
Edmonds James, Scratby	—	
Flegg James, Ormesby St. Margaret	—	
Ferrier Richard, Yarmouth	—	
Flowerday Robert, Ormesby St. Margaret	—	
Foster Richard, Scratby	—	
Gallant John, Ormesby St. Margaret	—	
Green Thomas, Scratby	—	
Hallock Charles, Ormesby St. Margaret	—	
Harvey Job, Ormesby St. Margaret	—	
Hannant Joseph, Ormesby St. Margaret	—	
Hull William, Norwich	—	
Hunt Matthew, jun., Hemsby	—	
Hubbard William, Ormesby St. Margaret	—	
Johnsons Richard, Scratby	—	
Kidman John, Ormesby St. Margaret	—	

	S.	C.
Leathe Thomas, Ormesby St. Margaret	—	
Leathe Robert, Ormesby St. Margaret	—	
Nichols Robert, Ormesby St. Margaret	—	
Read Christmas, Ormesby St. Margaret	—	
Read Robert, Ormesby St. Margaret	—	
Richmond Robert, Ormesby St. Margaret	—	
Richmond Edward Boyce, Ormesby St. Margaret	—	
Scarlet John, Ormesby St. Margaret	—	
Shrimplin James, Ormesby St. Margaret	—	
Tongate James, Scratby	—	
Tongate Benjamin, Ormesby St. Margaret	—	
Underwood Joseph, Ormesby St. Margaret	—	
Westgate Thomas, Ormesby St. Margaret	—	
Woodman Robert, Ormesby St. Margaret	—	
Woolston John, Scratby	—	
Woolston Robert, Scratby	—	
Woolston William, Ormesby St. Margaret	—	
Woolston Francis, Ormesby St. Margaret	—	
	36	18
Bosanquet Richard G., Ormesby St. Margaret		
Cole John, Honing		
Chapman William, Ormesby St. Margaret		
Cooper James, Cromer		
Gallant James, Hemsby		
Gedge William, Ormesby St. Margaret		
Gowen Robert, Ormesby St. Margaret		
Green Robert, Hemsby		
Gill H. William, Ormesby St. Margaret		
Humphrey Benjamin, Filby		
Lacon Sir Edmund Henry K., Bart., Hopton		
Manship William, Ormesby St. Michael		
Mendham Wace Lockett, Norwich		
Womack Arthur Lindoe, Blofield		
Woolston Henry, Ormesby St. Margaret		

Ormesby St. Michael.

	S.	C.
Bullimore Joseph, Ormesby St. Michael	—	
Caldicott Barnes, Ormesby St. Michael	—	
Chapman John, Ormesby St. Margaret	—	
Dunham Jeremiah, Ormesby St. Michael	—	
Fellowes William M., Ormesby St. Margaret	—	
Harrison William, Ormesby St. Michael	—	
Howes William, Ormesby St. Michael	—	
Larston John, Ormesby St. Michael	—	
Larston Samuel, Ormesby St. Michael	—	
Long Edward, Ormesby St. Michael	—	
Manship Benjamin, Ormesby St. Margaret	—	
Montague George, Swaffham	—	
Manship William, Ormesby St. Michael	—	
Munford William, Ormesby St. Michael	—	
Page Charles, Ormesby St. Michael	—	
Ransom John, Ormesby St. Michael	—	
Salmon William, Ormesby St. Michael	—	
Skoyles George, Ormesby St. Michael	—	
	15	3
Addy John, Ormesby St. Michael		
Cockeril Samuel, Ormesby St. Margaret		
Chapman William, sen., Ormesby St. Margaret		
Groom John, Ormesby St. Michael		
Lambert Henry, Martham		
Martin Hezekiah, Southtown		

Repps with Bastwick.

	S.	C.
Belson Richard Bell, Repps	—	
Boyce William, Ixworth, Suffolk	—	
Haddon William, Repps cum Bastwick	—	
Kidman Robert, Repps	—	
Laws James, Repps cum Bastwick	—	
Manship William, Repps cum Bastwick	—	

	S.	C.
Nichols William, Repps		
Postle Samuel Tolver, Repps cum Bastwick	—	
Powley John, Repps	—	
Rising Benjamin, removed to Somerton	—	
Thaine Noah, Yarmouth	—	
Wortley William, Martham		
Wortley William, jun., Repps		
	3	10
Flowerdew Charles, Repps		
Parker John, Filby		
Parker George, Filby		
Rising William, Somerton		

Rollesby.

	S.	C.
Annison Steward Richard, Rollesby	—	
Beck Benjamin, Rollesby		
Boyce John, Rollesby	—	
Browne Benjamin, Rollesby		
Clarke Isaac, St. Stephen's, Norwich		
Christmas John, Rollesby		
Chapman James, Rollesby	—	
Corban Charles, Great Juen-st., London		
Dunham John, Rollesby	—	
Ensor Smith Edmund, Rollesby	—	
Frosdick Daniel, Rollesby	—	
Kemp William, Rollesby	—	
Lincoln Richard, Rollesby	—	
Moore Luke, Rollesby	—	
Myhill William, Rollesby	—	
Norman Bowles Robert Richard, Gt. Yarmouth	—	
Parker William, Great Yarmouth	—	
Powley Robert, Rollesby	—	
Porter Robert, Burgh St. Margaret	—	
Ransome Edward, Rollesby	—	
Sowels Thomas, Rollesby	—	
Squires William, Ormesby St. Margaret	—	
	17	5
Annison Robert, Pakefield, Suffolk		
Clarke George Thomas, Hasboro'		
Harris George, Rollesby		
Kemp Robert, Rollesby		
Pritty Samuel, Pulham St. Mary		
Slack Thomas, Heigham, Norwich		
Tripp Thomas, Rollesby		

Runham.

	S.	C.
Aldis John, Great Yarmouth	—	
Brightwen George, Stamford-hill, Middlesex	—	
Cobb John, Runham	—	
Cory Charles, Burgh Castle, Suffolk		
Cory Robert Woolmer, Horsey		
Cory Alexander Turner, 49, New Bond-street, London		
Cufaude John Lomas, Great Yarmouth		
Dean William, Runham		
England Henry, Runham		
Fabb John Charles, Regent-street, Yarmouth		
Fabb William, Runham		
Gillett Edward, Runham-hall		
Gowen Robert, Runham		
Gowen Henry, Runham		
Hales Robert, Runham	—	
Howes William, Runham		
Kindles John, Runham		
Knights Edward, Runham	—	
Lamb James, Great Yarmouth	—	
London Richard, Runham	—	
Myhill William, senr., Runham	—	
Mingay Richard, Runham	—	

	S.	C.
Nursey Richard, Runham	—	
Palmer William, King-street, Norwich	—	
Reynolds William, Lound, Suffolk	—	
Reed John, Runham	—	
	18	8
Amis Edward, Great Yarmouth		
Barnes Jonas, Great Yarmouth		
Brightwen Thomas, Yarmouth		
Cory Samuel Barnett, Runham		
Cory Horace, 2, Albion Terrace, Limehouse		
Cory John Augustus, Durham		
Wayne William Henry, Much Wenlock, Shropshire		
Westgate Thomas, Ormesby St. Margaret		
Yaxley Richard, Great Yarmouth		

Somerton East.

	S.	C.
Clowes John, Great Yarmouth		
Varley Robert, Somerton East		

Somerton West.

	S.	C.
Annison Daniel, West Somerton		
Daniel Richard, Coombs, Suffolk	—	
Dawson James Frederick, West Somerton		
Dyble John, West Somerton	—	
Dyble James, West Somerton		
Hales Thomas, West Somerton		
Johnson Thomas, West Somerton		
Olley Henry, West Somerton		
Rising Robert, West Somerton		
Varley John, West Somerton		
	1	9
Grove Thomas Fraser, Ferne, Wilts		
Gedge John, Horsey		
Leach Stephen, West Somerton		
Rising William, Somerton-hall		
Trigg James, Hoddesdon, Herts		

Stokesby with Herringby.

	S.	C.
Bagge William, Stradsett-hall		
Bland William, Stokesby	—	
Cudden John Watling, Stokesby		
Daniel Knights Francis, Stokesby	—	
Empson Thomas, Stokesby	—	
Fearman Christmas, Stokesby	—	
Flowerdew William, Southtown		
Gunton William, Stokesby	—	
Myhill Robert, Stokesby		
Moore Aaron, Stokesby		
Palmer Edward, Stokesby		
Read John, Stokesby	—	
Smith Wiliam, Stokesby		
Steward John, Stokesby	—	
Waters Mark, clerk, Yarmouth		
Worship John Lucas, clerk, Stokesby		
Waters William, Herringby		
	6	11
Burroughes William, Stokesby		
Rowland John, Yarmouth		
Smith Edward, Stokesby		
Waters Mark, Mautby		

Thrigby.

	S.	C.
Brown Thomas, Esq., Thrigby-hall		
Brown William, Thrigby	—	
Skinner John, Thrigby	—	
	0	3

	S.	C.
Thurne.		
Brown Henry, Thurne	—	
Bishop Benjamin, Thurne	—	
Clark Samuel, Thurne	—	
Garrett William, Acle	—	
Gown James, Thurne	—	
Parker Thomas, Thurne	—	
Wigg Samuel, Yarmouth	—	
	6	1
Beverley William, Burgh		
Bolton Horatio, clerk, Oby Rectory		
Fellowes Henry, Kivestone-park		
Howes Samuel, Thurne		
Parker John, Filby		
Winterton.		
Amis James, Winterton	—	
Beare Spence Robert, Caister	—	
Brown Robert, jun., Winterton	—	
Davy Robert, Winterton	—	
Empson James, Winterton	—	
Fenn Robert John, Great Yarmouth	—	
Green John, Winterton	—	
Gunton Simon, Great Yarmouth	—	
Kittle James, Winterton	—	
King Benjamin, Winterton	—	
King James, Winterton	—	
Juby John, Winterton	—	
Juby William, Winterton	—	
Leech Edward, Winterton	—	
Larner Samuel, Winterton	—	
Rust James, Martham	—	
Sheales Samuel, Winterton	—	
Smith William, Lighthouse, Winterton	—	
Soulsby John, Winterton	—	
Womack William, Winterton	—	
	10	10
Banham Robert, Gorleston		
Brown Solomon, Winterton		
Clowes Richard Sept., Caister		
Durrant Edmund, Hemsby		
George William, Great Yarmouth		
Nelson Rev. John, Winterton		
Newman William, Winterton		
Yarmouth Great.		
Adams Robert, Great Yarmouth	—	
Adcock John, Great Yarmouth	—	
Aldred Charles Cory, Great Yarmouth	—	
Aldred Edward Cooper, Great Yarmouth	—	
Aldred Edward Reynolds, Great Yarmouth	—	
Aldred Samuel Boston, Holborn-hill, London	—	
Aldred John James, 4, Victoria-street, Holborn-bridge, London	—	
Aldred Samuel Higham, Great Yarmouth	—	
Ames Edward, Great Yarmouth	—	
Ames Abraham, Great Yarmouth	—	
Amis Samuel, Great Yarmouth	—	
Andrews Henry, Great Yarmouth	—	
Arbon George, Great Yarmouth	—	
Arbon Noah, Great Yarmouth	—	
Arbon Charles, Great Yarmouth	—	
Archer Clement, Rainbow-corner, Great Yarmouth	—	
Armes Daniel, Heigham, Norwich	—	
Atkins William, Great Yarmouth	—	
Ayers Thomas, jun., Great Yarmouth	—	
Ayers James, Great Yarmouth	—	

	S.	C.
Bailey Robert, Great Yarmouth	—	
Bailey James, St. George's-road, Great Yarmouth	—	
Baker John, Great Yarmouth	—	
Baker John, jun., Great Yarmouth	—	
Baker John, Queen-street, Great Yarmouth, Norfolk, 6, Inverness-road, Bayswater, in the parish of Paddington, Middlesex	—	
Bales John Barney, Great Yarmouth	—	
Baldwin John Diboll, Great Yarmouth	—	
Baldwin Charles, Great Yarmouth	—	
Baldwin William Diboll, Great Yarmouth	—	
Barcham William Daniel, Great Yarmouth	—	
Barker John, Great Yarmouth	—	
Barnby William Henry, Southtown	—	
Barnaby John Eager, Great Yarmouth	—	
Barnaby James, Mendham, Norfolk	—	
Barnes Charles, Great Yarmouth	—	
Barnes Jeremiah, Great Yarmouth	—	
Bartram Charles, Great Yarmouth	—	
Bartram Charles Logdon, Great Yarmouth	—	
Bartram John, Great Yarmouth	—	
Bartram Cubitt Engall, St. George's-terrace, Great Yarmouth	—	
Bartram William, 58, Southtown, Suffolk	—	
Barrett Thomas, Great Yarmouth	—	
Barrow Samuel, Great Yarmouth	—	
Barber Robert David, Great Yarmouth	—	
Bately Stephen Godfrey, Southtown	—	
Bately Benjamin, Great Yarmouth	—	
Bateman James, 12, Sussex-terrace, King's-road, Camden-town, London	—	
Bateman Matthew, Great Yarmouth	—	
Batley William, Gaol-street, Great Yarmouth	—	
Baxter Joseph, Great Yarmouth	—	
Bailey Joseph, Great Yarmouth	— —	
Bayfield William Henry, Great Yarmouth	—	
Beales William, Great Yarmouth	—	
Bean Robert, Tower-road, Great Yarmouth	—	
Beazor Martin, Great Yarmouth	—	
Bee James, Great Yarmouth	—	
Bee Robert, Great Yarmouth	—	
Beets John, Great Yarmouth	—	
Beecroft Peter, Great Yarmouth	—	
Beevor William, North Walsham	—	
Beckett James, Great Yarmouth	—	
Beckett Jasper Draper, Great Yarmouth	—	
Beloe Henry, Southtown	—	
Belson William, Row 86, Great Yarmouth	—	
Bellamy Winter, Great Yarmouth	—	
Bennett Edward, Norwich	—	
Benstead David, Great Yarmouth	—	
Bessey William Henry, Great Yarmouth	—	
Beverley John, Great Yarmouth	—	
Bishop Thomas, Great Yarmouth	—	
Blagg Thomas, 40, Southtown, Suffolk	—	
Blake Garson, Southtown, Suffolk	—	
Blake Joseph Starling, Queen-street, Portsea, Hampshire	—	
Blake William Barnabas, Great Yarmouth	—	
Blake Wm., St. Nicholas-road, Great Yarmouth	—	
Blake William, Great Yarmouth	—	
Blake Robert, Great Yarmouth	—	
Blake Robert, jun., Great Yarmouth	—	
Blogg James, Great Yarmouth	—	
Blogg Thomas, Great Yarmouth	—	
Blowers Henry Huson, Great Yarmouth	—	
Blowers Mark, Reading, Berkshire	—	
Blyth John Tolhouse, Great Yarmouth	—	
Bond Henry, Alma-place, Great Yarmouth	—	
Borrett Simon, Great Yarmouth	—	
Borking James, Great Yarmouth	—	

	S.	C.
Boulter Henry, Great Yarmouth	—	
Bowgin John, Southtown		
Bracey John Taylor, Great Yarmouth		
Bracey William, Great Yarmouth		
Bradbeer Samuel, Great Yarmouth		
Brewer John Dye, Great Yarmouth		
Bringalow William, Great Yarmouth		
Bristow John, Great Yarmouth	—	
Brock Samuel, Great Yarmouth	—	
Brooks Wilson, Great Yarmouth		
Brooks John, Great Yarmouth		
Browne John, Great Yarmouth		
Browne John, Great Yarmouth		
Browne Benjamin, Great Yarmouth		
Browne Charles, Great Yarmouth		
Brown John Hodds, Bethsheba-place, Great Yarmouth	—	
Brown Robert, Great Yarmouth	—	
Brown William Palgrave, Great Yarmouth	—	
Brown Richard, Great Yarmouth		
Brundish James, Great Yarmouth		
Buckle William, Great Yarmouth		
Budds William J., Gaol-street, Great Yarmouth	—	
Bullimore John, Great Yarmouth		
Bullock Charles, Great Yarmouth		
Bunn Thomas, Southtown, Suffolk		
Burrage John, Great Yarmouth		
Burkett William, Great Yarmouth		
Burtle James, Row 6, Great Yarmouth	—	
Burroughes William Norton, Great Yarmouth	—	
Burgess Thomas, Great Yarmouth		
Burgess Thomas, Great Yarmouth		
Burgess Richard, Great Yarmouth		
Burgess Benjamin, Great Yarmouth		
Burton Samuel, Southtown		
Burton Gent, Thorn-lane, Norwich		
Burton Charles, Great Yarmouth		
Burton James, King-street, Great Yarmouth	—	
Burton William, Great Yarmouth		
Buston John Truman, Great Yarmouth		
Buston John Truman, jun., Great Yarmouth		
Buston Hezekiah William, King-street, Great Yarmouth	—	
Bully Joseph Ablitt, Great Yarmouth	—	
Button John, Flixton, Suffolk		
Butler Robert, Great Yarmouth		
Byford George, Great Yarmouth		
Cannell Charles, King-street, Great Yarmouth	—	
Carter Daniel, Great Yarmouth		
Carrier William Porter, Gaol-street, Great Yarmouth	—	
Carrick Mark, East Dereham	—	
Carter William Charles, South Market-road, Great Yarmouth	—	
Ceiley Thomas, Great Yarmouth	—	
Chapman William, Great Yarmouth		
Chapman Robert, Great Yarmouth		
Chase James, Great Yarmouth	—	
Cheston Geo., St. Peter's-road, Gt. Yarmouth	—	
Child William, sen., Great Yarmouth	—	
Child Benjamin, Great Yarmouth		
Child Edmund, Southwold, Suffolk		
Child John Hardy, Great Yarmouth		
Child Robert, Great Yarmouth	—	
Church Samuel, Great Yarmouth		
Clark James, Row 144, Great Yarmouth	—	
Clarke Edmund, Great Yarmouth	—	
Clark John, Great Yarmouth	—	
Clarke Thomas, Great Yarmouth	—	
Clark Justinian B., Norwich	—	
Clarke William, Great Yarmouth	—	

	S.	C.
Clarke Richard, Great Yarmouth	—	
Clayton John, Great Yarmouth	—	
Clements George, sen., Queen's-place, Great Yarmouth	—	
Clowes George Washington, Great Yarmouth	—	
Cobb John, Charlotte-street, Great Yarmouth	—	
Coble John, Great Yarmouth		
Cole Thomas, Great Yarmouth	—	
Cole John Pile, Tower-gates, Great Yarmouth	—	
Coleman George, Great Yarmouth		
Cooper Henry Howes, Great Yarmouth	—	
Cooper Thomas, Great Yarmouth	—	
Cotton Charles, Great Yarmouth	—	
Cotton William, Great Yarmouth		
Cowles Reuben Frederick, Swaffham, Norfolk	—	
Cox William, Great Yarmouth	—	
Craske Samuel Woodward, North entrance, Great Yarmouth	—	
Crickmay Samuel Thomas, Great Yarmouth	—	
Crisp James, Great Yarmouth	—	
Crisp John Wiseman, Castle-meadow, Norwich	—	
Cromwell George, Great Yarmouth		
Crow Henry, Great Yarmouth	—	
Crow William, Great Yarmouth	—	
Cumby Moore, Lowne, Suffolk		
Dabenham Jonathan, Great Yarmouth	—	
Dale David, Aylsham, Norfolk		
Davey Frederick, Great Yarmouth	—	
Davey Daniel, Great Yarmouth	—	
Davie William, Great Yarmouth	—	
Davie William Cufaude, Cringleford		
Davidson James, Fishergate-street, Norwich	—	
Dawson Robert, Great Yarmouth	—	
Dawson Robert D., Great Yarmouth		
Dawson John, Great Yarmouth		
Debenham Abraham, Great Yarmouth	—	
Dendy Frederick, Gorleston, Suffolk		
Dickie James, Great Yarmouth	—	
Ditcham John, sen., Great Yarmouth	—	
Diver William Holmes, Great Yarmouth	—	
Diboll John Edward, Great Yarmouth	—	
Dorking Robert, Great Yarmouth		
Dowson Benjamin, Great Yarmouth		
Dowsing Richard C., Great Yarmouth	—	
Draper John, Great Yarmouth	—	
Draper William Henry, Great Yarmouth	—	
Draper Joseph, Great Yarmouth	—	
Dublack James Paston, Great Yarmouth	—	
Duffield John, Great Yarmouth	—	
Duffield Robert, Great Yarmouth		
Dunnell George, Charlotte-st., Great Yarmouth	—	
Durrant Robert, Great Yarmouth	—	
Durrant Edward, Great Yarmouth	—	
Durrant Jeremiah, Great Yarmouth	—	
Dyball Thomas, Great Yarmouth	—	
Dyer Daniel, Great Yarmouth	—	
Earl William, Great Yarmouth	—	
Earl Isaiah Furnace, Great Yarmouth	—	
Edwards Benjamin, Great Yarmouth	—	
Eggett Henry, Great Yarmouth	—	
Elliott George, Great Yarmouth	—	
Ellis Robert, jun., Great Yarmouth	—	
Emms Henry, Blofield, Norfolk	—	
Emms David, Great Yarmouth	—	
Etteridge John, Great Yarmouth	—	
Everitt William Henry, Great Yarmouth	—	
Everitt William Spencer, North Cove, Suffolk	—	
Everitt William, Cove, Suffolk	—	
Faulk Thomas, Great Yarmouth	—	
Fear James Clement, 9, High-street, Aldgate, London	—	

	S.	C.
Fellowes John Frederick, Pier Cliffe-lodge, Gorleston		
Fellowes John Henry, Southtown	—	
Fenner Robert, Sergeant, Chapel-square, Great Yarmouth		
Fenn John, Great Yarmouth	—	
Ferrier Richard, Burgh Castle, Suffolk	—	
Ferrier Richard, jun., Birkenhead	—	
Field Michael, Southtown, Suffolk	—	
Figgins John Harris, Great Yarmouth	—	
Fill Samuel John, Great Yarmouth	—	
Fisher John Goate, Great Yarmouth		
Fisher Thornton, Great Yarmouth		
Fisher William Thornton, Great Yarmouth	—	
Fish John, Great Yarmouth	—	
Fisk Joseph James, Great Yarmouth	—	
Flaxman Barker, Great Yarmouth	—	
Fleet Simon Raven, Great Yarmouth		
Forder Robert L., Great Yarmouth		
Foreman William James, Great Yarmouth		
Forrest Henry, Great Yarmouth		
Fowler Daniel Read, Great Yarmouth	—	
Fox William, Great Yarmouth	—	
Fox Orris, Dover-place, Great Yarmouth	—	
Fox Thomas, Great Yarmouth	—	
Fransham Robert Henry, Row 21, Great Yarmouth		
Freeman James, 8, Heigham, Norwich	—	
Freeman John, Great Yarmouth	—	
French Thomas, the younger, Great Yarmouth		
French John Hastings, Great Yarmouth		
Frere Edward B., Great Yarmouth		
Frosdick Christmas William, Great Yarmouth	—	
Frosdick James Thomas, Market-road, Great Yarmouth	—	
Fyson Joseph, Great Yarmouth		
Garwood Robert, Southtown		
Gedge William, Great Yarmouth		
George Thomas, Great Yarmouth		
George Henry, Great Yarmouth		
Gibbs Robert, Great Yarmouth		
Gidney Henry, Great Yarmouth		
Giles Joseph, Great Yarmouth		
Gillings James, Great Yarmouth	—	
Gillings John, Great Yarmouth	—	
Glanfield William, Great Yarmouth	—	
Goffin John, jun., Southtown, Suffolk		
Goffin Samuel, Great Yarmouth		
Goffin Thomas, Great Yarmouth		
Golding James Atkins, Great Yarmouth	—	
Gooch Thomas, Donor-place, Great Yarmouth	—	
Gooch Borrett, Great Yarmouth		
Gooch David, Great Yarmouth		
Gooch Thomas H., Donor-place, Great Yarmouth	—	
Goodrick George Thomas, Great Yarmouth	—	
Goodwin John, Great Yarmouth		
Goss William, Row 85, Chapel-street, Great Yarmouth		
Gourlay David Abraham, Great Yarmouth		
Gowen George, Great Yarmouth		
Gowen John, Great Yarmouth		
Gowing Stephen, Lowestoft, Suffolk	—	
Green William, Great Yarmouth		
Greenwood Edward, Great Yarmouth	—	
Greenacre Thomas, Great Yarmouth		
Grief William, Great Yarmouth		
Gunn Henry, Great Yarmouth		
Gyton James, Great Yarmouth		
Haines John, Great Yarmouth		
Hall Curtis, Eastgate, Peterborough, Northamptonshire		

	S.	C.
Hall John Barnard, Great Yarmouth		
Hall Horatio George, Fuller's-hill, Great Yarmouth	—	
Hall Richard Harradence, Fuller's-hill, Great Yarmouth	—	
Hammond Richard, Great Yarmouth		
Hammon Richard, Great Yarmouth		
Hannah Alexander, Southtown		
Harbord John, jun., Great Yarmouth	—	
Harbord William, Great Yarmouth		
Harbord William Charles, Great Yarmouth	—	
Harbert William, Great Yarmouth		
Harcourt George S., Great Yarmouth		
Harley George, Gorleston	—	
Harmer Robert H., Great Yarmouth		
Harper James, Great Yarmouth	—	
Harvey Robert, Great Yarmouth		
Harvey George, Great Yarmouth		
Harvey Robert Butcher, Great Yarmouth	—	
Harris John, Great Yarmouth		
Harrison Benjamin, Great Yarmouth	—	
Harrison James Hargrave, Great Yarmouth	—	
Harrison Matthew, Great Yarmouth	—	
Harrison John, Great Yarmouth	—	
Hastings Henry, Tower-gates, Great Yarmouth	—	
Hayward James, Great Yarmouth		
Hayward Edward George, Great Yarmouth	—	
Herrod Richard John, Great Yarmouth	—	
Hindry Edmund, New-st., Brompton, London	—	
Hinde Francis, Great Yarmouth		
Hewitt Daniel, Great Yarmouth	—	
Hindes Edward Mickleburgh, Great Yarmouth, Row 87	—	
Hobbs William, Great Yarmouth		
Hockley Charles, Great Yarmouth	—	
Hodskinson Frederick, Great Yarmouth	—	
Holmes Robert, Great Yarmouth	—	
Holt William, Great Yarmouth		
Holliday William, Great Yarmouth	—	
Holliday Daniel Henry, Great Yarmouth	—	
Holliday David Henry, Great Yarmouth	—	
Holley Thomas, Great Yarmouth		
Horn John, Great Yarmouth		
Hotblack Henry, Great Yarmouth	—	
Housago Henry, Great Yarmouth	—	
Howard William, Great Yarmouth	—	
Howard John, Great Yarmouth		
Howes William, Great Yarmouth		
Howlett Benjamin, Great Yarmouth	—	
Howlett Horatio, Great Yarmouth	—	
Howes William, Gorleston		
Hubbard John, Great Yarmouth	—	
Hudson Thomas, Great Yarmouth	—	
Hunn Edward, Great Yarmouth	—	
Hunn William, Great Yarmouth		
Hunt Henry, Broad-row, Great Yarmouth	—	
Hunt James, Brandon, Suffolk		
Hunter Henry Lovick, Great Yarmouth	—	
Hurst Thomas, Great Yarmouth	—	
Hylton John Bessey, Great Yarmouth	—	
Ives James Thomas, Great Yarmouth	—	
Ives William John Carter, 160 row, Great Yarmouth	—	
Ives Samuel, Great Yarmouth	—	
Ingram William, Great Yarmouth	—	
Ingram Charles, Great Yarmouth	—	
Isaac Edward, Great Yarmouth	—	
Isaac John Joseph, Great Yarmouth	—	
Ives Francis, Great Yarmouth		
Ives Charles, Acle, Norfolk	—	
Jay Benjamin, Great Yarmouth	—	

K

	S.	C.
Jay Edward Ward, Great Yarmouth		
Jay Henry, Great Yarmouth		
Johnson William, Great Yarmouth	—	
Johnson William, Great Yarmouth	—	
Johnson Job, Great Yarmouth		
Johnson Tobias, Great Yarmouth		
Johnson John, Great Yarmouth		
Johnson John, Great Yarmouth	—	
Johnson Edward Orfeur, Great Yarmouth	—	
Keeler James, Great Yarmouth		
Keeler John, Great Yarmouth		
Kemp Edward Curtis, Whissonsett, Norfolk		
Kerrison George, Great Yarmouth	—	
Key John, Great Yarmouth		
King Matthew, Great Yarmouth		
King George, Corton, Suffolk		
Kirby George, Great Yarmouth		
Kisbee Thomas, Great Yarmouth	—	
Lacon Henry James, Ormesby St. Margaret, Norfolk		
Lacon Edmund Henry Knowles, Hopton, Suffolk	—	
Lacey Robert, Great Yarmouth	—	
Lake Thomas Constable, Great Yarmouth		
Lake William, Great Yarmouth	—	
Lamb Robert A., Great Yarmouth		
Lamb William, Great Yarmouth	—	
Langley Abraham, Great Yarmouth		
Langley Samuel, jun., Gorleston		
Lane James Christmas, Great Yarmouth		
Lark James, Great Yarmouth		
Last James, Great Yarmouth		
Last William, Great Yarmouth		
Latter James, Great Yarmouth		
Lawson Benjamin, Great Yarmouth		
Laws William Durrant, Great Yarmouth	—	
Laws James, Great Yarmouth		
Lawn James, Great Yarmouth	—	
Layton Thomas, Great Yarmouth	—	
Layton Robert Martin, Thorney, Cambridgeshire	—	
Layton Hezekiah Martin, Southtown		
Layton George, Great Yarmouth		
Layton William, Great Yarmouth		
Layton William Benjamin, Great Yarmouth	—	
Leggett James, Great Yarmouth		
Lettis Thomas, the elder, Great Yarmouth	—	
Lessey Samuel, Great Yarmouth		
Lissamore James, Southtown, Suffolk	—	
Long William, Wood Norton		
Louttid William Alfred, Great Yarmouth	—	
Lubbock William, Great Yarmouth		
Maddeys Thomas, Great Yarmouth		
Maddeys James, Great Yarmouth	—	
Mallett William, Great Yarmouth		
Mann William, Great Yarmouth		
Marsh Samuel Charles, Great Yarmouth		
Marsh William, Great Yarmouth		
Martin George, Great Yarmouth		
Martins Robert, Great Yarmouth	—	
Maryson John, Great Yarmouth	—	
Marjoram Daniel, Great Yarmouth	—	
Maryson Francis, Great Yarmouth	—	
Maystone Robert, Great Yarmouth	—	
Mayes William, Gorleston		
M'Cullagh William Torrens, 23, Cadogan-place, London	—	
Miles James Talbot, Great Yarmouth		
Miller Charles, Great Yarmouth		
Miller John, 15, Brunswick-street, Hackney-road, London	—	
Mobbs William, Great Yarmouth	—	

	S.	C.
Mollett Robert, Great Yarmouth	—	
Money Thomas, Great Yarmouth	—	
Money Robert, Half-row, Fuller's-hill, Great Yarmouth		
Money Thomas Christmas, Great Yarmouth	—	
Money William, Great Yarmouth	—	
Moore Charles, Great Yarmouth	—	
Moore Thomas, Great Yarmouth		
Moore James Burward, Great Yarmouth	—	
Moore John Christmas, Great Yarmouth	—	
Morter Thomas, Great Yarmouth		
Morter Samuel, Great Yarmouth		
Morant Alfred William, Great Yarmouth	—	
Morley Edmund Norton, Great Yarmouth		
Moss Thomas, Great Yarmouth	—	
Moss William, Great Yarmouth	—	
Motts George, Great Yarmouth		
Nash John, Great Yarmouth	—	
Nash William, Great Yarmouth	—	
Naunton William, Norwich		
Naunton George, Southtown		
Naunton Libbis, Stalham		
Neale William, Great Yarmouth	—	
Neale Stephen, Great Yarmouth	—	
Neave Joseph Fleming, Great Yarmouth	—	
Neave James William, Great Yarmouth	—	
Newman Charles, Great Yarmouth		
Newark James, Burgh Castle, Suffolk	—	
Newark William, sen., Great Yarmouth	—	
Nicholls Edward, South-gates, Great Yarmouth	—	
Nicholls Thomas, Row 17, Great Yarmouth	—	
Nicholls John, Great Yarmouth	—	
Nickerson Robert, Great Yarmouth	—	
Nightingale Samuel, Great Yarmouth	—	
Norman John Howes, Great Yarmouth	—	
Norman John Arundle, Great Yarmouth	—	
Norton Alfred Crowe, Great Yarmouth	—	
Obee Obadiah, Great Yarmouth	—	
Olley William, Great Yarmouth	—	
Olley Henry, Great Yarmouth	—	
Orfeur John, Great Yarmouth	—	
Orford William, Great Yarmouth	—	
Osborn William, Great Yarmouth	—	
Outlaw James, Great Yarmouth	—	
Owles James John, Quay, Great Yarmouth	—	
Owles John, Great Yarmouth	—	
Owles Edward, Gillingham, Norfolk	—	
Page John Edmund, Great Yarmouth	—	
Page Robert, Great Yarmouth		
Page Robert, Great Yarmouth		
Palmer George Danby, Great Yarmouth	—	
Palmer Salmon, Great Yarmouth	—	
Palmer Henry Danby, Southtown		
Palmer William Hurry, Southtown		
Palmer James Hurry, junr., Great Yarmouth	—	
Palmer Edmund Reeve, Regent-street, Great Yarmouth		
Palmer Jonathan, Great Yarmouth		
Palmer Frederick, Great Yarmouth	—	
Panchen Charles, Great Yarmouth	—	
Parker Robert, Ormesby St. Margaret, Norfolk	—	
Parmenter Richard, Great Yarmouth	—	
Parmenter William, Great Yarmouth	—	
Parnell William, Great Yarmouth	—	
Paston Charles, Ber-street, Norwich		
Paston James, Great Yarmouth	—	
Paston Benjamin Tills, Norwich		
Patrick William, Great Yarmouth	—	
Paul Thomas, Great Yarmouth	—	
Pearson Martin, Great Yarmouth	—	
Peed John, Whittlesea, Cambridgeshire	—	

	S.	C.
Peed Samuel, Great Yarmouth and Cambridge	—	
Pell George R., Great Yarmouth	—	
Perry William, Great Yarmouth	—	
Pestell Henry, Great Yarmouth	—	
Plane John, Great Yarmouth	—	
Plane Thomas, Great Yarmouth	—	
Playford John, Great Yarmouth	—	
Phinn James Lilly, Great Yarmouth	—	
Pile William, Great Yarmouth	—	
Pillis William, Great Yarmouth	—	
Pitchers James, Neptune-place, Great Yarmouth	—	
Pizey Robert, Great Yarmouth	—	
Plummer Joseph Goulding, Great Yarmouth	—	
Plummer John Bruce, Great Yarmouth	—	
Plummer Henry, Great Yarmouth	—	
Pratt James, Great Yarmouth	—	
Preston Isaac, Great Yarmouth	—	
Preston Isaac, junior, Great Yarmouth	—	
Preston Edward H. L., Great Yarmouth	—	
Preston Charles Abbott, Great Yarmouth	—	
Preston Francis W., Tenbury, Worcestershire	—	
Proudfoot Edmund, Great Yarmouth	—	
Pulford George, Great Yarmouth	—	
Purdy Robins, Southtown	—	
Pye Richard, Great Yarmouth	—	
Pye Martin, Gaol-street, Great Yarmouth	—	
Pye Richard Allen, Great Yarmouth	—	
Quinton John, Great Yarmouth	—	
Rackham John, Great Yarmouth	—	
Rainer Francis, Great Yarmouth	—	
Ranney William, Great Yarmouth	—	
Randall James, Great Yarmouth	--	
Read William, Great Yarmouth	—	
Reading Isaac, Great Yarmouth	—	
Read Trivett William, Great Yarmouth	—	
Read John, Great Yarmouth	—	
Reddish James, Great Yarmouth	—	
Reeve Joseph, Great Yarmouth	—	
Remmonds James, Great Yarmouth	—	
Reynolds William Collett, Great Yarmouth	—	
Rice George, Great Yarmouth	—	
Richmond John, Great Yarmouth	—	
Rising Thomas, Out the White Lion opening, Great Yarmouth	—	
Rivett Richard, Great Yarmouth	—	
Roberts William, Southtown	—	
Robins William, Broad-row, Great Yarmouth	—	
Robinson John Frederick, Great Yarmouth and Hadleigh, Suffolk	—	
Rowland John, Great Yarmouth	—	
Rowland Robert, Great Yarmouth	—	
Royal James John, Great Yarmouth	—	
Rudd William, Great Yarmouth	—	
Rudd Joseph, Heigham, Norwich	—	
Rumbold Charles, George-st., Great Yarmouth	—	
Runacre James, Great Yarmouth	—	
Rust James, Great Yarmouth	—	
Rycraft Henry, Great Yarmouth	—	
Sacret Thomas, Great Yarmouth	—	
Sadler Joseph, Southtown, Suffolk	—	
Salmon John, Great Yarmouth	—	
Saunders John Gower, King's Lynn, Norfolk	—	
Scott William, Great Yarmouth	—	
Scott Henry, Great Yarmouth	—	
Scott James, King-street, Great Yarmouth	—	
Scott Samuel Artis, Queen-st., Great Yarmouth	—	
Scotten William, Great Yarmouth	—	
Sculley Edward, Great Yarmouth	—	
Seago William Rix, Lowestoft, Suffolk	—	
Self James, Great Yarmouth	—	
Sewell Edward, Great Yarmouth	—	

	S.	C.
Shakel John, Great Yarmouth	—	
Sharman James, Monument, Great Yarmouth	—	
Sharman John Close, Great Yarmouth	—	
Sherwood Robert, Belgrave-place, Gt. Yarmouth	—	
Shelly John Wilton, Great Yarmouth	—	
Shingles George Smith, Great Yarmouth	—	
Short John, Overstrand, Norfolk	—	
Shorten Samuel, George-street, Great Yarmouth	—	
Shuckford Isaac, Great Yarmouth	—	
Sillis William, Great Yarmouth	—	
Silvers Brighton, Great Yarmouth	—	
Simmons Philip, Great Yarmouth	—	
Simmons Edward, Great Yarmouth	—	
Simms Robert, Great Yarmouth	—	
Simms William, Great Yarmouth	—	
Simpson William Marfrey, Great Yarmouth	—	
Skinner James, Great Yarmouth	—	
Skinner William Barlow, Great Yarmouth	—	
Sloman Charles, Great Yarmouth	—	
Smith Thomas, Great Yarmouth	—	
Smith Edward, Great Yarmouth	—	
Smith Robt., Wrestler's-plain, Great Yarmouth	—	
Smith John Caporn, Great Yarmouth	—	
Smith Samuel, Great Yarmouth	—	
Smith William, Hopton, Suffolk	—	
Smith Edward, Great Yarmouth	—	
Smyth Spencer Thomas, Great Yarmouth	—	
Somerville William George, Great Yarmouth	—	
Spilling William, Southtown	—	
Springall Robert Christmas, Great Yarmouth	—	
Stagg John, Great Yarmouth	—	
Stanford Frederick, Darsham, Suffolk	—	
Stephenson Matthew, Great Yarmouth	—	
Sterry Nathaniel, Gorleston	—	
Steward Richard, Great Yarmouth	—	
Steward Christopher, Great Yarmouth	—	
Steward Arthur, Great Yarmouth	—	
Steward Charles Samuel Dale, Great Yarmouth	—	
Stolworthy Edmund, Great Yarmouth	—	
Stone Alison Davie, Southtown, Suffolk	—	
Stove Isaac William, Great Yarmouth	—	
Sturgeon John, Great Yarmouth	—	
Suggate William, Great Yarmouth	—	
Suggate Henry, Great Yarmouth	—	
Sumner George, Great Yarmouth	—	
Swan Henry, Great Yarmouth	—	
Swan William Diver, Great Yarmouth	—	
Swann George, Great Yarmouth	—	
Taylor William Huke, Great Yarmouth	—	
Tennant Robert, Great Yarmouth	—	
Teasdell John, Great Yarmouth	—	
Thomas John, Great Yarmouth	—	
Tompson George Edward, Boxted, Essex	—	
Thompson James T., Great Yarmouth	—	
Thwaites Alexander, Reading, Berks	—	
Tolver Samuel, Great Yarmouth	—	
Tomlinson Joseph, Great Yarmouth	—	
Topps Thomas, Great Yarmouth	—	
Trinham Samuel, Great Yarmouth	—	
Trory William, Great Yarmouth	—	
Trorey William, Great Yarmouth	—	
Tunbridge Richard, Great Yarmouth	—	
Turrell Charles, Great Yarmouth	—	
Tuthill John, Great Yarmouth	—	
Valiant Charles, Great Yarmouth	—	
Vaux Bowyer, clerk, Great Yarmouth	—	
Veale Robert, Great Yarmouth	—	
Veale Henry, Great Yarmouth	—	
Veale William Francis, Great Yarmouth	—	
Utting William, Great Yarmouth	—	
Wade John, Great Yarmouth	—	

S. | C.

Wade William, Great Yarmouth
Weles Charles Wm., Row 44, Great Yarmouth
Walc's Charles, Great Yarmouth
Waller William, Great Yarmouth
Walpole William, Southtown
Walpole William, Great Yarmouth
Ward Samuel, Blundeston, Suffolk
Waters James Denew, Great Yarmouth
Watson Joseph, Great Yarmouth
Watson George, Great Yarmouth
Watson John, Great Yarmouth
Wayth Daniel, Lowestoft, Suffolk
Wells Charles, Great Yarmouth
West John, Great Yarmouth
West John Davey, Great Yarmouth
West Thomas, Howard-street, Great Yarmouth
Whitby Daniel, Great Yarmouth
Whittleton George, Great Yarmouth
Wickham William Thos., Bethsheba-place, Great Yarmouth
Wilshack Harris, Great Yarmouth
Wilson Elijah, Great Yarmouth
Wiseman Peter, Great Yarmouth
Wiseman Richard, Great Yarmouth
Wisker John, Great Yarmouth
Withers John, Great Yarmouth
Woodhouse Samuel, Great Yarmouth
Woods James, Great Yarmouth
Woods Simon, Great Yarmouth
Woods Samuel, Cambridge
Woods George John, Norwich
Woolverton Charles, Great Yarmouth
Woolston William Woolage, Great Yarmouth
Woolsey Thomas, Great Yarmouth
Worts Robert, Great Yarmouth
Worship William, Great Yarmouth
Wright William, Great Yarmouth
Wright Richard, Great Yarmouth
Yallop George Steward, Gorleston
Yaxley Richard, Great Yarmouth
Yetts William, Great Yarmouth
Youell Edward, Great Yarmouth
Youell John, Great Yarmouth
Youngs Joseph Sidney, Great Yarmouth
Youngs Joseph, Great Yarmouth

350 | 323

Alcock Robert, Great Yarmouth
Aldis John, Great Yarmouth
Aldred Henry, Huddersfield
Allan John, Great Yarmouth
Ames John, Gaol-street, Great Yarmouth
Arbon James Noah, St. George's-road, Great Yarmouth
Arbon Daniel, Great Yarmouth
Arrowsmith Robert George, Ingrave, near Brentwood, Essex
Artis Samuel S., Great Yarmouth
Baldrey William, Great Yarmouth
Barnaby Robert Andrews, Great Yarmouth
Bateman George, Leamington
Batchelor Thomas John, Norwich
Beane Joseph, Caister
Beeching James, Great Yarmouth
Bird James Henry, Great Yarmouth
Bird William, Southtown
Bishop William, Great Yarmouth
Blake John Garson, Gosport, Hampshire
Blaud Arthur, Great Yarmouth
Bland James, Great Yarmouth
Bly John Henry, Gaol-street, Great Yarmouth
Blyth William, Great Yarmouth

S. | C.

Bolton William, Elm-hill, Norwich
Borrett James, Great Yarmouth
Branton John, Ipswich, Suffolk
Brereton Matthew, Great Yarmouth
Brightwen John, Thorpe
Brightman Henry Anson, Tynemouth
Brown William P. K., Great Yarmouth
Bunn James, Gorleston
Burroughs Robert, Great Yarmouth
Butcher Matthew, Great Yarmouth
Calvert Edmund Sexton Perry, Thames-street, London
Calvert William Henry, Thames-st., London
Calvert John, Thames-street, London
Carver James, Great Yarmouth
Christmas Cornelius Harley, Great Yarmouth
Clench John, 17, Prince's-street, Rotherhithe
Clifton Hezekiah Thomas, Great Yarmouth
Cobb James, Great Yarmouth
Coleby William, Great Yarmouth
Collier Charles, 20, Fitzroy-square, St. Pancras, Middlesex
Conyers James, Great Yarmouth
Crowe James, Bergh Apton, Norfolk
Crowe John, Great Yarmouth
Crucknell Henry, Great Yarmouth
Cushing Francis, Elmham, Norfolk
Dade Thomas, Broadway, Dorsetshire
Daniel Richard William, Comb's Rectory, Suffolk
Davey Thomas, Deptford, Kent
Davidson James, jun., Great Yarmouth
Ditcham John, jun., Great Yarmouth
Diver Isaac, Adelaide-street, Heigham, Norwich
Douglas James, Great Yarmouth
Drake James Roper, Great Yarmouth
Dunn John, Great Yarmouth
Eastick Spencer, Great Yarmouth
Easter William, Great Yarmouth
English Charles, North Market-road, Great Yarmouth
Fellowes William M., Ormesby St. Margaret
Field William, Great Yarmouth
Fish James, Great Yarmouth
Foreman Thomas, Great Yarmouth
Foreman James, Great Yarmouth
Frarey Robert, Great Yarmouth
Fulcher James Holmes, 34, Bridgewater-street, Liverpool
Fulcher James, Great Yarmouth
Fyson George, Bury St. Edmund's, Suffolk
George Samuel, Great Yarmouth
Gibbons William, Commercial-road, London
Gill Charles, Theatre, Norwich
Godbold William, Great Yarmouth
Godbolt James, Great Yarmouth
Goffin John, Great Yarmouth
Goffin Alexander, Great Yarmouth
Goose Robert, Great Yarmouth
Gostling William, Great Yarmouth
Gowen Henry, Runham
Gowing James Warden, Aldeby, Norfolk
Green John, Great Yarmouth
Greenwood Charles, Great Yarmouth
Gunton Walter Gabriel B., New Weston-street, Southwark
Gurney Matthew, Great Yarmouth
Harbord Griffin, Caister, Norfolk
Hardingham Stephen, Great Yarmouth
Harrison William, Great Yarmouth
Hickling Robert, Great Yarmouth

S. C.

Hennings Richard, Great Yarmouth
Hewitt Thomas Packer, Halvergate, Norfolk
High William, Great Yarmouth
Hills George, Great Yarmouth
Holl George, New Buckenham
Holt George Wells, South-quay, Great Yarmouth
Holt Wells, Great Yarmouth
Holstead Robert, London
Household Robert Burrows, Lynn Regis
Howlett Frederick, Great Yarmouth
Hubbock George, Ponder's-end, Middlesex
Humphrey George Dix, Great Yarmouth
Ibrooke Richmond, Newmarket-road, Norwich
James Charles, Heacham, near Lynn, Norfolk
Jephson Charles, George-street, Great Yarmouth
Jermyn James, South Gates-road, Great Yarmouth
Kemp James, Great Yarmouth
Kemp Robert Palmer, Coltishall, Norfolk
Kent Samuel, Brooke, Norfolk
Kerrison Roger Allday, Hill-house, Ipswich
King Thomas William, Herald's-office, London
Knights William, Row 121, Great Yarmouth
Lacey Robert, Great Yarmouth
Lamb James, Great Yarmouth
Lancaster James, High Holborn, London
Larke William, Great Yarmouth
Larter John, Great Yarmouth
Lemmon John, Southtown
Lewis William, Great Yarmouth
Lockhart Adam, Great Yarmouth
Mallett Samuel, Lowestoft
Mallett Robert, Great Yarmouth
Manship Thomas, junr., Martham, Norfolk
Mann William, George-street, Great Yarmouth
Martin Hezekiah, Southtown
Martin Henry, Great Yarmouth
Miles Richard, Great Yarmouth
Minter Samuel, Great Yarmouth
Morley Joseph, Great Yarmouth
Moss Thomas, Great Yarmouth
Munford Benjamin, Upton
Newman Isaac, Great Yarmouth
Newman Samuel, Great Yarmouth
Newark Henry, Great Yarmouth
Nolloth John, Great Yarmouth
Norman John, Great Yarmouth
Norman Richard Robert B., Great Yarmouth
Page Nathaniel Enget, Great Yarmouth
Parker Thomas B., No. 4, Crayford Cottages, Albany-road, Kent-road, London
Pearce William, Deptford
Peek John, Gorleston
Pettingill Walter Douglas, Great Yarmouth
Preston Samuel T., Brandon Parva, Norfolk
Press Thomas, Great Yarmouth
Punchard Isaac, Great Yarmouth
Ramsdale Joseph, Church-street, Southwark
Read James, Great Yarmouth
Reynolds John Preston, Necton, Norfolk
Rising Robert, Horsey

S. C.

Rising Thomas, Great Yarmouth
Rix Benjamin, Ipswich, Suffolk
Roate Robert, Great Yarmouth
Roberts Samuel, Gorleston
Runniff John, Great Yarmouth
Russell James Stewart, Great Yarmouth
Salt Francis, Southtown
Scott John B., Bungay, Suffolk
Sewell Edward, Great Yarmouth
Sharpe Charles Sharpe, Dover
Shardalow Benjamin, Thorpe St. Andrew's
Shephard Thomas Rump, Great Yarmouth
Sinclair Daniel, Great Yarmouth
Shakel John, Great Yarmouth
Slipper John, 92, Southtown
Smith Charles, Great Yarmouth
Smith John, Great Yarmouth
Smith William, Queen-street, Great Yarmouth
Stanford William Swan, Southtown
Steward Thomas Fowler, Great Yarmouth
Steward Charles, Blundeston, Suffolk
Steward Ambrose, Ipswich, Suffolk
Steward George, Knottingley, Yorkshire
Steward Robert, Southtown
Thompson Thomas, Great Yarmouth
Thompson James, Row 23, Great Yarmouth
Thorndick Henry Jarvis, King-street, Great Yarmouth
Todd Charles, Great Yarmouth
Todd George, Great Yarmouth
Tooke Thomas Hammond, Clifton, Bristol
Tooley Edward, South Market-road, Great Yarmouth
Travers Sir Eaton, Great Yarmouth
Turner Joseph Ellis, Great Yarmouth
Tuttle William, Regent-road, Great Yarmouth
Veale Henry John, Great Yarmouth
Williams John, Swanton Morley, near East Dereham, Norfolk
Wiseman John, Oby, Norfolk
Woodrow Edmund, Great Yarmouth
Woolston Benjamin, Great Yarmouth
Worship Harry Verelst, Great Yarmouth
Wragg John, Great Yarmouth
Wright Robert, Great Yarmouth
Yaxley Charles, Great Yarmouth
Yetts Joseph Muskett, 3, Old Jewry-street, London

Outvoters.

Costerton John Fisher, Great Yarmouth —
Cheston Chester, Clapton-square, London —
Curtis Richard, Martham —
Mason Robert, Yarmouth —
Pullyn Philip, Great Yarmouth —
Slipper John Armine, Ashby, Suffolk —
Teasdel Henry, Great Yarmouth —

4 3

Delph Samuel, junior, Swaffham
Manship Isaac William, Rollesby

POLLED FOR EACH CANDIDATE AT THE DIFFERENT DISTRICTS

IN 1832, 1835, 1837, 1841, AND 1858.

DISTRICTS.	1832.				1835.				1837.				1841.				1858.
	Cholmondeley.	Peach.	Keppel.	Windham.	Walpole.	Wodehouse.	Windham.	Gurney.	Wodehouse.	Burroughes.	Windham.	Gurney.	Wodehouse.	Burroughes.	Ffolkes.	Stracey.	Coke.
Norwich	821	868	970	935	951	1060	935	854	1154	1109	973	871	939	929	251	890	774
Loddon	...	...	...	...	...	...	...	...	...	...	...	...	295	300	72	197	271
North Walsham	619	633	580	621	686	740	605	554	728	690	633	574	715	712	153	463	590
Reepham	241	282	470	386	334	345	331	310	330	325	353	333	340	328	207	179	348
Long Stratton	520	518	731	718	576	638	610	591	701	677	677	634	639	635	312	489	521
Yarmouth	651	659	573	594	641	691	608	570	732	722	602	566	567	540	383	572	495
Total	2852	2960	3261	3340	3188	3474	3089	2879	3645	3523	3238	2978	3495	3434	1378	2720	2999

Total number of Electors on the Register in 1832, 7041; in 1835, 7281; in 1837, 8138; 1841, 8556; and in 1858, 7776.